Praise for the work of
ANNETTE BLAIR

An Unmistakable Rogue

"*An Unmistakable Rogue* brings to mind the best of Teresa Medeiros or Loretta Chase: funny, passionate, exquisitely lyrical."
—Eloisa James,
author of *Fool for Love*

"An innovative mix of family frolic and period gothic . . . fast-paced romance . . . plenty of sexual tension. Wonderful."
—*Romantic Times*

"Wonderfully written . . . captivating . . . engrossing . . . masterful."
—*Scribes World*

"Humorous . . . emotional . . . delectable."
—*Reader to Reader*

"What this story is filled with is love."
—*Romance & Friends*

continued . . .

An Unforgettable Rogue

"Never has a hero submitted to such sweet seduction while remaining very much the man in charge . . . Spicy sensuality is the hallmark of this unforgettable story."

—*Romance Readers Connection*

"After *An Undeniable Rogue,* I never expected to read such a wonderful story again. *An Unforgettable Rogue* proved me wrong."

—*Huntress Reviews*

"A beautiful blend of humor, pathos, and passion, with the added bonus of outstanding supporting characters."

—*Reader to Reader*

"Knight In Shining Silver Award for KISSable heroes. Bryceson 'Hawk' Wakefield is most definitely *An Unforgettable Rogue.*"

—*Romantic Times*

"Ms. Blair is such an awesome storyteller . . . *An Unforgettable Rogue* is a mesmerizing tale that sweeps the reader into the Regency era."

—*Scribes World*

"Annette Blair creates another memorable and refreshing love story . . . a charming read."

—*Jan Springer*

"I recommend *An Unforgettable Rogue* as an entertaining book in its own right, even more as part of the must-read Rogues Club series."

—*Romance Reviews Today*

An Undeniable Rogue

"A love story that is pure joy, enchanting characters who steal your heart, a fast pace, and great storytelling."
—*Romantic Times*

"An utterly charming and heartwarming marriage-of-convenience story. I highly recommend it to all lovers of romance."
—*Romance Reviews Today*

"Awesome! To call this story incredible would be an understatement . . . Do not miss this title."
—*Huntress Reviews*

"Annette Blair writes a very good story and has created some unforgettable characters in this excellent tale."
—*Romance Review*

"Annette Blair skillfully pens an exhilarating, humorous, and easy-to-read historical romance. You don't want to miss *An Undeniable Rogue*."
—Jan Springer

"Ms. Blair has a delicate touch with love scenes . . . none of her characters are insignificant."
—*Romance Readers Connection*

"A feel-good read that shines with warmth, wit, and passion."
—C. L. Jeffries, *Heartstrings*

The Kitchen Witch

Annette Blair

BERKLEY SENSATION, NEW YORK

THE BERKLEY PUBLISHING GROUP
Published by the Penguin Group
Penguin Group (USA) Inc.
375 Hudson Street, New York, New York 10014, USA
Penguin Group (Canada), 10 Alcorn Avenue, Toronto, Ontario M4V 3B2, Canada
(a division of Pearson Penguin Canada Inc.)
Penguin Books Ltd., 80 Strand, London WC2R 0RL, England
Penguin Group Ireland, 25 St. Stephen's Green, Dublin 2, Ireland (a division of Penguin Books Ltd.)
Penguin Group (Australia), 250 Camberwell Road, Camberwell, Victoria 3124, Australia
(a division of Pearson Australia Group Pty. Ltd.)
Penguin Books India Pvt. Ltd., 11 Community Centre, Panchsheel Park, New Delhi—110 017, India
Penguin Group (NZ), Cnr. Airborne and Rosedale Roads, Albany, Auckland 1310, New Zealand
(a division of Pearson New Zealand Ltd.)
Penguin Books (South Africa) (Pty.) Ltd., 24 Sturdee Avenue, Rosebank, Johannesburg 2196, South
Africa

Penguin Books Ltd., Registered Offices: 80 Strand, London WC2R 0RL, England

This is a work of fiction. Names, characters, places, and incidents either are the product of the author's imagination or are used fictitiously, and any resemblance to actual persons, living or dead, business establishments, events, or locales is entirely coincidental.

THE KITCHEN WITCH

A Berkley Sensation Book / published by arrangement with the author

PRINTING HISTORY
Berkley Sensation edition / October 2004

Copyright © 2004 by Annette Blair.
Cover art by Masaki Ryo/CWC International Inc.
Cover design by Rita Frangie.
Interior text design by Kristin del Rosario.

ISBN: 0-425-19881-2

BERKLEY® SENSATION
Berkley Sensation Books are published by The Berkley Publishing Group,
a division of Penguin Group (USA) Inc.,
375 Hudson Street, New York, New York 10014.
BERKLEY SENSATION and the "B" design
are trademarks belonging to Penguin Group (USA) Inc.

PRINTED IN THE UNITED STATES OF AMERICA

10   9   8   7   6   5   4   3

This book is dedicated with love and gratitude to:

Edie and Andy Anderson—for your hospitality and friendship. I will never forget those magic writing retreats on the mountain.

Janet Kuchler—for a summer home away from home, relaxing hours of pool plotting and laughter, late night talks, and for telling me to pay attention to the signs.

Rainy Kirkland—for dragging me to Salem in the first place, then for listening to my wild ideas—all my wild ideas—and saying, "You can do it, kiddo." Lucky for me, I always believe you.

One

LOGAN Kilgarven plucked a bright red leaf off the sleek black hearse in his neighbor's driveway. "What if she really is a witch?"

Jessie Harris laughed as she buffed the chrome hood ornament. "Melody Seabright is no more a witch than I am."

"Jess, I only moved into the apartment above her a couple of days ago, and already I've heard that she's flighty, unpredictable, and quite possibly a witch. After all that, you still think I should ask her to baby-sit?"

Jessie straightened, raised a speaking brow, and gazed at him through the top of her bifocals. "What would have happened to you," she asked, "if I had believed what people said about the town bad boy when you stood before me in juvenile court all those years ago?"

"Good point," Logan said, which didn't stop him from wincing at the mention of a past he'd tried for years to bury. Nevertheless, here he stood, back in good old Salem, Massachusetts . . . though he didn't suppose there was a better town in which to lay old ghosts to rest. He glanced over at his son, playing quietly in their backyard. No, nor a better place to raise a boy, either.

Logan took to studying the straight lines on the sleek sixties hearse Jessie had salvaged and refurbished. That was Jess, always trying to fix junk.

When Logan looked up, she was watching him, and he smiled, touched that she still worried about him after all these years. "If you hadn't given me a break, I'd probably be in jail today," he said, "and we both know it." He shook his head. "Are you going to remind me of that for the rest of my life?"

"I will if I have to."

Logan groaned. "Just don't do it in front of Shane, okay?"

After she finished polishing the hearse, he helped her put champagne and soft drinks in a cooler shaped like a coffin.

Jessie gave him a searching look. "I'll make you a deal. I'll swear off reminding you for about ten years—until after you tell him."

"Gee, thanks."

"I don't know if you'd be in jail right now," she said, considering. "But you might not be the respectable new executive producer at WHCH TV. Have I told you how proud I am of you? How glad I am that you came home?"

"A few times, on both counts," Logan said, shaking his head, but eventually he sighed. "I never intended to come back, you know."

"I know," Jessie said. "But you did want to give Shane a family, plus you thought a grandson would lure your mother into retirement; she knows, by the way."

"Ah yes," Logan said. "And I missed your meddling."

Jessie grinned. "It's not my fault you thought you'd find me baking cookies and waiting for you to need a sitter."

Logan laughed. "When we talked on the phone about the

possibility of my moving back and renting the apartment next door, I distinctly remember you saying—"

"That if you ever needed a sitter, I'd be nearby, and I am, but I can't sit tonight."

"Right. Mom made a similar promise, you know. And what do I find the first time I need a sitter, but her working a second job, again, and you . . ." He lifted the cooler into the back of the hearse and shut the door. "Giving world-class cemetery tours."

"I needed a new profession. Retirement didn't suit, and I wanted to have some fun. I mean, what else is an old judge good for?"

Logan checked his watch. "We were talking about leaving my four-year-old son with a woman who might be a witch. What am I gonna do? I need to be at work in twenty minutes."

"We were talking about leaving Shane for a couple of hours with a woman who loves kids, vintage clothes, and chunky doodle ice cream, in that order."

"Jess, this is serious."

Jessie shook her head. "I'll give you serious. You want someone who can connect with a boy whose mother gave him away? Melody's your girl."

Logan glanced toward Shane, on the jungle gym next door, to make sure he hadn't heard. "What's that supposed to mean?" Logan asked, his voice low.

"It means Melody can relate. Enough said." Jessie wagged her finger at him. "And you didn't hear that from me."

Logan ran a hand through his hair. "Great, just what I need, a baby-sitter with a dysfunctional background."

Jessie laughed outright. "Like yours was normal?" She swiped her hands on her jeans and picked up her car wax and buffing cloth. "Sometimes I think normal is dysfunctional."

"Maybe." Nevertheless, Logan felt the bite of her words

with an uncomfortable surge of guilt and regret. "Just for the record, I'm trying to do better by Shane."

Jessie nodded. "I know. Go for it, give Shane a break. He deserves it. You do, too. And so does Melody Seabright."

"Damn it, Jess. You're the one who taught me to think of somebody other than myself, and I do now—I think of my son—so you'll excuse me if I hesitate here."

"Look, I can't sit with Shane tonight, but Melody likely can. Ask her. She's great with kids, a regular nurturer, if you ask me, though she's only ever had me to practice on."

Logan sighed. Did he have a choice? He needed to get to work, and Melody Seabright came with the highest recommendation. "Okay. You win." He kissed her cheek and left her to finish prepping for her four o'clock "Boneyard Tour."

When he hesitated and looked back, Jess shooed him toward his house and the small foyer where Melody Seabright's door shared a landing with the stairs to his apartment above. "Shane," he called on the way. "Go upstairs and wash your hands."

In less than a minute, his son was racing past. *Fortunately for both of them,* Logan thought as he watched Shane dash up the stairs, *Jessie was the best judge of character he'd ever come across.* Nevertheless, Logan stopped short, not for the first time, at the sight of that purple door with its sprinkle of stenciled yellow stars.

This time, he knocked anyway.

Bracing himself as a series of clicking footsteps escalated behind the kooky portal, Logan still lost his breath upon sight of the goddess in stilettos who opened it. Hers was the kind of face that jumped out at you from the cover of a fashion magazine, though you knew in real life that she was flawed and imperfect. Except, she wasn't.

She had a body that cut him off at the knees, draped in a black fishnet tunic over red Capri pants and a matching halter top, but her black floor-length cape, lined in red satin, really threw him. Then she tossed her long, lush mane of ebony waves over one shoulder and gave him a hundred-watt smile. "Can I help you?"

The answer that came to Logan's mind had nothing to do with baby-sitting, and everything to do with the bad boy he used to be. Realizing it, shocked by it, Logan blanked. "Uh . . . nice door."

Her smile was spectacular, and the twinkle in her topaz eyes revealed a kaleidoscope of facets. "Thanks!"

Funny how Jessie had failed to mention that Melody Seabright was exactly the kind of woman who might once have knocked him on his bad-boy ass. Maybe it hadn't been such a good idea to let Jess and his mother find him an apartment, because his hot new neighbor had "flammable" written all over her.

She must have realized then that all the blood had left his brain and headed south, because she took the initiative and extended her hand. "Melody Seabright."

Logan's smile grew without permission, and as their hands met, and held, he could have sworn that a surge of pure electricity shot through him. "Logan Kilgarven," he said. "From upstairs."

"Logan. Hello. Welcome to the building. Come in, please—though only for a minute, I'm sorry to say. I've got an appointment at the Castle, and it's clear across town."

"The Castle?" he asked.

"Drak's place. Drak's Castle? You know, one of those grisly spook tours, Salem style. If you haven't been there, you have to go. I'm auditioning tonight as a female vampire for the fall tourist season."

"Thank God. For a minute there, I thought I'd rented in the red-light district."

"Hey!"

"No offense," Logan said, taking in the converted Victorian's original kitchen as he shut the door on the wings of a crisp fall breeze. "But have you looked in a mirror?"

"I don't have one in my bedroom, so I haven't had a chance." She opened a broom closet and regarded herself in the full-length mirror inside the door. She laughed, charming Logan, welcoming him in a way her words had not, as if they were . . . friends, a notion he dismissed in a quick bid for self-preservation.

"You think I might have a shot?" she asked.

"If you don't, they're nuts."

"Thanks." She sighed in relief and snatched her keys off the table. "Look, I gotta' go. Did you need something?"

MELODY watched the man's killer smile vanish as he stepped farther into her kitchen, despite her cue for him to go. A pity about his smile, though, that he didn't use it much. This was the first time she'd seen him as anything but a stuffed suit with a briefcase, and the view was fine.

He ran a hand through his thick, dark hair, as if he'd had plenty of frustrated practice, and let out a long, slow breath, and Melody got this rare image of herself softening his hard edges and relieving his stress by pushing him into an easy chair and draping something warm over him . . . her. She took a step back and wiped the picture from her mind.

"The thing is," he said, a plea in his look, "I *really* need somebody to watch my son for a couple of hours. I've been called unexpectedly back to work."

"I wish I could help," Melody said, "but I *really* need this job. Why don't you try Jessie, next door?"

"She's got a cemetery tour tonight." They shared a smile over their neighbor's new profession, and Melody found herself caught in the hidden depths of a stranger's eyes.

"I would never have asked you," he said, "if Jessie hadn't recommended you so highly."

"I'll have to thank her, but I can't help you tonight. I'm sorry."

"I'd be happy to pay you."

"Look, if a night with your kid's worth a month's rent, you've got a deal." She shook her head. "I'm sorry, honestly, but I've got some serious problems here. My roommate moved out without paying her share, I lost my job, and the owner of this place is a pri—pretty nasty guy who'd throw me out in a blink."

"You wanna talk serious?" An irked glint entered the man's startling blue eyes. "My son's mother decided she'd rather hang with a motorcycle stuntman than raise her son. So I've finally got him—and I couldn't be happier—but I've also got this new job with a boss who either doesn't understand single male parenting or disapproves of it."

"You're kidding?"

Logan slipped his hands into his pockets, jingled the contents, and grimaced. "He didn't come out and say so, but I got his message. Real men don't keep children in the workplace. So company day care is shot to hell—for the moment, at least."

"That's just not right. But didn't Jessie say you were born in Salem? I mean, don't you have any relatives? Someone who could baby-sit?" Melody inched her way toward the door.

"My mother's working tonight, not that she needs to, but that's a problem for another day. No, I'm flat out of good prospects. You're all I've got."

"Gee, thanks."

"Wait a minute," he said, a new spark in his eyes. "If you watch Shane tonight, I'm sure I can find you some kind of job at the station. Wha'd'ya say?"

"I'm sorry, but pumping gas is really not my style."

That fast, his killer smile was back, and so was Melody's lap-warming fantasy.

"Not a *gas* station," he said. "A TV station."

Melody's keys slipped from her fingers and hit the floor with a tinkling thud. "What?"

"WHCH, down the street."

"What kind of job are we talking here?"

"I'm only the executive producer, but—"

"Only?"

"Look, TV stations are always looking to hire somebody. Keep Shane, and I'll check tonight, I promise, though I can't guarantee you a position as exalted as a vampire."

Melody raised a disgruntled brow, even as her dishy new neighbor raised a placating hand. "Joke."

She knew for a fact that WHCH was looking for somebody to host a cooking show—their previous chef had been a real yawn. She loved cooking shows, though she'd practically slept through that one. "How long will you be gone?"

Logan checked his watch. "Say yes, and I'll be your slave forever."

Oh, the possibilities. Melody took another step back. His eagerness was as much of a turn-on as his pique. "How long?" she repeated.

"Two hours, three at the most," he said.

Melody mentally calculated the time it would take her to prepare one dynamite dinner, the kind that would make the man beg her to do his cooking show. "Sold, and take your time. I talked to your son out in the yard the day you moved in. Cute as a button, polite, too, but he doesn't smile much. How come?"

"He hasn't been with me long, and we're still getting to know each other."

"Better. You mean, you're getting to know each other better."

Logan ran that impatient hand through his hair again. "Can you baby-sit without the whole rotten story, or not?"

Melody snapped to attention and saluted. "Aye, aye, Sir.

Send him down, Sir. I'll make us dinner, Sir, and we can eat when you get back . . . Sir."

The handsome devil rolled his eyes, turned on his heel, and ran up the stairs, calling for his son to "hop to it."

MELODY got the "whole rotten story" out of Shane with nary a question or thumbscrew in sight. Four-year-old boys sang like canaries with chocolate chip cookies and milk before supper.

Shane talked nonstop, while Melody put a roast in the oven and turned the temperature up high, because the meat was still frozen. Though she watched cooking shows, she'd never had time to put any of the lessons to use. Takeout was quicker, but how hard could cooking be?

It took Shane a while to warm up to her. She didn't think he was naturally shy; his reticence seemed almost like a form of self-preservation. According to him, he hadn't lived with, or even known, his father for very long, which would account for his reserve around strangers.

Fortunately, he was a great kid, naturally friendly, *and* he knew how to measure dry ingredients, which helped a great deal when they started dessert.

After they put all the ingredients into the bowl, Melody turned on the mixer. "Don't get too close," she said, making a pinch-bug with her fingers and catching Shane's nose, "or you'll get caught in the beaters, and then what would your dad say?"

The boy giggled and flashed the smile Melody had been going for.

Unfortunately, the mixer didn't seem to be working right. The pokey beaters went therrrrump, therrrrump, while chunks of solid ingredients, clumped with butter, clung to them as they turned.

"Is it supposed to do that?" Melody asked.

"It's usually mushier," Shane said.

"Eggs! I forgot the eggs." Melody got the eggs out of the fridge, cracked one against the side of the mixing bowl, and dropped it in. Almost immediately, the beaters turned more smoothly, and the blending ingredients began to resemble a thick batter.

Shane grinned.

Melody wasn't so lucky with the second egg, and a few pieces of eggshell went in with it. "Drat! Catch that piece of shell. No, don't! You'll catch your fingers. Wait." She lifted the beaters so she and Shane could grab the shells before they were folded into the batter.

But the beaters took to spinning at warp speed, splattering batter all over, and Shane took to screaming.

Melody screamed, too, when she saw another slab of batter hit him in the face. Then the poor kid was crying, really crying, for her to turn it off.

By the time she pulled the plug, Melody was crying as well. "Where are you hurt, baby? Tell Melody where."

Shane kept shaking his head, and hiccuping, and swiping at his face, then he opened his eyes, and two dark little caverns swimming in tears stared accusingly up at her through a mask of yellow batter.

"I'll never forgive myself," she said.

He had batter in his hair, his ears. He was sneezing batter! After Melody carried him into the bathroom and washed him up, he admitted that the slap of batter had stung, and she cried again, in pure relief, because he was okay.

Shane patted her elbow. "It's okay, Mel. I'll take care of you."

Melody blew her nose. "How about we take care of each other," she said on a laugh.

"Okay, Mel."

After they went upstairs for Shane to change his clothes, they made friends with the mixer from hell, and during their second attempt, the batter actually looked like the picture in the cookbook. "Success," Melody said, as she poured it in a pan and placed it in the oven.

They got the hot fruit glaze right on the first try, another success, until Shane dipped a finger in for a scalding taste.

Melody applied a burn cream to the tip of his finger and covered it with one of her favorite cartoon Band-Aids. Then she wiped a few more tears and took him on her lap to cuddle. "Here," she said, bringing the wounded finger to her lips. "Let me kiss it better."

For a minute, Shane looked dumbfounded, then he buried his little face in her neck, and she stroked his baby-fine hair. "You all right, buddy?"

"I'm sorry, Mel."

"*You're* sorry?" She cupped his cheek and pulled his head back so she could look into his sad little face. "For what?"

"Being bad. Don't send me away."

"Send you . . . I might follow you home. Besides, you could never be bad. You're the best little boy that ever taught me to cook. Er, but don't tell your dad about the cooking, not until I'm better at it, okay?"

"Okay, Mel."

"Pals?"

"You and me?"

"Sure. You're such a good kid, I might have to borrow you from your dad once in a while, just so you can be a good influence on me."

"Okay, Mel."

"Do you know how to make gravy?"

"I watch Dad do it all the time."

"Good, let's try that next."

They decided to use a big pan and make a lot, because gorgeous old Dad liked extra gravy. But while Melody was stirring it, just the way Shane said Dad did, the gravy erupted without warning, bubbling down the stove like a hot lava flow.

"Yikes! Yikes!" In a panic as to how to stop it from taking over her kitchen, Melody lifted Shane off the chair he was standing on and moved him to safety.

While he repeated his new mantra, "Turn it off, turn it off," Melody tried a forward attack, but couldn't get close enough to the stove to reach the dial. So she went to the broom closet and flipped the circuit breakers—all of them—to cut the power to the stove . . . and plunged them into darkness.

A heavy silence fell, and lasted, for half a beat, until a spontaneous eruption of a little boy's giggles grew, and grew, and a crescendo of full-blown laughter, joyful and breathless, took over the apartment and filled Melody's heart.

After Shane finally caught his breath, Melody turned the circuit breakers back on, one by one, while he told her which room lit up. By the time they had enough light from the other rooms to see the kitchen, the gravy had cooled a bit and Shane fetched bath towels for her to clean up the spill.

Later, because she didn't have a potato masher, Shane tried to smash the boiled potatoes with the back of a big spoon, but during his enthusiastic attempt, the aluminum bowl, potatoes and all, bounced, upside down, into the sink. Shane looked so stricken, Melody twirled him off his chair and danced him around the kitchen. "I'm glad it was you," she sang, until she had him laughing again. "I'm glad it was youuuuuuu."

After an exhausting few hours, they surveyed the meal they had prepared. "What do you think? Awesome?" Melody asked. "Or yuck?"

Shane patted her hand. "It's okay, Mel, don't feel bad.

I'll teach you to cook, or Dad can, or he can cook for you. Then you can eat upstairs with us every night."

"That bad, huh?"

His grin was as deadly as his father's, and Melody wondered what old Dad would say about his son's chivalrous offer.

She was glad Shane had eaten the cookies before supper, though, because it was taking his father longer than they'd planned. They gave up waiting and tried to gnaw their way through the leather the recipe called Beef Burgundy, but that was useless. She didn't feel like eating dessert, but Shane dug right in . . . and promptly gagged.

Melody shoved a wad of napkins at him. "Maybe ginger, instead of cinnamon, and cherry pie filling instead of firm green apples, wasn't such a good idea, after all," she said.

Shane wiped his mouth, "Yuck!" he said, and giggled. Despite his batter-beating and sore fingertip, and the way dinner had turned out, a spark now lit his eyes, a glint of mischief and life that had been missing before. He'd had a good time playing chef, and she'd had almost as much fun as he had. But the results looked disgusting. Lord, she'd better get rid of the evidence before Logan returned. If he saw the mess she'd made, he would never—

"Hi, Dad. Me 'n Mel had fun. Look! We cooked!"

Two

MELODY turned on her heel, as every woman's fantasy man seemed to magically appear—jeans, soft and snug in all the right places, hair tousled, sleeves rolled up. Nothing uptight about dishy Dad tonight.

"Hey, sport," Logan said, hugging Shane against his legs as he cupped the boy's upturned head. "You changed clothes?"

Shane nodded, looking . . . worried.

"A spill, huh?" Logan said on a chuckle.

Shane relaxed. "Mel's washing my other stuff."

Logan looked up. "That wasn't necessary," he said, assessing her, Melody thought, from her steam-frizzed hair to her gravy-splattered mules.

"No problem."

"Sorry to walk right in," he said. "The door swung open when I knocked."

Gotta get that latch fixed, Melody thought.

Logan rubbed his hands together. "Something smells

g—" He focused on the table for the first time and stopped.

Appalled—that was the best word to describe the look on his face as he eyed her not-so-dynamite dinner, Melody thought. Drat. Was he turning a little green around the gills there? "Have you eaten?" she asked. "I can fix you some—"

"God, no."

"Not this," she said. "I've got—"

"No, nothing." He raised a hand so fast, she half expected him to form a cross with his fingers. "Thanks," he said, "but I'm beat. Let's go, Shane."

"Hey," Melody said. "You promised me a job."

"Oh, right. I forgot."

"You forgot!"

Logan chuckled. "I forgot to tell you that there's a secretarial job with your name on it at WHCH TV."

Melody stopped clearing the table and gave him a blank look. "A secretary?"

"A secretary doesn't beat a vampire?"

"We're not playing Old Maid, here. This is my career."

"Wearing a Halloween Costume for thirty days in October does not a career make."

"Thirty-*one*." Melody dumped a black clump that might once have been beef into the sink, shoved the petrified mass into the drain, and turned on the disposal.

Logan stifled his grin and waited for the labored grinding to stop. "Can you handle a computer?" he asked when she'd finished destroying the evidence. "We've got a data entry opening that pays—"

"What about the cooking show?"

"The what?"

"I'd rather be a TV cook."

Logan gingerly poked a cold, ugly, congealing casserole of something . . . gray and . . . purple? and lost the fight. The harder he laughed, the redder Melody got, until she was as bright as her man-eating Capri suit.

"You rat. You judgmental skunk. How dare you put me down. I blew a perfectly good interview to help you out."

Logan had to give her credit. She stopped raging to kiss Shane's head and tell him they'd had fun before resuming her attack on his rodent father. Shane even hugged her back.

"I don't doubt your ability because of your Dracula fixation," Logan said, surprised at his son's easy show of affection. "It's the fact that you can't seem to cook that concerns me."

"I can too cook. I just didn't have the right ingredients. I wasn't prepared, that's all. I'm a good cook, aren't I, Shane?"

His son looked a bit cornered for a minute, then he firmed his spine like a loyal little soldier, and damned if Logan wasn't proud. "Yeah, Dad, I only puked 'cause Mel said she probly—"

"That'll be enough, Shane," Melody said. "I can take it from here."

"Okay, Mel."

Logan had to bite the inside of his cheek to remain serious.

Melody raged, and she paced. She called him three kinds of weasels and gave him a dozen ridiculous reasons why she would be good on the cooking show. But when she paced toward him, her breasts bouncing jauntily in that red sling she was trying to carry them in, the buzz in his head became louder than the sound of her voice. And when she walked away from him, it took all his studied attention not to introduce her cute little ass to the palms of his eager hands.

"So, will you?" she asked, coming to a stop directly in front of him.

"I'm sorry; what did you say?" His stomach growled, while another part of his body reacted a good deal more strongly.

"Will you give it to me?"

The silence pulsed. Logan flushed. "Excuse me?"

"The interview. I'll watch Shane nights for a year, if you give it to me."

"Oh, the interview."

"What else would I? . . ." Melody narrowed her eyes.

Logan grinned, despite himself. "In the event I would even consider granting you an interview, you couldn't go dressed like that, you know."

"What's wrong with this?"

Besides the fact that he wanted to strip it away and suggest a friendly game of bone-jumping? "Nothing."

She looked suspicious. "What do you think I should wear?"

"I don't know. A dress, maybe?"

"A dress? Get real. This is the new millennium."

"You're interviewing for a TV show, Melody."

"Yes!" she crowed, as she did a sexy little happy dance and high-fived Shane.

That's when Logan realized he'd been screwed . . . without the perks.

Damn. She was good.

Logan took his son's hand. "Let's go, sport." At the door, he turned back to Melody. "I have to be honest with you, Mel. That outfit could probably get you the job." He wiggled his brows. "You'd sure get a raise."

"Skunk," she called after him, as she followed him out to the landing and watched him climb the stairs. "Shane," she said. "If your place gets to smelling too skunky, you can bunk down here with me."

"Okay, Mel. I'll go put on my pj's and be right back."

Logan shot Melody his most intimidating frown before turning to his son. "You will not. Your bed is upstairs."

"But me and Mel want to do a sleepover, Dad."

Logan took his son by the hand. It was all he could do

not to suggest that he'd like to come, too. Talk about your double meanings. Sheesh.

Five minutes later, Logan draped a lathered washcloth over his son's face like a pall and elicited a giggle.

Shane shook the cloth off of his face, caught it, tossed it back, and grinned. "Don't need it. Mel washed me up."

"How domestic of her."

"Yup, there's no more batter anywhere."

"Batter?"

"Yup, all gone."

"Uh . . . what say you wash up again, anyway."

Big sigh. "Okaaay."

Logan had not failed to notice, when he returned, that, although Melody had removed the cape and the fishnet tunic and traded her stilettos for clogs—going so far as to desecrate the Capri suit with a splattered apron—she had still looked stunning.

What a night. He was in lust, his son was in love, and in three days' time, he was going to put his job on the line and interview a witch—a witch who didn't know beans about cooking—for a cooking show.

What if she really is a witch? . . .

Logan had barely moved in before one of the secretaries at the station saw his new address and suggested he move out, fast. She said that Melody Seabright, his new downstairs neighbor, had recently made their six o'clock news, when she cast a spell on some guy who'd hit on her while she was giving a tour dressed as a witch. The guy claimed to have broken his ankle as a direct result of Melody's incantation, and he sued the tour company. That was how Melody had lost her most recent job.

But if she knew how to cast spells, why hadn't she bewitched herself into a better and more permanent job by now?

Logan handed Shane a loaded toothbrush, which he held

suspended halfway to his small smiling mouth. "Mel's neat, isn't she, Dad?"

"Neat," Logan said, grinning. The part of him watching his son's small happy face, and listening to him rhapsodize, wanted to kiss Jessie for her brilliant suggestion. The part that knew how dangerous women like Melody Seabright could be wanted to protect Shane from another one like his mother.

When Shane's perfect little teeth glistened, Logan followed him into a bedroom where Hogwarts ruled. "Tell me about your night with Melody," he said, hoping to get the scoop on the batter.

As Logan pulled the covers back, Shane imitated Mel's horrified reaction to her gravy boiling over, and her "Yikes" dance around the bubbling flow.

Oh boy, some cook, Logan thought. But his son had not giggled like this, or been this animated, since before the woman who'd given him life dropped him at Logan's front door with a curt, "I've had enough; you raise him."

For weeks after she split, Shane had asked daily when his mother would be back, until he stopped asking altogether. Logan tried to tell Shane that Heather had probably gotten tired of trying to hide him from Logan, but Shane wasn't convinced.

His fault, Logan knew. If he hadn't tried so hard to find Shane, his son's small heart might not have been broken. "C'mere, buddy," Logan said, angry and guilty and grateful all at once. "Give your old Dad a hug."

Shane slammed into Logan's legs.

With a lump in his throat, Logan lifted his son into his arms. "You're a hell of a kid, do you know that?"

Shane leaned back and grinned. "That's what Mel says."

"Then it must be true." Logan dropped him onto his bed, getting a laugh for his efforts.

"Can we buy Mel some measurin' stuff, Dad?" Shane

asked as he scrambled beneath the covers. "'Cause she doesn't got much. Or can she borrow ours? She might need to borrow me, too, sometimes, 'cause she needs me, 'kay?"

"We'll see."

"Not like Mom, I mean. Mel *really* needs me."

Logan tried not to show his surprise at that statement as he pulled the covers up to Shane's neck and kissed his brow, but the fist around his heart tightened. "I love you, son."

"Love you too, Dad."

Logan turned off the light.

"Hey, Dad?"

"Yes?" Logan flipped the light back on, prepared for the usual bedtime delay tactics, but his son was pointing toward the ceiling.

Logan looked up, saw nothing unusual, and looked curiously back.

Shane's index finger remained in the upright position. "Mel even has neat Band-Aids. See?" he said. "Can we get some like this?"

"Ah." Logan chuckled as he kissed him one more time, promising to buy a box of cartoon Band-Aids first thing in the morning. Turned out he did require a last drink of water—big surprise—before Logan finally made his way to his own room.

He chuckled as he sat on the edge of his bed. That boy was something, despite his unstable beginnings.

What had he meant by saying that Mel really needed him? What did "not like Mom" mean? Did a four-year-old boy need to be needed? Had Shane in his childlike innocence already replaced thoughts of his mother with Melody? After one night?

Logan tugged off his tie and thought with a great deal of guilt about everything Shane must have gone through, living with a mother who was always looking for the main chance.

He had to do better by that boy. The poor kid hadn't caught a break in the parent department, that's for sure.

Logan knew the stupidest thing he'd ever done was steal from that convenience store, though getting Heather pregnant had been the most irresponsible.

But now . . . now that he had Shane, he felt so . . . grateful. Grateful for having been irresponsible? Logan shook his head. It didn't make sense, but that's how it played out. And he wasn't sorry. He wasn't.

Then again, letting Heather run before he could marry her had brought him right back to stupid; he should have known she'd look for a rich ride out of town. When she discovered she was pregnant, Logan was suddenly too poor for her. No surprise there.

Of course she didn't tell her rich ride out that she was carrying a baby, Logan's or otherwise, so the guy eventually dumped her. Then she nailed another "in a long line of sugar daddies," according to the detective who found Shane.

After Heather signed the adoption papers, Logan signed his WHCH contracts. Now, for the first time, Shane was his. He might never have signed those contracts, or come back to Salem, if not for a son who needed a grandmother who needed to slow down. Then there was Jessie's theory that facing old ghosts was better than running from them, which remained to be seen.

Logan did wish he'd bought a house right away, though. Renting to make sure everything worked out with the new job was fine for a bachelor. For a little boy who needed security, another move sucked. Poor kid hadn't been able to catch a break his whole life.

What bothered Logan most at the moment, though, was Shane acting as if his break had finally come, just because Melody Seabright had opened her star-studded door. Melody . . . who seemed every bit as flighty as Heather.

Why couldn't Shane see that?

At least if Melody got a job at the station, she wouldn't have as much time to spend with Shane, which might be for the best. Not that Logan expected her to get hired. She might have managed to wear him down about the interview; his common sense had been skewed by a testosterone surge. But Ice Man Gardner was no pushover. He'd give Melody Seabright one hard look and she'd fast-freeze.

Logan almost felt sorry for her.

THREE days later, Logan left Shane with Jessie and backed his Volvo out of the detached garage, muttering all the way. When he'd knocked on Melody's door, she wasn't ready—big surprise—so here he sat, cooling his heels, when he was due at work in ten minutes. So what if she had an interview at the station this morning? She could have gotten there on her own. Why he had offered to take her in with him, he couldn't think. Then again, thinking around Melody was proving to be difficult.

"Hustle it, Mel, you're gonna' make me late," he called, as she came down the steps. Then he got a good look at her and stopped thinking altogether.

She slid into the passenger seat and fastened her seat belt, while the scent of something exotic and sensual further fogged his brain.

"Good morning," she said. "Don't you love Salem in the fall?"

He was tired, late, irritated, and now he had to keep from touching the vision beside him, even as she raised his temperature and stirred his senses. "You're not wearing *that,* are you?"

"If that isn't a typical male—"

"You wouldn't know typical, if it bit you in the butt—"

"Hey, watch it!"

Logan took a calming breath. "Right. Sorry. I haven't been sleeping well," because she was wreaking havoc with his libido twenty-four/seven. "Look, if you really want this job, that getup's probably not—"

"You said I should wear a dress."

"Where did you find it, the attic?"

"The Immortal Classic. Why? Is there another vintage dress shop in town called The Attic?"

"I'm out of my depth, here," Logan said to no one in particular.

"Well, drive, why don't you? I thought you said we were late."

Logan sighed and vowed this was the last time he'd drive her anywhere. "Listen, Mel, Jagger Harrison Gardner, the man who'll probably do the interview, is—"

"More of a tight ass than you are?"

"Succinct, and correct, in one."

"So?"

"I just wanted to be fair and give you one last chance to change your clothes and make a good impression from this side of the century."

Logan watched her brow furrow as she perused her off-beat navy suit. The tight-waisted jacket flared provocatively at her hips, that feminine touch offset by wide padded shoulders and mannish lapels. Though to give her credit, her mouthwatering, alabaster cleavage shot masculine all to hell. The slim, straight skirt, slit to her thigh, ended just above her ankles. Funny, he'd never found ankles alluring before. And did the top of that slit reveal a garter at the edge of one sheer, silk stocking? Ah, hell, now he wouldn't be able to get out of the damned car.

"I love this outfit," she said. "A suit is perfect for an interview, especially this suit for this interview."

Logan gave her as impartial an assessment as he could, given his current physical discomfort. "I like your hair piled on your head like that," he said to turn his thoughts. "But I've never seen anything like that suit before."

"This is a turn-of-the-century walking suit in pristine condition, and I'm not changing, so you may as well go ahead and drive."

"Your funeral."

JAGGER Harrison Gardner, the station's general manager, not so affectionately known as the Ice Man, liked to say he was "a young fifty." He was rich, and he had power, and not a day went by that he didn't remind somebody of the fact.

Logan acknowledged that Gardner was getting his reminder out of the way early this morning, when he waved off the director of human resources and commanded Logan to "stay."

This was going to be an ugly three minutes.

Melody stepped out of the powder room and stopped Gardner cold.

Then again, maybe not.

She flashed that smile of hers—the one calculated to raise male temperatures, and other anatomical parts—as she came toward them and extended her hand. And when Gardner's hand touched hers, Logan could have sworn he heard the sound of ice beginning to crack.

Witch or not, Melody could make magic just by walking into a room.

They followed Gardner to his posh corner office, where he invited them to sit on a white, silk, crescent sectional that curved around a circular glass coffee table.

There, Gardner examined Melody's cleavage for so long, he had to lick his drooling chops. When the older man finally picked up her résumé, Logan gave her a "tough break" look. After all, she'd held seven jobs in the past year.

But the boss tossed the small sheaf back onto the table with no more than a cursory glance.

Wait a minute, Logan thought. Hadn't his own résumé been placed under a microscope?

"Tell me, Miss, er, Seabright," Gardner said. "What makes you feel qualified to host a cooking show?"

Bingo, Logan thought, as he sat back to await her answer.

"Please," Melody said, with a little too much sugar for Logan's palate, "call me Mel." Then she stood and began to pace, swinging her cute little ass, and taking full advantage of that thigh-high slit. The stilettos didn't do her any harm either. She gave his boss an over-the-shoulder glance, using her amazing mink lashes to good advantage, before she turned to face them. "As to my qualifications, Mr. Gardner—"

"Call me Jag."

What? Logan sat straighter.

Melody grinned, first at Gardner, then at Logan, and it was all he could do not to grin back. What was happening to him?

Melody Seabright, that's what.

"Well, Jag, there are any number of factors that contribute to the success of a TV show. I'm photogenic, for one." She gave him a full leg-out-of-the-slit pose to prove it. "And a certain charisma is key, which I believe I have. Showmanship, talent, sincerity, believability, and sex-appeal, are also essential, as is a *gimmick.* Since this is Salem, Massachusetts, I worked up an idea for a show called *The Kitchen Witch.*"

Stopping across the table from them, Melody bent over to tap her résumé with a perfect lavender fingernail, her breasts teetering on the brink of a spillover—pulling out the big guns, so to speak. "As you can see," she practically purred, "I used to work for Bewitched and Bedeviled Tours, during which time, I was required to portray a witch.

"On your own six o'clock news," she stressed, "your anchor reported that I did such a good job, one man swore I had actually bewitched him, and he sued the tour company." She placed her hands on her luscious little hips and gave them a slight quarter turn, just enough to raise the testosterone level in the room to dangerous proportions. "Is that talent, or what?"

"It's a load of crap is what it is," Logan muttered.

"What did you say, Kilgarven?" Gardner asked.

Logan ignored the militant spark in Melody's eyes. She'd heard him clearly enough. "She should be able to cook, too."

"Of course," Melody said, shocked that anyone could doubt her. "Or I could cast a spell." She zapped them with her smile and moved her hands and hips in a swami-like fashion, as she turned in a slow, seductive circle, wielding the wand she'd pulled from her purse.

> "*Abracadabra Melody Bright*
> *Will do what it takes to spice the sauce right*
> *Rosemary, allspice, brandy, and wine,*
> *Do, Mr. Gardner, make the cooking show mine!*"

The wily witch ended in a flourishing bow, cleavage at half mast.

Rattled, Logan ran a hand through his hair.

Gardner gave her a standing ovation. "You'll make a great cooking show host."

"But she can't cook," Logan said, certain that bringing in a noncooking witch to interview for a cooking show was going to come back and bite *him* in the butt.

"I will?" Melody said, as Gardner's words registered. "I got the job?"

Gardner chuckled. "Who could do it better?"

"A cook!" Logan repeated, but who was listening to him?

Three

"I thought about ways we might advertise," Melody said, throwing Logan a chiding look for his last-ditch effort at bringing her cooking skills, or lack thereof, to Gardner's attention. "And I think we could utilize any number of magical phrases, such as: "Culinary Saucery with . . . or Magic in the Kitchen with . . . *The Kitchen Witch.*"

With dollar signs in his eyes, Gardner grinned and rubbed his hands together in agitated anticipation. "I can practically taste syndication. *The Kitchen Witch* out of Salem, Massachusetts." He turned on Logan. "Why didn't you come up with something like this, Kilgarven? Shame on you."

Logan came out of shock with a jolt, as Gardner took Melody's hands, stepped back, and gave her a salivating once-over. "You certainly came well prepared," he said, shaking his head. "But suppose I'd had in mind to cast you as something other than a witch?"

Melody gave him a feline smile, stepped back, pulled a few fan-like combs from her hair, and let the entire mass of black magic tumble in waves to her waist. "Jag," she purred. "I can be anything you want me to be."

Logan could practically see the boss's pupils dilating while the blood in his system took a U-turn.

Ice Man in heat.

After that performance, they'd be nuts to cast Melody as anything but a witch.

"A witch, definitely," Gardner unknowingly echoed. "I'll have your contract drawn right up."

"Before you do . . . Jag," Melody said, with another efficient sweep of her long, dark lashes. "Since the idea is mine, I'd like to retain the rights to the show's name and format, and my persona." She fluffed her hair with laughing exhilaration. "We're gonna make an awesome team."

For a moment, Gardner was struck dumb. "Uh, um . . . the contract." He had so much trouble pulling his gaze from Melody's Rapunzel-like tresses, he nearly walked into the wall.

Three Mile Island had nothing on Melody Seabright.

When the door shut behind Slush-Man, Logan stood.

Melody gave him a smile that turned part of him to pulp, the rest to rock. "I got the job!" she screamed and threw herself into his arms.

Oh, this was nice. This was fine. Logan stroked her back and skimmed a possessive hand along her hip.

She leaned back in his arms, her smile still dazzling. "Well? Say something."

"I'm . . . in shock?"

Melody lost her smile and stepped from his arms. "Especially since you tried to screw me."

Logan wanted her back and despised himself for it. "If I had tried, I'd have succeeded."

"Why Mr. Kilgarven, I do believe you're hiding a streak of wild behind those predictable pinstripes of yours."

If you only knew. "While the soul of a hustler beats

beneath your turn-of-the-century prim." Shane's mother was exactly the same—a sexy shell of coy charm over an empty, hard-as-nails core. Melody was more of a threat, however. Because she had the mesmerizing ability to appear so disarming, one tended to forget her missing heart.

"Don't look now," Logan said. "But you just took a job under false pretenses."

"Bull. I conceived the show myself, every detail, and I earned the job with pure showmanship. Hot damn, I'm good."

"What happens when you can't cook?"

"I'll be such a magical cook, I'll have you begging to taste what I make."

Logan scoffed. "Save the smoke and mirrors for your audience." But she was right. In front of the cameras, showmanship would get her further than cooking skills any day. Except that, when her first meal went down the disposal, and Gardner remembered exactly who recommended her for this interview, Logan's job, and his son's secure future, could end up in the sewer as well.

When Gardner came back with the contract, he named a salary and benefits package that made Melody squeak with joy. And well she should, Logan thought. The package was damned near as good as his own.

Maybe she was a sorceress, after all. Melting an Ice Man was no easy task.

"Just one more thing," Melody said, after she read the contract, and before she signed.

Here comes the deal-breaker, Logan thought. She got away with the rights, but now she was getting greedy and she'd blow the bankroll.

"I'll need Station Day care for my little guy." Her smile went soft. "His name is Shane, and he's four. I checked out your day care center yesterday, teacher credentials and all, so I know it's a top-notch facility."

Logan's jaw went slack, as did Gardner's.

"And will your . . . little guy be coming and going with you?" Gardner asked tightly. "Or with Mr. Seabright?"

"There is no Mr. Seabright," Melody said. "Except my father."

Gardner's tension vanished. "Fine, fine. Let me show you your office."

Humble pie tasted a lot like crow, thought Logan, reeling, blindsided by Melody the quick-change artist, sexiest witch in Salem, as he followed her and Gardner down the hall.

"This is the office," Gardner said. "Even without windows, I don't think it's too bad. What do you think?" Gardner asked Melody, while Logan remained dazed and astonished over the fact that she had arranged day care for Shane.

"Awesome," Melody said.

Logan focused on the office—butterscotch camel-back sofa, honeyed oak tables . . . "Wait, this is my office."

Gardner grinned. "Until the one next door is refurbished, you'll share."

FOUR and a half hours later, Logan watched Melody limp into "their" office. "What happened?" he asked, rising from behind his desk.

"I just took a hundred-mile tour of the station in spikes." She moaned and dropped into the overstuffed, comfortable as hell, butter-soft leather chair, to which he silently bid a fond farewell.

"I must have met every single person who works at WHCH," she groaned. "I even met some guy from one of our affiliates. Westmoreland, I think his name was."

Logan got her a Perrier from the fridge beneath the wet bar and twisted off the cap.

"You're a doll," she said, accepting it and taking a parched sip.

"I'm a man whose been cut off at the . . . office," he responded dryly.

"Your office, I know. Logan, I'm sor—"

He held up a hand. "I'm kidding." He sat across from her and leaned forward. "Lose the heels."

She pushed her spikes off, with a groan for each new ache, and rubbed one foot with the other. "Thanks."

"Give 'em here," Logan said, liking the fact that he'd surprised her. But when he took her feet into his lap to massage them, he was caught off guard, seduced by lavender toenails and a gold toe ring. Damn. Feet were not supposed to be sexy, and his reaction only got worse as he massaged them, because she moaned, and wiggled, and sighed . . . in ecstasy, damn it. She even squeaked a couple of times from somewhere deep in her throat, a sound that sent sparks straight to "the big guy." Logan imagined that she might sound something like that if he were deep inside her and—

"Lord, I'm in heaven," she said, closing her eyes, in rapture once more. "I may never move from this spot."

In heaven himself, or maybe it was hell, Logan wouldn't be moving anytime soon either, but for a different reason. If he hadn't been sure before, he knew now that having Melody around twenty-four/seven would make for the kind of stimulation he'd once lived for, sought out at every turn, the kind he should be running from, far and fast.

"I can't wait to tell Shane I got the job," she said, rushing Logan up for air as quick as she'd dragged him under, giving him a good case of the bends with the jolting reminder of his goals and responsibilities. Damned straight, she'd be a distraction, the kind he did not, repeat, did not, need, a sizzling, confusing disturbance with both an enervating and an energizing effect on him. Hell, she was a regular bunny with boundless batteries as far as his libido was concerned.

But just when he thought he had her pegged, when she'd proved that, like Heather, she'd use sex for her own selfish benefit, she'd gone and got Shane into day care.

Did she knowingly use sex? Even now, with her eyes closed and her features serene, she seemed oblivious to everything around her. Yet he was caught, immobilized, captured by the sight of her—body riding low, skirt riding high, bare feet in his happy lap, proving, without question, the existence of stockings and a garter belt . . . a navy one.

In a bid for sanity, Logan called her name and waited for her to look at him before speaking. When she did, her topaz eyes guileless and wide with innocence, he took a breath to keep from drowning in their seductive depths and tried to remember what he wanted to say.

Oh, yes. "Sharing my office is nothing compared to what you did for me and Shane," he said, rubbing a thumb over her toe ring. "I can't believe you got him into day care, even researched it. I honestly don't know how to thank—"

"Don't thank me until we figure out what to do about him calling me Mel, and you Dad."

Logan grinned and massaged a beautifully sculpted arch. "I thought about that while you were gone. We can drive in together," he said, rescinding his earlier avowal, for his son's sake, never to do so again, "and split up in the garage. You can walk Shane to day care, and I'll come right up. At the end of the day, we can reverse our route. Shane won't expect anything different, because I'll be driving."

"And if somebody hears him call me Mel?"

"Pull them aside and tell them you want him to outgrow that stage at his own pace."

"Clever, and devious."

"Not really," Logan said, thinking the words applied to him in at least one discomforting way. But did they apply to her? "Day care service should be mine by rights," he went on. "We're just picking our battles."

An hour later, Logan chuckled as they drove from the station parking garage, while the boss stood beside his own car watching them. "Man," Logan said, "he's gonna hate himself when his T-level goes down and he realizes he let you walk away with the rights to the show." He gave her a wink. "I gotta tell you," he said. "That took *cajones*."

"High praise." Melody grinned. "What part of the interview do you think got me the job?" she asked. "The incantation, maybe?"

Logan nearly drove off the road. "So, the spell was real?"

Melody did a double take. "You got a problem with spells, Kilgarven?"

He shrugged. "Can you spell your way into a job?"

Melody laughed. "I'm here to tell you that I can spell my way out of one."

So, Logan thought, maybe the incantation had been nothing but a ploy to derail cooking questions, not that she would ever admit as much to him.

"I don't mind admitting," she said, "that I had an easier time coming up with the show's name and format than I did finding something to rhyme with *mine* that made sense. Even then, the charm was lame. But I think it might have done the trick."

"Mine," Logan said. "Twine. Entwine." He gave her a dangerously searching look. "Entwine your limbs with mine?"

After a long, hot beat, he looked back at the road, sorry he'd opened that mixed bag of magic tricks, glad she didn't have the *cajones* to respond this time, because she looked as if she might be up for it. Oh boy.

"It does rhyme," she said after a pulsing minute, "but it's not what I was going for, interview-wise."

"Sure it was. Bewitchment, seduction—they're exactly what you were going for, just a bit more subtle. Gardner's gonna take you up on that invitation, by the way."

"You son of a— Stop the car! Stop, I'm getting out."

Caught off guard by her fury, Logan reached out to try and keep her from unhooking her seat belt. "I'm sorry. Truce. Truce," he said.

Logan swung into the Hawthorne Hotel parking lot to calm her and clear up the misunderstanding without getting into an accident. "Mel, Mel." He unhooked his own seat belt and took her fumbling hands from the latch on hers, then he removed her grasp from the door handle and finally hit the child-proof locks.

At the resounding click, Melody stopped struggling, almost, but not quite, conceding defeat, her breath coming as fast as her fury. "Do you really think I would . . . that I would? . . ."

"No. I realize the way that must have sounded, but it's not what I meant," Logan said. "It's just that I know the drill." He moved close enough to smell springtime, reminding himself that for women like Melody and Shane's mother, revving up and putting out were two entirely different matters. "You were just using your assets, playing to Gardner, nothing more, and I know that. I even appreciate your talent, but I'm warning you that he might not be as wise to the ploy as I am," because Heather had used him, not Gardner, for "tease" practice. "I wasn't saying you'd follow through," Logan added. "Honest."

Melody stilled and took a breath, as if she might or might not believe him. "I don't know what you mean by 'the ploy,'" she said, "but I don't think you have a very good opinion of me. Fine. That's your choice, and I've been warned. But you know what, Kilgarven? Just because I look like . . . I do . . . doesn't mean I'm missing a brain. You have talent, you use it to get a job. That's the way it goes. I got a job on a TV show by using some damn fine showmanship. So sue me, but stop looking down your nose at me for using what I've been given."

That bit of wisdom worked like a stun gun, probably because she made sense, which made Logan feel like a jerk, which he deserved. The fact remained that she couldn't cook, but this was not the time to bring it up. "You're right," he said. "Again, I'm sorry."

"Listen," she said, poking him in the chest, still carrying a furious head of steam. "One: Assets can sometimes double as liabilities. Remember that. Two: The drill, if that's what you want to call it, was me demonstrating how I would use sex-appeal on the show, and if Gardner got confused, then I'll straighten him out."

Oh, she'd straighten him out all right, Logan thought. That was the problem.

"Three: I'm going to have to be able to work with that man, a lot of men, without you getting all bent out of shape."

"I know." Logan shook his head. "I'll be cool from now on. Scout's honor."

"Were you a scout?"

"Sure." *Until they threw me out.*

WHEN they pulled into the driveway, Shane came running over to the car from Jessie's. "Hey, Mel, wanna come to my pirate cave picnic next Saturday to watch the tall ships come in? You don't have to cook or anything, but if you want to, I can help."

Melody ruffled Shane's hair. "Thanks, buddy." She turned to Logan. "You're going to watch the ships from a cave?"

Logan supposed he should be sorry that Shane had taken it upon himself to invite Melody, but an imprudent, adventurous part of him wanted to spend time with her, too. Working side by side, driving into work together should be temptation enough, he supposed, without hanging together on the weekends, but Shane had asked. "We practically front Salem Harbor," he said, "so with a pair of binoculars, we should be able to see the ships after they clear Winter Island and before Marblehead gets in the way. Better than fighting the tourists."

"The pirate cave is nearby?"

"That's what he calls our turret." Logan pointed to the top of their old Victorian. "I haven't been able to convince him that a cave isn't likely to be surrounded by windows." Logan stepped closer to Melody, as Shane followed something hopping in the grass back toward Jessie's. "I won't let him go up alone, because there's a door to the widow's walk up there. Even with it locked, the thought of him having access to the roof makes me crazy. What do you think about me using a leash on him, Saturday?"

Melody grinned, which was Logan's intent, and a nice change from the mood of their ride home. "Seriously," he said, "it'll be a fine vantage point. Watching the ships make their way toward Boston Harbor gave me the perfect excuse for a supervised pirate cave picnic. Join us."

"I don't want to crash your party, besides I won't know anyone else there."

"Just Jessie, me, Shane, and my mother. It'll be fun. Come on."

"In that case, it does sound like fun. I love the tall ships, and I've never been up in the turret. Can I bring something for lunch?"

"Just your appetite. My mother's in charge of the picnic. She's a great cook."

"As opposed to me?"

"I didn't mean that. Look, just to make you feel better, I'll be first in line to sample what you cook during your run-through in a couple of days."

* * *

"PIGS wouldn't eat this slop."

Logan heard the comment as he stepped onto the set after he'd missed Mel's preliminary run-through.

Gardner stood with his hands on his hips looking a bit dazed. "Where's the black cat I got for a walk-on?" he asked. "I think the poor thing ate some."

"Hey?" Chuck yelled into a headset. "Anybody see a dead pussy?"

Silence, and the acrid scent of smoke, hung in the air like a pall, and everywhere Logan looked, somebody was cleaning a mess. The oven door hung open at such an odd slant, Logan was afraid to ask what happened. He *knew* he shouldn't have met with the Nutty-Yum people today. He should have cleared his calendar and been here for Melody. Speaking of whom . . . "Where's Mel?" he asked. "Anybody seen Melody?" he shouted.

"Can't have gone far," said the soundman through the mike. "Broom's still here."

"Cute," Logan said, running his hand through his hair. "But is she all right? She didn't get hurt, did she?"

"Relax, Logan, she's fine, maybe a bit upset."

"Upset? Why?"

The guy shrugged. "Because her chicken exploded?"

Four

"HER chicken *exploded?*" Logan looked around, waiting for someone to explain, but nobody did. Wait a minute. Chickens didn't just explode. Though with Mel, you couldn't be sure. "What the hell happened here anyway? And why are you all hanging around? Doesn't anybody have work to do?"

"Hey, Logan, come see this," Gardner called, with a laugh. Poor guy hadn't refrozen properly since Melody came on board.

Logan went to find the boss examining the remains of . . . damn, that might actually have been a chicken. "Son of a—" Logan bent on his haunches to get a better look. "What in the world? Hey, somebody shoved a firecracker up this bird's butt! Okay, who's the wise guy?"

Tim Kaiser came over. "This was *supposed* to be Mel's initiation, Logan."

"You mean like when you locked me in the shower? That kind of initiation? Do you initiate everybody?"

"Only the people we like."

"Lucky Mel." Logan ran a hand through his hair. "What did she do when the clucker blew?" Damn. He was starting to find this funny, which would not be a good thing, if Melody didn't.

"She ran off the set."

"Couldn't you have initiated her another way?"

"Hell, Logan, we didn't think you'd like us to lock her in the shower with, say, Hal or Woody."

"Good thinking." His people already knew he had the hots for her, though *she* hadn't seemed to figure it out yet. "I'll go and look for her."

He found Melody in their office, lights off, face down on the sofa, and sat beside her to stroke her hair. She purred like a kitten, raising his temperature, urging him on. Neither of them spoke.

Just sitting in the dark, running his hand along her witch's mane of sable curls felt erotic as all hell, never mind that stroking it lured him all the way down its incredible length to the curve of her fine bottom beneath . . . and he was a lowlife, getting hard when he should be consoling her.

"I like that," she said.

Wonderful. "Me, too." She had obviously no idea how much, which was another puzzle; Heather would have known and used the knowledge to her advantage. Logan shook his head, grateful he sat in shadows too dim for her to see either his confusion or his physical reaction.

"Gardner doesn't have the *cajones* to fire me, himself, does he?" Melody asked in a small, pathetic voice.

"He doesn't, actually, but I'm not here to fire you, so you can stop feeling sorry for yourself. I should probably fire the crew, though."

Melody raised herself on an elbow. "The crew? Why?"

Logan tried not to show his amusement. "For stuffing a firecracker up your chicken's butt."

One minute she was lying down, the next she was standing over him hauling him to his feet by his necktie. "What did you say?"

"Hey, you're choking me."

"Your crew did what?"

"Mel." Logan pried her hands free and loosened his tie. "They want to be your crew, too. That's why they played the joke on you. They want to be friends."

"Are they insane?"

"Think of this as similar to when a little boy puts a snake inside the desk of the girl he likes."

"You know, I'm glad I wasn't born in this town. You're all kind of spooky."

"Well you'd better go out there and show my fellow spooks that you can take a joke, or life's going to get pretty dull around here." Logan switched on the light, and his heart tripped when he saw that she had been crying. Without a thought, he opened his arms and she stepped in, which he liked, except that he liked it too much, especially the way she folded herself into him, as if he were all the protection she needed. Oh boy. For both their sakes, Logan relaxed his hold and took a half-step back, but Melody followed and clung.

Not good. "You want me to go and make everything better?" he asked, baiting her to let go, half-hoping she'd hold on.

She buried her face in his shirt and nodded.

He raised her chin, so he could see her. "Will the real Melody Seabright come out fighting?"

"Don't." She batted his arm. "I'm . . . fragile."

As an army tank. "I don't know why you'd think you screwed up, you being such a great cook and all."

With a gasp, her head came up.

"Gotcha!" Logan crowed.

Hands flat on his chest, Melody pushed him away. "Rat!"

"That's my girl. Now go fix those raccoon eyes, and we'll go back to the set. The gang is waiting to welcome you, officially." As she went to do his bidding, Logan looked down at his white shirt, at the splotches of black eye makeup on it, and rolled his eyes.

"I gotta like this, right?" she called from the private bathroom attached to their office. "I mean, I'm not supposed to smack anybody around, am I?"

"We all go through it, Mel." Logan heard the echo of his words and knew he'd opened a bag of tricks better left sealed. Damn.

"What did they do to you?" she called a couple seconds later.

Logan considered a bald-faced lie. In the end, he chose a partial truth. "They locked me in the shower."

Melody came out with a perplexed look on her face and an open lipstick in her hand. "You can't lock a shower."

"No, but you can set up a barrier to keep the door from opening."

"So . . . what?" she asked, closing the long slender tube and tossing it on her desk. "Did you spend the night in the shower?"

"A couple of hours." They started down the hall side by side.

"In a shower? Alone? Glory, all you could do in a—" Melody stopped walking. "Wait a minute. You weren't alone, were you? Guys who'd blow up a chicken wouldn't lock you in a shower alone. How much fun could that be?"

Logan kept going and didn't answer.

Melody followed him toward the set, waiting for him to elaborate, and when he remained suspiciously silent, she almost laughed. "What was her name, Logan?"

Still no answer.

"I'll take that as a memory we don't want to share," she

said as she passed him by, making sure he couldn't see her smile.

When she got to the set, half the crew stood milling about, looking as forlorn as if someone had swiped the last beer.

She'd ruined their gag, stolen their laugh track. Now how was she supposed to— "Hey, I heard there was a chicken down here, needed mouth to mouth."

Nothing.

"Somebody wanna' razz me?" she said. "Go ahead. I can take it." But only silence and long faces greeted her. Logan was right, if she didn't handle this, life on the job would become too boring for words, in which case she might have to cast a few spells for kicks. No wait, spells were good—they could add color and depth to the show, providing she had a crew.

"Listen, guys, I appreciate that you wanted to . . . um . . . welcome me to the station and all. I'm flattered. Incredibly. And, okay, the gag was cute, funny even. Poor chicken. Ha ha. But let's get something straight right now. In the future, anybody comes near *me* with a firecracker, I'm out'a here!"

They cracked, broke into laughter. Whew. Melody didn't know what she would have done if they hadn't. Some of them even applauded. She acknowledged the compliment with a theatrical bow, and while she had their attention, she raised her hands for silence. "One last thing. Who'll be my bud and tell me who got locked in the shower with Kilgarven during his initiation?"

"That was Nikky from Human Resources," Chuck yelled.

Ah, camaraderie. Nothin' like it. Melody turned to share the moment with Logan, but he was walking away, shaking his head.

"Hey," Tim added. "Don't forget that Logan and Nik

didn't come out for nearly two hours, even though we freed 'em in one."

Glory, what'd they do, clock 'em? "When was that?" Melody asked.

"A few weeks ago, just after Logan started," Woody said.

"Yeah," Tim added. "Nikky's still smiling."

As the chuckling crew returned to cleaning the mess they had caused, Gardner came up behind her and placed his hand a little too firmly on the small of her back. Melody stepped away.

"They meant well," he said.

"Yeah. They were kind of sweet, I guess."

He checked his watch. "Workday's over. Need a lift?"

"Thanks, anyway, Jag, but I've got stuff to do on the show."

She did have some details to look over, so did Logan, and as much as she wanted to know about the episode with Nikky, Melody kept her mouth shut while they worked at their separate desks in companionable silence for almost an hour.

More than once during that time, she thanked the stars for her luck. With her lemon chicken blown to smithereens, nobody had to taste it. Now she would have more time to practice. She also thought that Logan had been a surprisingly good sport, for a stuffed suit, both with her initiation and his own. Not for a minute could she imagine her father putting up with any of it.

When she shut down her computer and began putting things away, Logan slammed a hand on his desk. "Damn it," he said. "I can't stand the pressure. Grill me and get it over with. You wore me down. Ask me about my initiation. About Nikky. Go ahead; ask me anything. I'll tell you whatever you want to know."

Melody chuckled as she stood and opened the bottom drawer of her desk. "Like father like son. Easy marks, the both of you. Remind me not to waste my money on thumb-screws. You didn't even need chocolate chip cookies." She pulled out her purse and shut the drawer. "Thanks anyway, but if I want to know, I'll ask Nikky." She slung her bag over her shoulder. "Finished Shane's paperwork?" she asked, taking it from his desk and looking it over. "I need to drop it off in day care. Meet you in the garage in ten minutes."

FRIDAY began a lot like the day of Melody's interview. Logan knocked on her ridiculous purple door, again, and Melody wasn't ready, again. This time, however, she told him to come in. When he did, she shoved a huge boxy garment bag into his arms. "Take this to the car, will you? Then come back for that big brocade bag over there, but be careful, because the zipper's busted."

She was bossy, all right, but when she was wearing that red Capri suit, he'd carry *her,* if she told him to, and her garment bag as well. "When did I get demoted to bellhop?" He groused on principle, so she wouldn't take him for granted.

"Blame Gardner," she said. "He wants to see some of the specialized outfits I'll be wearing on the show. You have no idea what a chore it was to gather all the necessary underwear for these things."

"I would have been happy to help. You should have called."

"Let me guess," Melody said. "The Victoria's Secret Catalog is prime reading material in your house."

Logan heaved a sigh, heavy with regret. "Not since Shane moved in."

"Yeah, well, life's a bitch."

Logan left with his arms full and a grin on his face, charmed despite himself. "Hey Shane," he called from the bottom of the stairs. "Step on it."

Wired in anticipation of his first day of day care, Shane played twenty questions all the way to the station. Then the chatterbox gave Logan a stranglehold neck hug and a kiss on his ear before getting out of the car with Melody.

Logan appreciated the silence after that, despite the touch of anxiety he was feeling over his son's new adventure. Though he would be close by, compared to when Shane stayed at Jessie's, Logan knew his son was feeling some anxiety of his own, and Logan wished he could protect him from all of it.

THE minute his dad's car disappeared from sight, Shane bit his lip and looked up at Melody, his fear as clear as the deep blue eyes—his father's eyes—through which he looked to her for support.

Melody wondered what she thought she was doing. Another in a long line of nonmaternal women, she barely remembered her jet-setting female parent who had likened motherhood to a nightmare. But when Shane shivered and swallowed as if his throat had closed, Melody knew her fears were nothing compared to his.

Poor baby; he was waging a battle between bravery and fear, anticipation and dread. She knew exactly how he felt. If he cried, she'd sit right down and cry with him, except that he needed her to be strong. Their hands met midreach, and she bent and pulled him into her arms—so tiny, so . . . in need of protection . . . and all he had was her, poor thing. "I'm here, buddy."

"I know, Mel."

"Do you know how lucky you are?" she asked. "Day care is wicked cool."

He tried to contain his shiver. "*Wicked* cool?"

"Um hmm." His bravery gave Melody the strength to rise, take his hand, and begin walking him down the hall.

"Eighteen children about your age are waiting to meet you, you lucky boy." She wished her voice wasn't shaking. "You're gonna have a blast while your Dad and I slave away upstairs."

"Where, upstairs?"

"Right above you, two floors up. Mrs. Williams will call if you need me—there's an elevator straight to day care, and I'll be down before you can count to ten."

"I can count fast. Will you be close enough? Dad, too?"

"Promise."

Shane slowed when he saw a little girl kiss her mother good-bye, and he dropped Melody's hand to wrap his arm around her legs. "I don't like getting dropted off."

Melody cupped his little head and felt his shiver run through her. "I don't gotta live here, right?" he asked, looking earnestly up at her.

Melody squeaked and knelt once more, pulling him close. "Of course not. You live with your Dad. Nothing's changed, except Jessie gets to give Boneyard Tours during the day, and you get to play with kids who don't need liniment afterward."

As if on cue, a dozen or so children spilled into a glassed-in playroom. "Look at that," Melody said. "They're having fun already."

Shane took it all in, and when laughter erupted, he nodded and straightened. "Look, Mel, it's filled with all my new friends that I haven't met yet."

Melody's tears hovered so near, she could taste salt. "Yes, darling, it is. You can meet them as soon as you're ready."

Shane nodded and squared his shoulders. "Okay," he said, raising his chin. "Let's go meet them."

IT wasn't until Logan pulled into his parking space that he realized he'd been left to fetch and carry enough luggage for a European jaunt. He got out of the car swearing. He'd be damned if he'd make two trips just to haul a load of Mel's fluff.

After several aborted attempts, he finally managed to carry everything at one time, aware that his struggle was nothing short of pigheaded.

In the garage elevator, he lost his grip on one of the bags, caught it, and wrestled the damned thing up and under his arm. God help Mel when she got to the office, because he was going to be setting down some rock-solid rules for the future.

When the elevator opened on his floor, Logan heaved a sigh. Almost there. *Just a hall and a half to go,* he thought as he trudged on.

"Hey Hansel, where's Gretel?"

Logan was halfway through the partitioned secretarial offices, when the wiseass remark forced him to consider the smiles he'd been getting. He stopped and turned in the direction from which he'd come . . . and saw the trail he'd left behind. A freaking rainbow of bras, bikinis, stockings, even a pair of G-string bikinis—a treasure trove of man's favorite playthings—littered the floor behind him. "Damn!"

Tim Kaiser stopped at the opposite end of the trail. "Way to call a meeting, man. Cool. Do we get to keep the crumbs?"

"Shut up and help me pick this up."

Six men dove for the goodies. On second thought— "Don't touch!" Logan shouted.

A cumulative groan rose from the station's male population.

"Tim," Logan snapped. "Come and get this damned garment bag and take it to my office. The rest of you, back to work."

With more than a few wistful looks and a great deal of speculation, his eager helpers drifted away.

Retracing his steps and clearing his trail took Logan an agony of scorching minutes. When he finally bent on his haunches to pick up the last of the crumbs, a man-skewing black lace teddy, the elevator beside him opened and a pair of choice legs, feet encased in red spikes, stepped out and stopped before him, and Logan primed himself for battle.

"You kinky little devil," said the wicked witch of the east, spiking his guns.

Nearby, a gaffer with a death wish chuckled.

Five

"NOT a good time to push, Melody," Logan said as he rose, juggling a brimming tapestry bag and a black merry widow.

She dangled a pale gold bra before him. "I knew you were in trouble when I saw my favorite under-wire sticking out the elevator door in day care."

Logan snatched it from her hand and stuffed it into his breast pocket. "Shane settle in okay? I was worried."

"You weren't alone, but he'd already made a friend by the time I left."

"Have you been crying?"

"Nah."

"You sure he's okay?"

Melody's smiled blossomed. "He's great."

"Thank God." With a relieved sigh, Logan ran a hand through his hair and caught a garter in the nose. Reminded of the spectacle he presented, he swore.

"I *told* you the zipper was busted."

Logan noticed, in his peripheral vision, a curious throng hovering just out of range. To keep them from hearing, he got up close and personal, and his body jumped to attention, aggravating him the more. "Just hustle your sweet little ass down the hall and into the office," he said. "Do not say a word. Do not pass go. Do not collect $200."

"Aye, aye—"

"One more word . . ."

Mel shut her mouth. Lucky for her, she knew when to fold.

Side by side, they walked, she as sedate as could be, while he carried the large bag of heavy-duty lingerie strategically placed before him.

Both of them nodded and smiled to the people they met along the way . . . until Melody leaned close. "I gotta tell you, Kilgarven, that bra in your pocket really pops with navy pinstripes, but when you trip over the garter belt dangling from that bag, you're not gonna look half so dignified."

AN hour later, Logan was still fuming. Did Melody simply stumble on trouble, or did she suck adversity up like Super-Magnet? He was beginning to think that he would find her picture next to *loose cannon* in the dictionary.

Man, if the office grapevine didn't spontaneously combust today, it never would. Half the staff had watched the sexy witch and her erotic assortment turn him into the kinky devil she considered him . . . horny.

He had never been as humiliated, or stimulated, over anything in his life, and he couldn't seem to release the volcano of frustrated ire boiling inside him. He might have, if he'd been given the satisfaction of strangling Melody after their erotic parade, but the opportunity had not presented itself.

Then again, he could be arrested for what he really wanted to do to her. Logan sighed in self-disgust. Hard to believe that he had come to pride himself on his impeccable reputation as a serious businessman, as a man in control . . . until Melody Seabright had opened her door and turned him into a ticking time bomb of thundering testosterone.

Time to vent might at least have helped him get over the flaming humiliation, but no, when they got to their office, who did they find but Gardner waiting for them.

Seeing the boss had prompted Logan to snatch the yellow bra from his pocket and shove the male-thrumming wisp into the brocade bag. Then he grabbed the red garter belt Melody had kindly rescued before it tripped him and deposited the bawdy hoard into their bathroom. The Ice Man did not need another meltdown. His libido had already cost the station a fortune in residuals.

God knew, Mel's outfits were turn-on enough; nobody should have to suffer the added discomfort of knowing what she wore beneath them. Her fashion show had long since begun and as if to prove his thoughts, she came out modeling yet another seductive little number for Gardner's lecherous perusal.

Logan's heart sped, his palms sweat. Yes, he was a lecher as well, a frustrated one. He'd seen and touched, even inhaled the perfume on most of the gossamer and lace that caressed every hidden inch of Melody's soft, porcelain skin.

He bit back an oath and shifted in his seat. If he had a modicum of self-respect, he would leave the room, the station, maybe take a job in another country. He might have to sign into a detox center, though, or be locked away for good, to get Melody Seabright out of his simmering blood.

But Logan didn't make a move, not to stand and leave, nor even to turn his head. He didn't so much as bat an eye, because he didn't want to miss one incredible moment of Melody's scintillating fashion show—no matter the cost to his pride and self-respect, never mind his poor deprived body.

Maybe he was a masochist, sitting here anticipating more of her fascinating torture. He must be sick, letting himself be titillated by the array, imagining the possibilities—like sticking your fingers into a light socket, again and again, just to test the buzz and relive the zap.

He should put some space between them before he was lost for good. So what if his son adored her? So what if she'd solved his day care problem? Shane needed stability and security, neither of which Logan could equate with Melody Seabright.

Look what she did to him. She morphed him—despite his best efforts to remain unaffected—tempted him to disgraceful behavior, and had him coming back for more. One look from her, and he lost his grasp on the staid and practical executive producer he'd worked so hard to become, and became that bad-boy troublemaker from the tenements again.

Man, he hated that. He'd been slapped with too many reminders of his failures over the years. He didn't need any more.

Bad enough his mother insisted on staying in the tenements, though he could now afford to get her something better, like a house or condo of her own. Bad enough he was the one who'd turned her into a workaholic in the first place—stealing from a convenience store at twelve years old, no less—to the point that he couldn't get her to stop working. Now here's Melody with the ability to knock him back on his ass as well.

Logan didn't know which of them was worse, Mel or his mother, but his mother, he had to keep around.

MELODY felt the stab of Logan's penetrating gaze like pins in a voodoo doll. He hadn't so much as blinked at the twenties flapper dress she'd modeled, or the fifties strapless, and they looked awesome.

Big deal, carrying her clothes into the station had caused him embarrassment. Sure, he was pissed. He had a right. But get over it, already. His anger, she discovered she could handle, but his disinterest bothered her a great deal—more than it should, she supposed. Like she wanted anything to do with another pin-striped tight ass.

Nevertheless, Melody stepped directly in front of Logan and nudged his foot with the toe of her forties platform shoe, until he looked up and "saw" her.

"Tell me what you think of this one," she said, drawing his gaze by rotating her hips close enough for her polka dots to cross his eyes.

No comment. She'd gotten his attention, though. That tick in his cheek was a dead giveaway.

Melody moved a straight chair to the center of the room.

As much to snap him out of his snit as to reveal the surprise at the front of her dress, she raised a foot, placed it on the chair seat, and leaned in. On cue, the dress slid open, front and center, to reveal her bent leg to her thigh, her shoe's three-inch heels and thin ankle straps, adding pure sex to the pose.

Logan paled and swallowed.

And that's what you get for sulking, Melody thought. "This is a shirtwaist designed by St. Laurent in the seventies," she said, "to reflect the style of the forties. I think red polka dots on black fits the show perfectly and might work for the pilot. The unique style sends a subliminal, "Watch me make magic," kind of message.

Gardner rose and walked around her, examining her from every angle. "There's a lot I like about this one, though it doesn't have the same allure as that straight black dress with the foot of beaded fringe at the hem."

"The flapper dress, you mean." Melody turned to Logan,

pleased to note that he had not taken his gaze from her. "What do you think?" she asked.

Logan shook off his trance and loosened his tie. "Who knew that polka dots could be so . . . so—"

"I know," Mel said, unable to stifle her grin. "Kind of snappy, kind of understated. Lively, you know, without being . . . fluorescent."

Finally, she'd set Logan's smile free, and God what an improvement. He sat forward, in the game again. "I don't expect we'd want all black, or all dresses for that matter," he said, not seeming to expect an answer, but more to clarify his thoughts. "I don't think uniformity of any kind would fit our flamboyant witch." His wink made Melody feel worlds better. Then he stretched his legs, crossed them at the ankles, and slid his hands into his pockets. "That flapper dress, by the way, would better suit a show where you prepare something formal—say, a New Year's Eve dinner party."

"Excellent," Melody said, surprised and impressed.

"But if we're talking pilot, here," Gardner added. "And market-testing the audience, I don't think we want off-the-wall flash, either, not yet. Give us another turn-around, will you, Mel?"

Melody did two slow turns, and given their twin expressions, she knew that Logan and Gardner had stopped examining her as men but were now regarding her with an eye toward audience appeal and ratings.

"That's the dress," Logan said with the air of a man who's aware he's made a good decision. "For my money, that number is first-show, secure-the-market perfect."

"Agreed," Gardner said looking pleased. "Melody, my little witch, you're a natural. Now all we have to do is find a theme song." He checked his watch. "Listen, I've got a lunch appointment, and I won't be back afterward, but thanks for the fashion show, Mel. You helped me with another idea. See you both on Monday. Have a great weekend."

"Another idea?" Logan said as he watched Gardner walk down the hall. "He means another fantasy."

"Fantasy?" Melody responded from beside him. "You're talking about his reflection in the mirror, right?"

Logan turned a raised brow her way. "I'm impressed. You already have him pegged." Then he gave himself a symbolic slap upside the head. "What am I talking about? You had him pegged before you met him. How did you know that a stage production interview would work?"

Melody shrugged. "One: I was applying for a stage production. Two: He's a man, so I tried to stimulate his male . . . thinking."

"You *were* playing up to him, but you got upset when I said so."

"Because you implied that I'd put out to get the job."

Logan winced. "I didn't, but forget I brought it up." He stepped near enough to enslave her with the sexy, spicy scent of him and shook his head. "Let me tell you again how sorry I am for giving you that impression." He seemed so earnest, so . . . He made her forget everything except some deep-seated need inside her to touch him, something primitive and almost, but not quite, stronger than her will to resist.

Their eyes met, and held, as if he sensed her struggle. She wished he'd open his hand and cup her cheek, lean in and touch his sculpted lips to hers. She wanted him to give her a reason, any reason, to touch him back.

When he did, finally, lean close, Melody's heart tripped, and her insides pulsed in anticipation. Then he grinned, his eyes crinkling with mischief, shattering the taut thread of need inside her, distancing them without separating them, and Melody was grateful.

"Care to tell me which of those soft, skimpy little numbers you're wearing under there?" he asked with a sexy rasp that might have turned her weak at the knees, if she weren't so shocked by the question.

With a gasp, she stepped back and shook her head, denying the request, marveling over the kind of teasing that did not fit her pinstriped image of him, though it unnerved her in a new and different way. He had best not step out of stuffed-shirt mode too often, she thought, too close to caving for her own good.

"I've already seen everything," Logan coaxed.

"Not while I was wearing it, you didn't."

"Hey, I'm willing." The tension eased with Logan's laugh, but Melody was left off balance and wanting. "I'm ready," he said.

Me, too, she thought, stepping away. "Sorry about my booby-trapped bag," she said, going for safer ground.

"Booby-trapped is right." Logan went to pour a lime seltzer and offer it to her. When she shook her head, he sipped it thoughtfully. "It wasn't your fault, not really. You did tell me the zipper was broken."

"Truce, then?" she asked.

"Sure . . . if you tell me whether you're wearing the red or the black—"

"In your dreams, Kilgarven."

"Right," he said. "Definitely. Can't blame a guy for trying, though. How about lunch?"

"I can't," Melody said, pondering his response. Definitely? Was he dreaming about her the way she had been dreaming about him? She grinned, her spirits uplifted by the possibility. "Sorry, I already have a lunch date."

Logan raised a brow. "Okayyy."

"Don't you want to know who I'm lunching with?"

He turned to shuffle the papers on his desk, pretending disinterest, Melody thought. "Your dates are your business," he said.

"Big of you."

He stopped and gave her a cocky grin. "Hey, I'm a big guy. Anytime you want proof . . ."

"Proof, I can get elsewhere."

That threw him.

Her turn to smile. "I'm lunching with Nikky."

"Shit!"

MELODY did not return before Logan closeted himself in with Max Peabody, the station owner, and his daughter Tiffany, an educated, cultured young woman with a calm, finishing school polish. A perfect turn of events, Logan thought. He needed a new focus, and an education major could be just the ticket.

Logan gave Tiffany a genuine smile and listened to her enthusiastic, if entry-level ideas on how to promote *The Kitchen Witch.*

It didn't bother him that Melody had a lunch date. He wouldn't care if she said she dated one of the crew, but the fact that she planned to swap stories with Nik had thrown him. Sure, he and Nik had shared a blazing, mutually agreeable, no-strings . . . hot and sweaty bout of sex. Okay, so several bouts, which only revealed a healthy sex drive on both their parts. No problem, no looking back. Melody should try it sometime. Several times. With him. Hey, Nik might be piquing Mel's interest right now. Logan grinned.

Tiffany bristled just enough to draw his attention.

"What?" Logan said.

His mind had been drifting while she had been talking. Oops. Logan hoped he'd at least kept her in his sights.

Hey, what was with the gleam in Max's eye?

"So," Tiffany said. "You'll come, then?"

"Sure . . . but you'll have to remind me of the details closer to the date." Logan took a chance with ambiguity . . . and got away with it, apparently.

He didn't know what his problem was. Peabody's daughter was attractive and available. She seemed honestly to enjoy his company, and she must like children, or she wouldn't have studied early childhood education. Logan figured he should take her out for his son's sake, if not for his own, but he couldn't seem to come to the point of asking.

Perhaps he could start slow and offer to walk her to the elevator, but he kept blanking on her name. Once, he nearly called her Melody.

As the meeting dragged, Logan's gaze strayed to the clock more often than it should. Not that he was anxious to see Mel; he just wanted to know what Nik said.

As it happened, finding out had to wait, because the next time he saw Mel, she was standing in the parking garage, outside day care, Shane's hand in hers.

They looked good, as if they belonged together, her and Shane, laughing and chatting, and he was an idiot, Logan thought. Melody would never stay around for the long haul. She was made of glitz and sparkle, bright as magic itself, smoke and mirrors, a flash in the pan.

His son was simply enjoying the show. Any kid would.

Mel was like a sea squall—made of nothing but air, but mighty powerful all the same.

Tiffany was more like a spring day, a staying kind of woman, smart, nurturing, stable, a keeper. Tiffany would make a good mother, a good . . . wife? Logan guessed he'd have to think about that.

Okay, so maybe he enjoyed Melody's magic as much as Shane did. She was sweet, her laugh a treat, but she was also flighty, unable to hold a job, flashy, feisty . . . habit forming . . . and Shane adored her. Logan shook his head as he stopped the car in front of them.

If he thought Shane had been talkative that morning, his early energy hardly compared to the enthusiastic, ongoing monologue he delivered on the way home. Craig, Scott, and Torrie were the names his son repeated most often. They had welcomed him into their exalted circle and taught him any number of new and exciting "games," not all of which pleased Logan.

Shane was especially proud of the fact that they had gotten away with playing while they were supposed to be napping.

At a red light, Logan looked into the rearview mirror and made eye contact with his loquacious son, the sight of him, happy and easy going, still new enough to be a source of pride and not a little gratitude. "Guess you had a good time today, sport."

Shane beamed. "It was bitchin', Dad."

Six

THE word *bitchin'* echoed in the silence, and Logan slid his gaze toward Melody without turning his head, as if such a word from the mouth of a four-year-old did not make him want to jump the seat, shut down the car, and stunt Shane's formative years. Damn it, he didn't know the first thing about being a father.

Melody turned to look out her window, but not before Logan caught her grin. "You're a big help," he muttered.

Her only response was a muffled squeak.

"This is serious," he said.

"Everything with you is."

"What's that supposed to mean?"

"It means, lighten up." Melody nodded toward the back-seat, and Logan checked his rearview mirror only to find his son playing a palm-sized video game, as if he had not just dented his father's confidence.

Melody leaned close, distracting Logan with her fresh vanilla scent. "All kids do it," she said, bringing him back.

"Yeah," he said, ceding the point, remembering how he'd passed Cussing 101 with honors . . . except that Shane was not supposed to be like him. Logan scowled.

"Tell me you're not gonna punish him or something." Melody kept her voice low, her expression mirroring his. "Way to make the word important, Dad."

Damn it, he wasn't any better at this parenting business than Shane's mother. Good God, what if he was as bad as his own father?

"Glory, Logan, lighten up," Melody said again, watching him.

Logan raised a brow. "Glory?"

"Hey, you'd rather I say something like—"

"Never mind. I've resorted to *freaking,* myself, since you know who moved in."

Melody smiled. "Seriously, ease up on him, will you. It's not like he robbed a liquor store or something."

Logan did a double take, nearly missed the turn, and laid rubber as he chose a hard right over a wrought iron fence. Damn! "Sorry about that," he said, three fast heartbeats later, as he glanced in the rearview mirror to catch Shane's grin. "You okay, buddy?"

"Do it again."

"Great," Logan said.

Melody regarded him assessingly. "What was *that* about?"

Logan shrugged. "You okay?"

Melody rolled her eyes. "Sure, roller coasters are my favorite, especially at rush hour."

Logan smiled despite himself. She wasn't a sea squall in their lives; she was a roller coaster, his honest-to-God favorite ride. Hell, no wonder he liked her; spending time with her made him feel as if he was at an amusement park. Figured, what he liked best about her drove him the craziest . . .

fine for a punk juvie with no responsibility, not so fine for a conscientious father.

Logan sighed. "It's the whole discipline thing," he admitted. "Being on the giving end as opposed to the receiving end took me by surprise. Guess I wasn't ready. Sometimes this parenting business worries me."

"Being *with* him, raising him, listening to him . . . your daily presence . . . that's what counts, Logan, take it from me. He can depend on you for anything, and he knows it."

"But he's never needed discipline before."

Melody leaned close. "That's nothing to write home about."

"What?"

"He's been too good," she whispered. "Normal is better."

"Now I've heard it all."

Melody frowned. "You got a problem with normal, Kilgarven?"

"No, but I have a problem with the Melody Seabright version. Hell-o-o—" Logan lowered his voice. "He had a *bitchin'* day at nursery school, remember?"

Melody grinned. "Gotta love a precocious kid."

"Oh, I love him. That's the easy part." The fist around Logan's chest eased, though. Shane could be precocious at times. Probably best if they didn't make a case out of this. Otherwise, the kid might use the word just to get a reaction.

With relief, gratitude, and not a little surprise at the help Mel had been, Logan gave her a wink. "As for precocious, I'd say it takes one to know one."

"Those are not my genes he's carrying," Melody said, taken off guard by a wash of longing. The thought of a child—with Logan's genes and hers—had actually crossed her mind, a mind obviously taking flight.

By the edgy look on Logan's face, it seemed entirely possible that he sensed her longing, or thought the same.

Either way, he seemed no more comfortable with the notion.

Like both of her parents, she was a loner, and she liked it that way. A child of hers would be in deep trouble. The way things stood, she had no one to screw up but herself when unemployment reared its ugly head. Fantasizing about a child—of hers and Logan's, no less—was nothing but a backasswards step into her Barbie and Ken years, way back when Daddy took care of everything . . . by paying all the bills . . . and staying far away.

She might be confused about Logan—likely due to a temporary, if flaming, case of lust—but neither he nor Daddy would be taking care of her anytime soon. She could take care of herself, thank you very much. She would prove that to Logan, as well as her father, if she had to.

Besides, hadn't she decapitated Ken in a fit of temper and lost his head? If that didn't have some kind of deeper meaning, she didn't know what did.

Logan pulled the car into the driveway, and Melody sighed. Thank God they were home, and not a moment too soon.

At her door, he halfheartedly invited her for backyard burgers, but she gave him an out, and herself time to come to terms with her odd fantasies, raging hormones, and ticking body clock.

The minute her door shut behind her, Melody stepped out of her spikes and heaved a sigh heavy with relief. Nothing like the sanctuary of her own apartment. For supper, she chose a meal suited to her mood: cheesecake, chips, and chunky doodle ice cream—the three C's—from the food group "comfortus grantus"—guaranteed to make every problem easier to handle.

In her living room, she unhooked her bra beneath her melon shell, slipped the straps over her hands, then freed herself from the underwire, via the shell's vee neck. Sighing in supreme contentment, for the week of hard work behind her and the weekend ahead, she dropped into a big, cushy, chintz chair, and munched. Sometimes, life could be serene.

From upstairs, she heard the echo of running feet and a warbling Shane-giggle. Swift upon its heels came a deep and sexy man-laugh, and Melody went all warm and soft inside. Father and son playing together.

Shane had stepped as easily into her heart as he had into her kitchen, melting her to her soul. Must be his rusty freckles and mahogany cowlick, not to mention the endearing replica of Logan's half-grin. Yep, she had fallen hard, a surprise for a nonnurturer like her, but she guessed it had been easy enough; he was a great kid, though lost in a lot of ways. When his father left that first night, she'd seen Shane's eyes darting to and fro, as if he were prepared for the worst. She'd recognized the fear he kept hidden, that he'd be left behind for good. She wished she could reassure him, make him feel secure in his father's love, though Logan was doing a pretty good job of that, whether he knew it or not.

For that reason, among others, Melody feared that if she weren't careful, she might find herself falling for Shane's yuppie-pin-striped dynamite dad as well. And if she and Logan weren't a toxic combo, who was?

Logan's motto was "plan, work, prosper, invest wisely." He embraced routine, while she liked to change course on a whim.

So, why the sizzle every time he got close? Why listen for his step, crave his smile?

Because she was an idiot, that's why.

Her philosophy had always been "live, love, enjoy, grab life by the cajones and make it sparkle," because really, if you didn't do that for yourself, who would? Never mind that her life usually turned out more like "get a job, get fired, get a new job."

She had followed the same pattern with boarding schools. Like clockwork, as Daddy predicted, she'd screw up, clean up, and try again. Good thing she liked change, because change seemed to find her at every turn. Her job at the station was the biggest and best change ever, she thought, wondering how long it would last before she screwed that up, too.

For half a beat she thought the job might actually impress her father—as in make him proud of her—then she shook her head on a derisive snicker and picked up her cheesecake.

Logan was a lot like her father—though Logan not only played with his child, he had now lived in the same house with Shane for two full months in a row. That would have been a record for her father.

Nevertheless, she and Logan were incompatible, unsuitable opposites, and they didn't have much in common, either. Bad, bad, bad.

Just like her parents. For the short duration of their marriage, Daddy had traveled in one direction, Mom in the other, until Mom's fatal diving accident when Melody was six.

If *she* was ever foolish enough to have children, Melody wanted more for them. She supposed she wanted them to have a dad like the easy-going Logan, the free spirit she sometimes glimpsed behind the briefcase. She wasn't surprised she was attracted to a man who read to and played with his child, even sometimes sang him to sleep, according to Shane.

Hey, a man who didn't abandon ship under fire of heavy lingerie couldn't be a total tight ass. Also in Logan's favor there was that totally cute, tight ass to consider.

Melody smiled, picked up her chunky doodle dessert, crossed her ankles on the coffee table, and savored her first creamy bite. Logan Kilgarven was surely not for her, and she could take that fact to the bank.

On the other hand, she could still picture him in her mind's eye, stuffing her garment bag into his trunk this morning. Nothing wrong with appreciating the view.

ON Saturday, the tall ships were due to start arriving at two, and Logan had said to come upstairs around one-thirty.

At one, Melody was still cleaning the mess she'd made while sorting through her clothes the morning before. She was also trying to find the strapless bra and seamless bikinis she usually wore under her two-piece playsuit, which was perfect for the pirate cave picnic, though she might have taken them to work by mistake. As she dialed Logan's number, she gazed out the kitchen window in time to see Shane dash across the backyard. Logan picked up on the first ring.

"Did you see my yellow bra and bikinis in the bag I left in the bathroom?" Melody asked.

"I assume you want Logan," a woman said. "This is his mother. Do you want me to look?"

Melody lowered her brow to the wall near her phone, shook her head, and felt the blaze on her cheeks. After a warm minute, she told herself that someday she might actually see the humor in this. Maybe. "Mrs. Kilgarven. Hi. This is Melody Seabright from downstairs."

"You just missed Logan," the woman said. "He went to get the ice cream he forgot to buy."

"Just like a man."

"I'd be happy to help you find what you're looking for," Logan's mother said, amusement lacing her voice.

"Shane went with his father, didn't he?" Melody asked, though she knew the answer.

"Of course."

Melody sighed. She *had* seen a shadow precede Shane's dash through the yard. "Why don't you come downstairs for a cup of coffee, Mrs. Kilgarven, and let me explain my opening remark."

The woman chuckled. "Phyllis, please, and I can hardly wait."

When Logan and Shane got back from the Stop-N-Go-Broke, where they charged two grand for ice cream, laughter from the other side of Melody's door stopped Logan cold, one foot on the stairs. A frisson of alarm shivered his spine and raised his hackles. Familiar laughter, well, familiar voices anyway. Couldn't be his mother; Phyllis Kilgarven hadn't laughed in years. Jessie, maybe? Yes, that was Jessie's voice all right. No, maybe it was his mother.

A premonition of doom swamped him. Suppose Melody had cornered them both, which scared the hell out of him. Because he was smart. And paranoid. His mother and Jessie together could wreak havoc, he knew from long experience. Throw Melody into the toxic blend, and . . . oh God, there went his organized world.

Logan regarded Melody's door, panic increasing with every star. Ignoring the thud of his heart, he'd barely knocked before it opened, slow and torturous, as if by an unseen hand, macabre, menacing.

The sight that greeted him stopped his blood. The most dangerous women in the witch capital of the world sat at Mel's retro fifties enamel table, heads together, surrounded by a spill of salt, a harried lime, and a quarter bottle of tequila.

Logan held the door for support. "Please tell me that bottle wasn't full when you started."

They all three giggled. Great. "Hello to you, too," he said, eyeing Melody's sexy red cover-up, short and saucy, an outfit that in any other circumstance would make him want to take a closer look . . . examine the goods, cop a feel.

He regarded the bright-eyed trio and raised a sober brow. "Ready to party?"

Melody grinned. "We started without you."

No foolin'.

His mother raised her glass his way. "You kinky little devil."

Ah, crap.

Mel raised hers. "A toast to *long* office legends. Uh, I mean long-standing."

"Hey," Jessie nudged Melody's shoulder with her own. "I thought you said, 'long-staying?'"

The tequila triplets burst into laughter.

Logan touched his throbbing temple. Too late to put himself up for adoption, but he might have to move . . . to another galaxy. "Damn."

Shane gasped. "Dad, you said a bad word."

"I had provocation, son."

Shane's face lit up. "If I get a poor vacation, can I call Roddy Simms a dick-head?"

All laughter, all sound, stopped.

"Shane," Logan said. "We need to have a talk."

"Right after our pirate cave picnic," said Shane's grandmother, who rose to propel him by the shoulders into the hall and out of harm's way. "Melody, why don't you get dressed and come on up," she said. "Logan, let's go."

"Yep," Jess said, giving Logan a loaded wink and taking Shane's hand. "Let's go make Jessie's famous marshmallow salad."

"Do we gotta put fruit in it?" Shane asked.

Logan waited for them to hit the stairs before he shut Melody's door and turned on her. "Please tell me you didn't tell Jessie and my mother about Nikky."

"You mean they didn't know? Shame on you for keeping secrets from your mother. And Jessie, too, why she's like—"

"The thorn in my freaking side! Tell me, do you tell your mother about all your . . . your—"

"Many and varied sexual exploits?" Melody snorted—a measure of the tequila in her blood. "Hah, she should have lived so long."

Logan's stricken look made Melody sorry she'd shocked him, but she wanted out of the subject and fast. "You never told me what a delicious sense of humor your mother had."

"My mother? You're kidding? What did you say that she found so amusing?" Logan began to advance, tripping Melody's pulse with the promise of retribution sparking his eyes and creasing his brow. "Do I have to teach you to keep what's between us . . . between *us*?" he asked.

The wicked purpose in his expression sent Melody scrambling from her chair. She took a step back for each one Logan took in her direction, and when the wall stopped her retreat, he raised a brow . . . and grinned. "You gonna tell her about this?"

"This?" The word emerged as a squeak.

"This," Logan repeated, inhaling her, as if she were a flower for heaven's sakes, and skimming her brow with his lips, as he reached beneath her short, scarlet robe to stroke the sensitive skin above her knee and—oh, nice.

"And this," he said as he stroked higher.

Nicer.

"If you're gonna be telling tales, Melody Seabright, I think you ought to know what you're talking about."

Skittish as a cat on the inside, Melody held her breath so as to appear still as stone on the outside. Logan stroked beneath her robe, slowly upward, until he cupped her bottom in both hands, nothing between her skin and his palms but a scrap of silk.

"So," she said, in view of their positions, her breathing shallow. "You wanna dance?"

Logan's chuckle seemed to come from deep inside as he pulled her against him and planted nipping kisses on her temple, her earlobe, her hair.

Melody's mouth parted, opened of its own accord, the tender skin of her inner lips abraded by his bristled jaw one minute, soothed by the silk at the hollow of his throat the next. He smelled spicy delicious, tasted salty sweet, and felt better than she could have imagined.

Caught in a swirling current of excitement and apprehension, Melody didn't know whether to push Logan away and escape, or pull him closer and revel in the "dance." While she tried to decide, he tongued the pulse at the base of her throat, released a button, two more, and licked the pale skin between her breasts deeper into the vee of her robe.

To add to her needy frustration, her knees about gave out as he made a stroking foray with his talented hands to a torturous spot just shy of her center. All the while, he kept her prisoner, kept her from buckling, and with his mouth, he gave a great deal of nibbling attention to a spot just shy of her lips . . . and if he damned well didn't reach either of those destinations pretty damned soon, Melody was going to scream.

Logan pulled without warning from the kiss, his gaze assessing, and she almost howled, but before she could, he opened his mouth over hers, hard and greedy, and she swallowed the unexpected trill of satisfaction that rose in her throat.

Melody reveled in the potency of his promise as Logan pulled her tighter against him, rough, needy, arching hard into her. He cradled and settled her in all the right places along a torso, lean and firm . . . everywhere. A perfect fit, a dance in place, rocking, stroking, crests against hollows.

"Dancing" with Logan Kilgarven felt . . . dangerous, like riding a heathen sea wave. Somewhere in the back of her brain, Melody knew she'd wipe out, that it would hurt, bad, but she didn't give a damn, because the high was higher than she thought she could go.

When Logan fitted his ponderous length firm against her center, Melody closed on him to capture him with her thighs and keep him there, rocked him against her, promised more with muscles pulsing warm and wet.

She did some exploring of her own over his tight, soft-washed jeans and black T-shirt, skimming her hands down his back and across his nice firm butt, making him moan even as he kissed her with staggering skill.

She tried to keep her head and remember her goal: to find out firsthand whether Nikky had been exaggerating Logan's assets. It did not seem possible from this angle, yet just to be sure, Melody slipped her hand between them and grasped his thick rigid length.

Logan groaned, became larger, firmer, thicker. Glory! *Not* an exaggeration.

Melody held and kneaded his burgeoning promise—she couldn't help herself; there was so much to work with—while Logan encouraged her in a voice gone hoarse and rough with coaxing. Her back against the wall, their hands and bodies moving with primitive purpose, they danced to a quickening rhythm that could end only one way.

"Hey, Dad!" The door flew open and hit the wall.

Logan and Melody jumped apart.

Mel screamed.

Logan hit his head on a cupboard and swore.

Seven

"AWESOME! Scared'ya, didn't I?" Shane was all big eyes and tickled surprise.

Aroused to painful proportions, Logan had turned his back, bent over double, and braced his hands on the counter, swearing below his breath.

Melody clutched her robe closed. "We were um . . . uh . . . We were—"

"Trying to sneak up on a mouse, son, from different directions, but you scared us, and the sucker got away."

Melody bit down on a giggle and could not look at Logan.

"A mouse?" Shane gazed eagerly about the floor. "Want me to help?"

"Shane?" Logan said. "You wanted something?"

"Oh, yeah. Gramma Phyl said, 'Cool it and come upstairs. Dessert later.' "

Melody's giggle finally escaped as she went into her room and shut the door. While dressing for the pirate cave picnic, she wondered how to get herself abducted later by Long John Kilgarven.

WITH the party in full swing, Logan mixed another batch of margaritas. That meltdown in Melody's kitchen had been an aberration, a fall from grace, a mistake. He remembered thinking so at the time, even as he approached her and prepared to teach her a lesson. But as if he had stepped from his body and watched from afar, he'd seen his hand, pale against the tan of Melody's leg, imagined the silk of her, warm against his palm, and knew there was no turning back. Almost as if the choice had been taken from him . . . as if he had been . . . bewitched.

What if she really is a witch? The question resonated in his mind. Logan frowned and shook his head. Though the silk and scent of her would not stop teasing him, mind and body, he would resist the witch from now on. So what if she'd tasted of lime Popsicles with a kick. He would not fall back into his bad-boy habits. And taking Melody Seabright to bed would be a sure and painful plummet, a mistake he could not afford. He would not attempt to entice her into staying after the party, as he might once in his blighted life have done, not with Shane in the house, not that he thought she would. He would not; he could not. He had a son to raise, a son who needed a stable family life, not a horny, reckless father.

Allowing himself to become attracted to Melody would be . . . worse than risky, Logan thought. It would destroy all he'd worked to achieve for his son. Forget that he hadn't become this stimulated this fast since . . . had he ever become this stimulated this fast, beyond the first rush of puberty?

Shane's mother had surely enticed him in a way he remembered, seriously scary, since Mel excited him in a way that made Heather seem like a dud in comparison.

Talk about an ice bath. If a woman more dangerous than Shane's mother wasn't a natural deterrent, nothing would be. Logan handed his mother and Jessie each a second drink, while Melody taught Shane to use his new binoculars from inside the windowed octagon turret. Of course, Melody kept her mind focused solely on his son, while Shane's sick father kept his attention on Melody's perfectly rounded bottom as she bent over the boy.

Logan wondered if a celibate order of monks for fathers existed—something like AA, but for single fathers addicted to sex lives.

"Melody? Mellie-Pie, are you up there?" Logan's speculation ended with that boisterous call from somewhere below.

"Daddy?" Mel said, standing straight.

"Can I come up?"

"Daddy?" she shrieked.

Right behind her, Logan watched Melody fly down the stairs then stop before some big guy with a fake smile—must be Daddy.

Logan went down to introduce himself and invite Mr. Seabright to the picnic.

"I can't believe you came," Melody told the very proper older gentleman—as different from her as magic is to reality—as they made their way up the stairs.

"But I told you I would. Did you forget again?" Mel's father patted her hand in a patronizing manner, while Logan bristled on her behalf, and Melody's expression spoke more of promises broken than forgotten.

Chester Seabright pulsed with as much vibrant life as his daughter, though he stood a great deal broader, taller, and a bit too starched in his charcoal pin-striped suit—the style Logan favored, actually, though more expensive—and he seemed to lack Melody's sensitivity in a very big way.

Logan introduced "Judge Jessie Harris" to him first, to

impress the man for some reason, but Jess took exception. "I've retired from the bench," she said shaking Chester's hand. "Now I give spine-chilling cemetery tours in my own private hearse."

"That must have called for quite the adjustment," Chester said, his tone not altogether approving.

"It makes for a nice change, actually." Jessie reclaimed her hand with a wry grin. "Change can be good. It's called balance." She gazed at Logan through the top of her bifocals, a sure sign he was in trouble, before she regarded his mother, then Melody. "Balance," she repeated. "I know a few people around here who should try it sometime."

Logan and Melody glanced at each other, then away. They'd damned near made a radical change, but Logan wouldn't have termed it a strike toward balance so much as one toward a tumble, ass over heels, down a very steep rabbit hole.

Chester politely refused the margarita Melody offered him and requested a martini, instead.

Figured, Logan thought, realizing he'd disliked Chester Seabright on the instant, but not sure why. Jessie, he saw, in true form, tried to reserve judgment, to give Melody's father the benefit of the doubt, while his mother acted like a calf-eyed schoolgirl with her first crush. After about fifteen minutes of that, Logan sidled up to his not-so-subtle parent, confiscated her margarita, and replaced it with an iced soft drink. "Bat those baby blues at him one more time," he whispered, "and I'm gonna ralph all over you."

His mother gasped and burst into laughter. What was wrong with her today? Laughing, flirting? Was there a full moon or something? Oh, crap. Full moon over Salem. In this company, that could be a howl.

When a couple of Melody's oddball friends showed up, the day took an even spookier turn, if that were possible.

"Everybody," Melody said, her hands on Shane's shoulders. "This is my friend Vickie. She owns The Immortal Classic, the vintage dress shop where I buy my clothes, and she's doing very well with it, too. And this is Kira," she said, indicating the woman dressed all in black.

Vickie, looking like a shy Russian peasant, nodded a general hello.

"Oh," Kira said, hands on hips, "so Vickie's your friend and I'm not?"

Melody blushed, a phenomena Logan would like to examine at his leisure, but Kira of the wild red hair, svelte black dress, and multipierced ears with more hoops than a circus, winked as she took his hand and gave it a firm shake. "Do you believe in magic?" she asked.

Shane broke into a giggle just then, a jubilant sound—because Melody had taken to tickling him—and Logan had to admit, if only to himself, that magic seemed entirely possible.

"I don't really expect an answer," Kira said at his studied silence. "I just like to make people of a certain temperament consider the possibility of magic. Works better than prunes."

His mother barked a laugh, which did not help her cause one bit, Logan thought, even as Jessie bit off a smile, and the music for "Do you Believe in Magic?" began to play in his head.

Shy as she appeared, Vickie went to Chester and offered her hand. "I want to thank you, Mr. Seabright, for your investment in my dress shop. I could never have gone into business without your help."

Chester Seabright, that starched, holier than thou businessman, damned near blushed. "I'm n— You're . . . welcome . . . Vickie. I'm, er, glad I could help." He and his daughter exchanged a sharp, meaningful look, Chester's expression fulminating, Melody's sparkling with mischief.

"Don't worry," Kira said, recapturing Logan's attention. "We're not party-crashing. We just came to borrow some lavender and lemon balm for a quick spell."

"Oh, from my herb garden," Melody said. "Love and healing, right? Sure. Come on."

"Nice meeting you," Kira and Vickie chorused, as they followed Melody down the stairs and toward her kitchen garden out back.

After Melody left, the party went dead—as if the life had been snuffed from it, and Logan wondered if anyone else had noticed the sudden reduction in energy at her absence.

When she returned, Shane insisted Melody look at the ship coming in. Then Jess had to tell her about last night's Boneyard tour. Then, when Mel finally started in his direction, her father stopped her. Logan was finally forced to raise a fresh margarita and wiggle the glass to catch her eye and lure her over.

"Kira's a witch," she said, coming up to him and accepting the drink.

No kidding, Logan thought, watching her give the same enthusiastic attention to the salted rim of her glass that she'd given to their kiss in her kitchen earlier. "She is, huh?" He'd lost track of the conversation.

"Yep, a real one."

Oh yeah, now he remembered. And what about you? he wanted to ask, less aroused but still caught in her spell. Are you a witch, too? It had not escaped his notice that Melody knew as well as Kira which spells the herbs were used for. "Why do you keep an herb garden?" he asked.

"For cooking, of course."

Logan's laughter did not endear him to Melody, but her witch and ditz friends, her suspect herb garden, not to mention her let's-make-magic approach to life, did help strengthen his resolve to keep his distance, especially from her talented mouth.

Only two tall ships passed by Salem Harbor before full dark, just enough, thank God, to thrill the four-year-old pirate among them. Then they all went down to the living room, where Melody's father sat beside her, complimenting Logan on his "expensive" cordovan leather sectional before taking his daughter's hand. "Mellie, I think about you all the time."

Melody's soft, full-hearted smile made her topaz eyes shine, as if she'd been given a great gift. "Really, Daddy?"

Chester nodded. "Every month when my accountant reminds me that you're not cashing the checks I send you."

Melody's pleasure dimmed, and Logan caught the flash of hurt she tried to hide. "I told you, Dad, I don't need your help. I'm doing fine."

Logan's respect for Melody rose a double notch. She *was* doing fine, though he was concerned about how long that would last.

"So you give my money away?" Chester didn't so much ask his daughter a question, as chide her for her answer. "In my name, no less," he said to the company at large, "to heaven knows who all, and his cousin's worthless brother besides." He patted Melody's hand with the first show of fatherly affection Logan had seen. "Who's going to come knocking on my door asking me for more money this week, Mellie-Pie? 'Free the Warthogs?' or 'Iguanas for the Homeless?' "

Logan stifled a chuckle, no less entertained than his mother, while Jessie didn't look the least surprised at any of it.

"So, let me get this straight, Mr. Seabright," Logan said. "I take it that you sometimes send Melody money to live on?"

"Sometimes? Try, every month, and it's more than enough to live on. It's enough to . . . live pretty damn well on. She doesn't need those pathetic jobs she takes."

"Damn it, Daddy!"

"Dad, Mel said a bad word."

Good for Mel. "Provocation, son," Logan said.

Shane thought about that for a minute, but when he started to speak, he caught the warning in Logan's look, and shrugged.

Logan returned his attention to Mel's father. "So, Melody chooses to provide for herself, does she? I find that commendable." Logan gave her a thumbs up, garnering a grin from her and a grimace from her father. "And she gives your money to charity?"

"Worthless charities, and worthless dress shops doomed to failure. Hell, she's throwing my money away." Chester looked at Melody in much the same way Logan had just regarded Shane, as if she were a recalcitrant child. "Care to explain yourself?" he asked her, "while we're on the subject."

Melody raised her gaze to the heavens before focusing on Logan, rather than on her father, the twinkle in her eyes subtle, but undeniable. "Kira got a job as a fund-raiser at The Salem Museum of Witchcraft and needed a few donations to her credit." She shrugged. "Daddy's checks were just sitting there, gathering dust, so I got the bright idea of signing one of them over to the museum."

"Six thousand dollars," Chester roared, loud enough to make Shane step in front of Melody and square his shoulders.

"Six grand. Did you ever hear of anything so, so—"

"Worthwhile?" Melody supplied. "Really, Daddy, it's an institution with an admirable mission and a sound fiscal plan. So is Vickie's dress shop." She turned to Logan. "For some reason, Daddy went ballistic." Her chuckle seemed to escape of its own volition.

It would be easy to think that Melody had been pissing Daddy off for attention, like Heather had done with her father by dating Logan, Logan remembered, but it seemed clear that Melody had started by helping a friend and that annoying her father had been an unexpected plus.

"I have better things to do with my money," Chester groused to no one in particular, as he rose, looking harried, and emptied the martini shaker into his glass. "You'll like this one, Mellie," he said, his grin wry. "A woman walked into my office this week with a prego twelve-year-old in tow, and doesn't she tell some receptionist, in front of half my staff, that she wants to talk to me about what I've done."

Logan choked on his drink, Jessie completely lost it, which got his mother laughing, too, and Shane wanted to know what a 'ceptionist was.

"Oh, Daddy," Melody said, half laughing, half concerned. "I'm guessing she came from The Keep Me Foundation?"

Chester Seabright did not appreciate being the entertainment, and yet Logan saw a quick flash of something that could almost be termed *longing* in the way he regarded his daughter just then. It made him wonder if Chester didn't want Melody's approval as much as Mel wanted her father's.

Logan caught his mother's eye and knew that she had noticed the same thing.

"You weren't rude, were you?" Melody asked her father. "Not to them?"

"Rude!" Chester shouted. "I'm never rude."

"Right," Melody said, pulling the dish of cashews closer. "But The Keep Me Foundation does great work, Dad, with teens who want to keep—" She tousled Shane's hair. "It pays the obstetrical bills, gives the young women a place to live, before and after, and an education, so that they can provide for their little ones. They even help new mothers find apartments and get work and baby-sitters."

"It's bad enough you won't take my money," Chester said, missing the point entirely, "but do you have to give it away in *my* name?"

"Well, I don't want them coming after me for more. I don't have any money."

Her father sat beside her and patted her knee. "You're a looker, sweetheart, but I sure wish you had some brains in that gorgeous featherhead of yours."

Logan's mother grimaced. "Chester," she said. "Melody was joking; she doesn't deserve that."

Way to go, Mom.

Melody scooped up the last of the cashews.

Logan slid the bowl of popcorn her way. "Mel *is* gorgeous," he said. "I'll grant you that, sir, but a featherhead? The star of the new *Kitchen Witch Show* on WHCH TV? I don't think so."

"Mellie?"

Melody eyed the popcorn. "Hardly a star, Dad."

Logan caught her watching him, not sure if he'd pleased her by sticking up for her or annoyed her by putting her father in his place. Either way, the guy deserved what he got. But when Logan looked more closely, he saw that his defense had warmed Melody in a way that warmed him right back. She pushed the bowl of popcorn aside.

"Star or not," Chester said. "Using her assets to advantage hardly makes her bright."

"What is it with men and my assets?" Melody snapped. "And you can both just stop talking about me as if I weren't here."

"Not bright. Brilliant," Logan said, knocking the wind from her sails. "Melody is brilliant. She came to the station with a sound business proposal and every aspect of the show worked out—title, persona, wardrobe, marketing. I'm telling you, she wowed management, big time."

"You sound as if you were there," Chester said.

"Hell-o," Melody said in two annoyed, but intrepid syllables. "*I'm* still here."

"Well," her father snapped. "Was he there, or not?"

Melody sighed. "He's the producer, Dad."

"Aha!"

Logan rose from his chair. "I take exception to the insinuation in your tone, sir."

"Yeah," Shane said, taking a similarly defensive stance. "Just 'cause Mel didn't have no more apples and the cherries made me puke—"

Logan put his hand on Shane's shoulder and gave it a gentle squeeze. "Right, son. Time for dessert. Why don't you go get the ice cream out of the freezer while we finish our discussion."

"Okay, Dad." Shane raced toward the kitchen but slid into a turn just their side of it. "We got chunky doodle!" he announced before resuming his sprint.

"I'm telling you, sir," Logan continued. "Melody is magic in front of the cameras—" An idea hit him, and he grinned. "Wait, that's it! Magic. Kira's odd greeting could be our theme song. Can't you hear them playing 'Do You Believe in Magic?' as your intro, Mel?"

"I like it," she said in surprise. "Do you think Gardner will?"

"Yeah," Logan said. "I do."

"You, on television?" her father said, erasing her smile. "I don't know, Mellie. I'm afraid you'll make a fool of yourself, of us all, really. Better think twice before you do something so . . . so public."

"Right, Dad." Melody shook her head and got up. "No ice cream for me, thanks. I'm going to call it a night. This has been a long week." She hugged Jessie, then Phyllis, then she forced a smile and took her father's hand to pull him from the sofa. "Let me walk you to your car, Dad."

"Chester, stay," Logan's mother said, and Chester sat down again.

Both Logan and Melody frowned as Logan accompanied her to the door. "You okay?" he asked, stepping into the stairwell with her and closing his door to shut out the sound of the party behind them.

Melody shook her head, as if she didn't want to talk about it, as if she couldn't get any more words past the lump in her throat.

After seeing her father wear her down, Logan wondered if Daddy didn't have something to do with her string of failures, sort of a subconscious "that's what he expects, so that's what he'll get" kind of thing. "Mel?"

"I'm fine." She smiled half-heartedly. "Just beat."

Logan didn't believe her, and he didn't want to let her go feeling the way she did. He indicated that she should precede him down the stairs.

If she ate when she was upset, she must be twice as upset, if she could stop pre-chunky doodle.

Eight

MELODY wondered why Logan came out onto the landing with her, but when he took her arm halfway down the stairs, she stopped and turned with the question on her lips.

With a slight pressure of his hand, however, and a silent invitation in his eyes, he urged her down. So she sat, there in the enclosed stairs—too surprised to deny him—shoulder to shoulder with the man who'd swept his talented hands over every intimate part of her only a few hours before. Melody shivered at the memory.

Logan shrugged out of his zippered sweatshirt and placed it over her shoulders.

Oh God. She could love a man who . . . took care of her? *Not.* She needed sleep, a good night's rest, that's all. Her defenses were down. She didn't really want to put her head on Logan's shoulder or feel his arm around her. To be safe, though, she sidled away and leaned against the wall to face him and keep her distance.

Silence settled around them, soft and comfortable. The

unlit stairway felt . . . intimate, not quite dark, but not light either. Slatted mahogany walls, a yellowed ceiling, doors, closed at either end, cocooned them. A hideaway, cozy, clean. Melody gave the step above them the white glove test, minus the glove. "Shane did a good job this morning."

"Part of his chores," Logan said, and they shared a smile. "I admire your charity work," he added, changing the subject so fast, and to something so . . . personal, that Melody didn't know what to say. Screwing up, she could deal with, but compliments threw her.

"I'm guessing that pissing Daddy off in the process was a bonus." He winked. "Extra bang for your buck, so to speak?"

"Pissing Daddy off . . ." She shook her head. "*That,* I'm good at."

"You're good at a lot of things; you just haven't found them all yet."

Melody did a double take to see if he was being serious. "How tactful of you." She thought about the amorous incident in her kitchen and wondered how good he would have found her, if they hadn't been interrupted—thank the stars they were.

Logan must have caught her blush, because he raised a questioning brow, but she wasn't going anywhere near that subject, not with him, not yet. Not ever. "Pissing Daddy off is easy," she said.

"But you work so hard at it."

"Nah, I'm a natural. And he's an easy mark, stuffed suit with a briefcase, no sense of humor, obsessive, solemn, sedate, bor—" She stopped, but the words hung thick in the air between them. After a minute, she shrugged. "Oops."

"I am *not* like your father."

Glory, Logan had gorgeous eyes, Mel thought, especially when they flashed fire, like now. "Did I say you were? It's not my fault if you see a similarity . . . or three."

"Gee, thanks." Despite his sarcasm, he smiled. "So you're saying that any man who carries a briefcase and wears a suit is not the 'one' for you."

"I'm saying there isn't 'one' for me. I don't want 'one,' thank you very much. I've got all I can do to take care of me. What about you?"

Logan shook his head. I've made more than my quota of mistakes for one lifetime, thanks."

A roar of laughter from upstairs caught their attention. "Giddy up," Shane ordered. "Giddy up, horsey."

"Your father must be giving Shane a pony ride," Logan said.

"Hah! Not my father."

"Jessie," they said in unison, leaning into each other.

"My father's probably talking business and boring your mother to tears."

"She didn't seem bored to me, not with anything he said. She seemed disgustingly interested."

"They *were* flirting with each other, weren't they? I thought so, but I figured I'd had too many margaritas."

Logan shook his head. "I have never seen my mother flirt in my life . . . until today."

"Creepy, isn't it," Melody said, "thinking of our parents as sexual beings?"

"Oh yuck, as Shane would say. Did you have to go that far?"

Melody laughed, tickled at this lighthearted aspect of Logan the tight ass, but his regard changed to one more in keeping with her briefcase-toting image of him. Serious. "Speaking of sexual beings," he said.

Melody stilled, realized how close they sat, and though Logan gave her plenty of time to move away, she couldn't for the life of her do so. Then the arm she craved, his hard-muscled arm, slipped tight around her, pulled her close, and those lips she remembered as cool and soft met hers. A gentle kiss, barely there. A lingering need, stoked but unmet, breaths mingling.

One kiss more. Another.

"Sleep well," Logan said, pulling away, seeming as reluctant, and relieved, as she.

He stood with her, touched the corner of her mouth, coaxed it upward into a smile, then watched her take the last few steps to the landing. He nodded as she turned the knob.

"Night," she said and went inside.

So much for getting kidnapped by Long John Kilgarven, she thought as she regarded her kitchen with new eyes, remembered her earlier wish, and knew that her not getting abducted would serve them both better in the long run.

Melody opened the refrigerator, looked inside, and shut it again. A screwup and a perfectionist had no possible future together. None. They might have pretty damned good sex, though.

Their hot kitchen affair had certainly held a great deal of promise. Hell, it had been the best part of her day. Though there had been a few other highs before the evening ended. Logan approved of her giving her father's money to charity, for example. Who knew? He'd gone too far in trying to make her feel better when he called her brilliant, of course. She was never that, but she had conceived the idea for the show and everything that went with it.

Perhaps she wasn't so much of a featherhead, after all. Maybe she did have a bit of a mind for business. Logan had implied as much when he defended her. Logan had defended her. She wondered if his knight-in-shining-armor act would turn into as heavy a burden for him as the false veneer of confidence he'd laid on her.

Melody pulled a bag of chips from the cupboard and carried it into her room, eating as she went. Too bad she'd needed defending. She sighed and stepped out of her shoes. At her desk, she pulled out a drawer to look at her father's checks, but her mind couldn't wrap itself around the hurt and frustration they represented.

Slamming the drawer gave her some satisfaction. But signing them over to The Keep Me Foundation tomorrow would give her a great .deal more. Every kid should be wanted by at least one parent, she thought, popping another chip into her mouth. And what poetic justice that one of her parents should fund the cause.

She would tell the development officer that her father might like to meet some of the babies, too. Melody chuckled as she sealed the potato chip bag, washed her hands, and began to undress.

After she finished in the bathroom and turned off the lights, she settled into bed to ponder a certain blue-eyed producer and relive the way she'd felt in his arms, twice in the same day, once frantic and hot, once tender and sweet. "Long John Kilgarven," she whispered into the darkness. She had raised the devil in him for sure, and now she didn't know what to do about it. She knew only that the attraction between them sizzled, a dangerous hiss and sputter that she should deny, or at the least, ignore. Except that she couldn't seem to do either. She wanted him to touch her again, to see how far he would go. She wanted . . . to quote one of her boarding school teachers . . . to play with fire.

WHEN Logan returned to his apartment, he found his mother wearing her sweater and carrying her purse. "Where are you going?" he asked. "I thought you were staying over." He'd looked forward to the chance to talk to her about retiring.

"I changed my mind," she said. "I want to talk to Chester, so he's taking me dancing."

Dancing?

"Sure am," Melody's father said. "Let's go, Phyl."

Phyl? Logan swallowed his annoyance and kissed his mother's cheek. "Maybe you can stay over next weekend."

After everyone left, Shane postponed the inevitable by eating one spoonful of ice cream between each chunky doodle ice sculpture he created. Eventually the caramel and chocolate melded and turned the mixture a nutty dull gray, and when he tipped his bowl to drink the rest, ice-cream soup ran down his shirt, his chair, and puddled on the kitchen floor.

"That's it. Bedtime, sport."

"Ah, Dad."

But tonight, Dad meant business. He read one story, ruffled his son's hair, kissed him twice, and tucked him in. He couldn't get his mind away from the fact that Melody's father seemed to drain the life out of her. He couldn't forget seeing his mother flirting for the first time in his life, either, or the fact that she was no more aware than Melody was of the effect she had on men when she flirted.

Logan ran a hand through his hair. Melody. You had to respect a woman who threw her father's guilt money in his face by signing it over to charity—charities, plural—to which he would never contribute on his own.

After Logan finished straightening up and doing the dishes, he got into bed, still thinking about Melody, the feel and scent of her, until he finally grabbed the remote and the TV listing to get her out of his head.

When the phone rang, he saw that somehow the eleven o'clock news had come and gone. "Huh? Hello?"

Jagger Harrison Gardner, as station manager, should have been the one to go into work when a burglar alarm went off in the middle of the night, but Jag wanted Logan to get out of bed and go meet the police at the west entrance.

Logan hung up and swore. "That man would pass the buck, if God were next in line."

Logan cursed again as he tossed the covers aside and

rose. He shouldn't be called a producer, he should be called a jack-of-all-trades, or of whatever trade Jagger Harrison Gardner didn't feel like doing, or taking responsibility for. Logan didn't even want to be a producer. He wanted to make documentaries, not ride shotgun over other people's creativity, or lack thereof. He certainly did not want to do station walk-throughs at half-past freaking midnight.

As he pulled on his jeans, he remembered that he needed a sitter. Man, he hated to wake Mel. She'd seemed so tired when she said good night, but she had promised she'd sit if he needed her, and he honestly did. Besides, he wanted to make sure that she felt better.

It took quite a while to get her to answer her door, and when she finally did, she looked groggy enough to be walking in her sleep.

Logan couldn't stop his grin.

She looked like a little girl with her wild, fly-away hair tumbling to her shoulders, though that's where any likeness to childhood ended. Her long, shapely legs were as bare as her feet. Her breasts sat proud and free, her nipples making hard points against a soft tan T-shirt, long enough to cover essentials and short enough to inspire dreams. A Salem favorite, the shirt depicted a witch, artfully inviting him "in for a spell."

Logan's body said a quick and emphatic yes; his saner self knew better. "You have no idea how much I would like to take you up on that invitation," he said, making Mel's sleepy brow furrow in confusion. "But I've been called in to work. Can you—"

"Problem?"

"More like some cat tripped a burglar alarm. Routine."

That was all the explanation it took before Mel nodded and started on her comatose way up the stairs. Logan shut her door and followed, thoroughly enjoying the splendid view from down below.

Enjoying it too much. Not good, the way his body reacted to the sight and scent of her. Downright dangerous, as a matter of fact. As soon as he made sure Mel found his sofa without breaking her neck, he would grab his keys off the dresser and—

Melody about stopped his heart when she made straight for his room and crawled into his bed. Ignoring his jumbled covers, she lay on her belly, raised a knee, hugged his pillow like a lover, and went back to sleep.

For an eternity of throbbing beats, Logan's heart sped and his palms sweat, while he stood mesmerized in the doorway of his bedroom, staring at Melody Seabright's little silk-clad ass out there jump-starting his libido.

Logan wiped the sweat off his brow. This had to be the wildest turn-on of his life, he thought, especially now that he knew the way her skin felt against his. She looked like a gift from the gods, and man, did he ever want to unwrap the package.

Too bad he couldn't, especially while she slept. If he did, he would be taking advantage. A lowlife. Extremely low.

Logan's sigh of regret filled the room.

Then he brightened. He should cover her up, so she didn't catch cold. Good idea. As he approached her, Melody shifted in the bed, about stopping his heart, and ended up facing the wall, aiming her cute little bottom his way.

Logan savored the sight—Melody Seabright half naked in his bed—a dream come true. No, a nightmare, since he couldn't touch, anyway. Besides, he had to leave.

Too bad he couldn't seem to move. Did bewitchment have a residual effect? he wondered. Because he would swear that something—something strong—kept him from moving his legs.

Calling himself a fool, Logan tested his theory and, of course, he could move. Funny thing, though, he didn't end up stepping away from Melody at all, but toward her, and the closer he got, the stronger the pull.

The burnished glow of her sleek skin made a sharp contrast to the white of his sheets and the black of her scant bikinis, as she lay there all sleep-warm and strokable, his palm itching to make contact.

"Best just cover her up, Kilgarven," he whispered, hoping the sound of reason in the quiet room might make an impression. Right, he thought, cover her and be done with it. But when he grasped the blanket to pull it over her, he caught her foot, and she shifted and sighed. "Logan," she said in a breathy, seductive whisper, so low, he might have missed the plea if he hadn't been leaning over her. At least, he *thought* she'd said it. Wished she had.

"Mel?" No answer. "Melody?"

"Logan?" she said—no doubt this time—then with a whimper and a purr, she wiggled her bottom, as if to bring it to his attention.

And hadn't she succeeded in a fine upstanding manner, or so his body thought. Logan wondered which rose the more upright, her ass or his dick?

Did he believe in magic? Hell yes. He had a feeling he was looking right at her, and if she didn't tell him exactly what she wanted, he'd be doing a whole helluva lot more than looking. "Mel, speak to me. Please."

"C'mere," she said, as she curled into a ball, shocking him out of mind, moving in such a way as to make room for him, as if she wanted them snug as spoons in a kitchen drawer. Oh boy. Logan's imagination went on red-alert. He thought about the possibilities of climbing in with her . . . and got a hard affirmative nod from the big guy.

Once he would have accepted her unspoken invitation in a New York minute. Logan junior thought it a fine idea, but his other brain said he should think about it. Logan nearly laughed. Hell, he'd been thinking about it since he met her.

But no matter how hard he tried, he couldn't come up with one solid reason, not one, for walking away. The two of them were consenting adults after all. Melody had issued an invitation, and he needed to accept or decline. A man would have to be an idiot to walk out on such an amazing offer.

He might have changed his bad-boy ways, Logan thought, but that didn't make him an idiot. Melody's impatient whimper at that precise moment made his decision for him. At the least, he could test the curve of her bottom and commit it to memory, at the most—

As if his hand had a mind of its own, Logan reached for her.

She fit his palm as if she'd been created with his fantasies and desires in mind. Not too small, not too big, truly a wondrous bottom, the kind that made you believe in the presence of a greater being, one with an eye toward perfection.

As Logan cupped and stroked that world-class bottom, as he made his caressing way over her hip and around toward her center, Melody sighed and whimpered, a reward beyond bearing. She repeated his name, moved beneath his hand, each sexy purr, each lithe movement of her hips telling him she liked to be touched, that she was as sensuous as she was sexy.

Logan almost wished he didn't know.

Nine

THE closer Logan stroked toward the heat of her, the heavier and harder he became. Every beat of his heart echoed in his brain as he placed a knee on the bed. Melody rolled to her back, offering new and amazing possibilities, and he damned near came.

Then he froze. Her eyes were closed. Though she had reveled in his touch, called his name, urged him on, turned him on, she had been doing so in her sleep.

As if he stepped into an ice bath Logan shivered, his erection vanished, and his heart took to beating double time. Embarrassment rushed him in heated waves. Night sounds became apparent in proportion to his returning sanity—the wind, crickets, tree frogs, chiding him in harmony.

Logan swore beneath his breath and grabbed his keys off the dresser, regret in his soul and guilt in his gut. He had just experienced the best, and worst, turn-on of his life. He had also just come as close to irresponsibility as he'd allowed in years.

He'd gotten into the habit of remaining in control, but letting his passions rule him was not the kind of control he could afford. Once, that had been everything, but not now.

Thank God, Melody hadn't awakened to discover what a lowlife he really was. "Jerk, scum, idiot," he called himself as he took his jacket from the closet, his words bringing a measure of sobriety . . . and gratitude for close saves.

Logan looked in on Shane, then checked his watch and saw that nearly half an hour had passed, while he had been lusting after his son's sitter, for pity's sake.

That he wanted to make love to Melody didn't bother him. Lust was natural. But the fleeting idea of sleeping beside her, and worse, waking beside her, frightened the hell out of him . . . as if he needed her.

It was time to remember that Melody Seabright spelled trouble with a capital *T*. Logan groaned inwardly just thinking about the trouble he could get into with Melody, how close he'd just come. She exuded a madcap abandon that bordered on reckless. So what if she was there for Shane night and day? So what if Shane adored her to the point Logan feared his son would move in with her if he could?

Shane didn't know what was best for him. His father did. And joining Melody in that bed would have been one of the worst mistakes Shane's father could have made . . . and he had already pulled off some world-class beauties. The worst had been getting a sexy number named Heather pregnant, though the result was a gift he didn't deserve. Now he had to protect his son from another potential mistake— Melody. Logan groaned. What had he done to hook up with Heather and Melody in the same lifetime?

His worry crystallized. Suppose Melody was every bit as flighty and unreliable as Shane's mother? Suppose she hurt Shane as badly as Heather had?

Logan checked his watch again, swore, and took the stairs two at a time. Shane started crying before he hit the landing. Logan ran back up. By the time he got there, Melody was sitting on the edge of the bed, coaxing his son awake with gentle words.

Shane opened his eyes, blinked a couple of times, focused on each of them, one on each side. No hesitation, no second thoughts, he reached for Melody, and Logan's heart sank.

"I thought you went to work," Melody said as she rocked his son in her embrace, stroked his hair, and kissed his brow. "Shh, baby, it's okay."

"I was on my way out when I heard him."

"He's too sleepy to stay awake long. We're okay. You can get going."

"Yeah, I'm . . . running late." At the door, Logan stopped and turned. "Mel, do you walk or talk in your sleep?"

Melody winced, a dead giveaway. "What did I do now?"

Logan shook his head, easing the concern in her expression. "You didn't do anything." He had nearly done something terrible, for which he would never forgive himself, but she had not been responsible. "I'll be back as quick as I can," he said.

Logan berated himself all the way to the station, until he remembered that Shane had been crying for his mother, and that when it came to a choice, his son had gone to Melody for comfort, not his father. Logan slammed his hand on the wheel. "Serves you right, Kilgarven."

What had not happened with Melody in his bed had been for the best, Logan knew. He could not get involved with anyone, especially not Melody Seabright. It had taken him years to become a man in control, but it had only taken her a few weeks to break that control, and he had no one but himself to blame. He was going to stay away from her from now on.

* * *

MELODY slipped off the forties walking dress she'd just modeled for Gardner, regarded herself critically in the mirror, and wondered what was wrong with her.

She was wearing the underwear she'd been looking for on the morning of the tall ships party, just another unwelcome reminder, among many, of her shortcomings.

As if that day hadn't gone bad enough, she'd capped it by having an erotic dream about Logan . . . while sleeping in his bed, no less. Glory, he had been doing amazing things to her. Worse, she had wanted him to do as much, and more. The dream had been so real, she remembered waking eager and ready for him. So real, the feel of his big, capable hands haunted her still.

Later that same night, as she'd waited for Logan to return from the station, she'd realized that she would have to stay away from him, but no need. He had apparently decided to stay away from her, as far away as he could get, given the fact that they traveled to work together, and shared an office and a house.

As a matter of fact, steering clear of someone became pretty damned obvious when you tried to pull it off in close quarters. Logan's ploys to avoid her were getting embarrassing.

What had she done to drive him away?

It didn't matter. She didn't miss him. She wanted him at arm's length. She would not fall for a conservative, pin-striped workaholic. Though she'd had no say in the matter, her father amply filled the role of token tight ass in her life, which made one too many.

So what if Logan smelled of cloves, tasted of sex, and kissed like . . . God, and he stood so . . . tall, and . . . masculine, and his hands on her felt—

Melody broke a nail trying to tug her stubborn blouse off the hanger. "Damn it." She pulled an emery board from her makeup kit as the bathroom door opened.

Melody squeaked, and Logan gaped, devouring her with hungry eyes, which damned near improved her mood. "Do you not know how to knock?" she snapped.

"I distinctly remember that the door stood ajar," he said, his frank appraisal stroking her like a caress, so that where his gaze lingered, Melody sizzled.

"Oh," she said, feeling like an idiot, because she remembered why the door hadn't closed properly, and it was all his fault. He had annoyed her by walking out in the middle of her impromptu fashion show, and she'd slammed the bathroom door so hard afterward, it had bounced open again.

He regarded her now, with appreciation, and her pulse kicked into overdrive.

"That color makes your eyes sparkle," he said.

Melody looked down at herself, surprised. Like a doe in headlights, she stood unmoving, in nothing but a pair of lace bikinis and a strapless underwire, which he liked very much, judging by his evident reaction.

Melody raised her chin, proud of her power, and stood her ground. She'd teach him to ignore her. "Lemon chiffon," she said, striking a pose.

"Huh?"

"The color is lemon chiffon."

"Oh."

"Hey, Mel," Woody yelled from their empty office. "Somebody called to say your kid's waiting in day care."

"Damn!" Logan whispered, quietly shutting the door, as if to protect her modesty. "Get dressed."

"Go ahead." Melody stepped into her lime Capris and nearly lost her balance. "Get Shane," she said, hopping on one foot. "I'll catch up with you."

"Right. Good idea."

*   *   *

WAITING for the elevator took more patience than Logan could muster. God Mel had looked . . . tasty, like a dessert he'd like to savor. "Damn." He'd felt himself harden and all but tremble with need when he saw her. He was in worse trouble after staying away from her for nearly a week than he'd been when he saw her fifty times a day.

He looked up and wondered how long the elevator had been sitting there with the doors open. He just made it inside before they began to shut. When he saw Melody coming down the hall, he dove for the "open" button, hit "close" instead, and swore, but she managed to slip between the gap in the doors anyway.

"Cranky today, are we?"

"Can it, Mel."

"Aye, aye—"

"Mel . . ." Logan hated when she tried to hide her amusement, like now, because it charmed him as much as it irked him, damn it. Annoyed with himself for letting her get to him, hoping no one saw him dive for the "open" button like a hormone-ripe teen, he inhaled the subtle, intoxicating scent of the day. Orchids. Okay, so he'd been sniffing the perfume bottles she kept in the office medicine cabinet. Man, had she turned him into a sick bastard, or what?

The elevator jolted to a teeth-jarring stop as the lights flickered and went out, and Melody fell against him, her thick waving mane stroking his cheek, toying with him, sending him spiraling into alert mode.

Logan wanted to bury his face in that hair, bury himself in her.

To his relief, and dismay, she regained her balance and moved away. "What happened?" she asked.

Logan grasped the railing to keep from pulling her back. He might not be able to see her, but he knew, his body certainly knew, that she stood nearby. "How the hell should I know?"

"No need to snap. I didn't take that long."

"It's not you."

"It must be me. You've been avoiding me."

"No I haven't."

"Have."

"Have not."

Her rude noise made him smile in the darkness. "You most certainly have," she snapped. "For the last four days."

Five. "Why? Does it bother you?"

"No. Yes. Maybe a little."

Melody felt the warmth from his body radiate through her clothes and stroke at her core. He touched her hair—oh God—moved it from her brow, his breath warm at her temple. Had she moved closer? Had he?

She closed her eyes, her sigh of contentment so obvious in the silence, she was grateful he couldn't see her flaming cheeks.

The elevator whirred to life then stopped again, so fast, the lights barely flickered.

"Damned electricians. I hope your office is finished soon."

"Anxious to get rid of me?"

"Anxious to get back to normal," he said. "Nothing personal."

Nothing personal, Melody thought, wishing he'd kiss her. "You don't think this is another initiation, do you?"

The silence lasted long, pulsed, as did she. Logan's hand at her jaw both startled and enervated her, his torso touching hers turned her molten, as if the missing electricity shot through them both.

Logan's breath fanned her lips, made them tingle as if he'd caressed them. Melody sighed as his mouth came for hers, a whisper of breath, promising more, promising . . . everything.

The lights came on, blinding in their intensity, and the elevator arrived in day care in two sobering beats.

SHANE chattered like a magpie on the way home, which relieved Logan considerably, as it eased the sexual energy sparking between him and Melody. He didn't want to dwell on what had not happened in the elevator, what should never happen.

"Dad, Dad, in the road. Stop the car! Dad!"

Logan caught his son's terror in the rearview mirror, and pulled right over. "What's wrong—"

"I saw it, too," Melody said as she opened her door and bolted. Even as Logan called her back, she stepped into a stream of two-lane traffic moving at a fair clip.

Horns honked. Cars stopped. The tour trolley screeched to a halt. One guy drove his truck up on the curb and ended nose-down in a holly hedge.

Only the women drivers seemed miffed; the men were too busy watching Mel move. Man, she really did have a figure that could stop traffic. She looked like an ad for rainbow sherbet in her raspberry spikes, sexy lime Capri pants, and lemon chiffon top, traffic frozen around her, as if she were true north.

Logan looked at his son then, and swore inwardly at the pure adoration Shane directed her way. There she stood, teaching him to play in traffic, and he looked as if she had just saved the world.

Two men got out of their cars and started toward her, then a police car pulled up beside her. Logan wanted to go to her rescue, but he didn't want to drag Shane into what might become a scene, and he couldn't leave him alone in the car.

Reduced to watching from a distance, Logan felt as if he were letting Mel down. He'd probably end up dropping Shane at Jessie's, though, so he could go and bail her out. Honest to Pete that woman could get herself into trouble.

To Logan's surprise, however, not two minutes later, she made her way back to the car with a full male escort—two cops and two civilians. Logan didn't appreciate the way one of the cops guided her with a possessive hand to her back, as if she couldn't make it on her own. She'd gotten out there by herself, hadn't she?

Watch it, buddy, Logan thought as he stepped from the car, waited, then opened the passenger door for her to get in. "Bozos," he said beneath his breath as he shut it and watched them walk away. He'd give Mel a piece of his mind later, he thought belting himself back into the driver's seat. For now, he'd get her the hell out of there and away from the ogling hordes.

Mad at her for jumping into traffic, madder still at the men who drooled on her, it took Logan a minute to focus on the kittens she and Shane were cuddling. Then he saw the small brown paper bag in her lap. "Jeez," he said. "Is that what you saw in the road? A bag of kittens?"

Shane's eyes spilled over tears as he nodded. "They were gonna get squished, Dad. Mel had to save 'em."

Logan looked at Melody, and she looked back, daring him to deny it. He shrugged, and she nodded. "Pet store," she said. "Now. We need kitty formula and an eyedropper, or maybe a baby bottle. A little one. I'll ask the clerk."

Logan started the car, while Melody wrapped both kittens in Shane's sweater and handed them to him. "Hold them, but be gentle, and keep them wrapped so they're warm. Your dad is going to stay in the car with you while I go in the pet store and get what they need. Okay?"

Shane nodded. "Mel?"

"What, baby?"

"Where's their mother?"

"Pet store," Logan announced as he pulled into the lot, and dropped Mel at the door, glad they'd been so close, she hadn't had a chance to answer Shane's question. "Go ahead, Mel," he said. "We'll be watching for you when you come out."

She nodded and left, looking as relieved as he felt.

"Dad?" Shane said a minute later. "Where's their mother?"

ON Logan's coffee table, Melody spread an assortment of baby formula and rice cereal, eye droppers, mini baby bottles, kitty vitamins in a tube, pet blankets and warmers, not to mention kitty litter, a scooper big enough for the kittens to sleep in, and a litter box.

"Did you get enough?" Logan asked.

"Stuff it, Kilgarven," she responded dryly.

"I want to call them Ink and Spot," Shane said.

"Good names, sport," Logan said.

One kitten mewled incessantly, while the other looked terrifyingly near to giving up the fight. If they lost one, his son would never get over it. "What can I do to help?" Logan asked as he followed Mel into his kitchen.

"I need a bowl and the smallest funnel you can find."

Logan swore and started rummaging. "You shouldn't have—"

Melody slammed a can of formula on the counter. "You think I should have left them there to die?"

"No, but stepping into traffic with—"

"Screw the traffic. We've got to keep them alive."

Logan shut his mouth and ran a hand through his hair in concerned, and wholehearted, agreement. Between them they silently mixed a miniscule amount of baby cereal with the formula and enlarged the holes in the nipples. Melody took the sluggish kitten to feed, the one with a white spot on the tip of its stub tail, and she let Shane feed Ink, its frenetically starving sibling.

It took a while to coax Spot into suckling, but Melody didn't give up. She sat on the sofa and rubbed its throat and crooned forever, before being rewarded with a first tentative pull on the nipple. She looked at Logan then, letting her relief show. He felt the same, perhaps more so, and they shared a moment of complete communion—gratitude, relief, with an underlying contentment that smacked dangerously of domesticity.

"Ink drank it all," Shane said, snapping Logan back to a safe reality.

He leaned over and kissed his son's head. "She's had enough for now. She's purring in her sleep."

Shane beamed. "You saved 'em, Mel!"

Logan straightened and frowned. "Melody acted without thought to the consequences, son."

Melody's head snapped up. "Excuse me?"

"Your actions were reckless and dangerous," he said. "You do realize that your life is more important than a—"

"Don't even say it."

"You *know* I'm right."

"I know you're a narrow-minded suit, with a . . . necktie where your heart should be."

"I know that *you* taught my son to run into a street full of speeding cars."

Ten

THE realization took Melody's breath away, but she knew the minute Logan said it that he was right. She had taught Shane a dangerous lesson. "Oh my God."

The small wide-eyed boy watching them looked worried . . . because they'd been arguing in front of him, of course. She hadn't realized that either. "Your dad is right," she said, as Shane came over and stopped in front of her. She took his hand and tugged him closer. "I should never have rushed headlong into moving traffic like that. It was reckless and dangerous."

"But you had to save Ink and Spot."

"I should have gone about it differently," she said. "More carefully."

"Different, how?" he asked.

Melody stumbled over her answer. She couldn't think what she should have done different.

"Mel could have found a policeman to stop the traffic for her," Logan said, giving Melody a sidelong glance before hunching down in front of his son, there at her knee. "You have to promise me, sport, that you'll never, ever, step into traffic."

"Not even when I'm like, twelve, and grown up?"

Logan smoothed his son's cowlick with a depth of fatherly affection that made Mel's chest ache. "Cars going that fast are deadly," he said, his gaze intense, "and I don't know what I'd do if something happened to you. I need you, son, and not like Mom, either. I mean, I *really* need you."

Shane's eyes widened, and he stepped into his father's ready embrace.

Melody bit her lip and swallowed, focusing on the drowsy kitten in her lap, aware that something significant had just passed between father and son, something she did not understand, a soul-deep kind of connection that she yearned to experience, though it frightened her to the pit of her belly.

"When I'm sixteen," Shane said, as he pulled from the embrace, "then can I? If another baby animal without a mother needs help."

Melody placed the half bottle of formula on the end table. "Don't ever do what I did today, sweetheart. Please."

"Maybe when he's thirty," Logan said, petting the kitten in her lap with his index finger. "Thirty is old enough."

"Right," Mel said, amazed at how tiny the kitten appeared in proportion to Logan's large, well-shaped hand, glad Logan no longer seemed angry with her.

"But what if I see a baby animal in the road before I'm thirty?"

"I'll rescue it for you," Logan said.

"Or Mel can. You and Mel can do it 'til I'm old enough, right?"

Logan and Melody regarded each other, the knowledge that their paths would diverge years before, heavy and unspoken between them. They nodded tentatively, both to appease a wide-eyed boy who had a great capacity for love and to keep him out of danger.

DRESS-REHEARSAL day arrived at four in the morning for Melody. She'd told Logan she was so nervous, she wanted to go to work a couple of hours early, to make sure everything was all set, which was true . . . as far as it went, but she had essential errands to run on her way, so she fired up her vintage VW.

For the first show, Gardner had decided she would cook an Early New England–style dinner, which worked for her, but whatever she cooked, she knew she would need help to pull off a rehearsal.

Before Jessie and Logan's mother could leave for work that morning, she needed to pick up the Boston baked beans and brown bread from Jessie, and the cider baked ham from Phyllis. Melody's friend Vickie had agreed to prepare her grandmother's famous hashed squash, an Old New England favorite, and Kira had donated a steamed cranberry pudding to the cause.

All of Melody's friends had come through for her, for which she would remain supremely grateful, though each of them, in their own ways, had hinted that they would not "bail her out," to quote Vickie, "a second time." Melody knew they were right. She did need to learn how to cook for herself. She had even suggested to Jessie and Phyllis Kilgarven that she would like to have cooking lessons. But Jessie said her Boneyard tours were picking up, and Phyllis mentioned dating Melody's father rather steadily—which news Melody would not be the one to impart to a certain male Kilgarven, of the long, tall variety.

"I will learn to cook," Melody repeated to herself as she carried a huge glass casserole dish bearing a crusty, cider baked ham onto the set at six that morning. And she would, though not before her first show, unfortunately.

All she needed to do was get through dress rehearsal, and she would be halfway to making it through her first show. How hard could it be to sprinkle herbs on a ham, stab it with cloves and throw the meat into an oven? She didn't actually need to cider-marinate the ham she was pretending to prepare. Who would know?

After her fake preparation, she would simply take Phyllis Kilgarven's finished ham from the oven. Voilà!

The live show would be a different matter, of course, but she would deal with that in due course, like the day after tomorrow.

PIECE of cake, Melody thought the following night. Her rehearsal had gone great. Perfect. The crew had applauded. Tiffany Peabody—who seemed to dislike Melody, as much as she liked Logan—had scowled, which pretty much proved it was good. Gardner had beamed, and Logan had groaned in ecstasy when he tasted the ham. "Almost as good as my mother's," he'd said, and Melody forced herself to turn away, so she didn't smack the half-wit and tell him the ham *was* his mother's.

In less than forty-eight hours, she would be shooting the first *Kitchen Witch* show live, she thought, as she practiced making the ham in her own kitchen, while praying that her first would not be her last.

For the tenth time, she smoothed Logan's mother's ratty old recipe, so she could read it better. Phyl couldn't have been kidding when she said she knew the recipe by heart. Who could follow this old thing, with half the instructions bonded by edible glue? Every time Melody tried cooking it, something different went wrong. Tonight it was the glaze, as in: She could stand a spoon erect in it.

Tomorrow, she would have to cook the meal successfully, throughout the course of the show, in order to teach her audience, in live segments, how to do it themselves. Oh God. What would she do if the meal she prepared on live television ended up resembling the dinner she and Shane had murdered the first time she took care of him?

She could still picture herself that night dancing around the kitchen yelling "Yikes," with Shane trying not to giggle. She remembered his gentle, "Yuck," and, "Oh no."

Too bad she couldn't bring him on the show with her, she thought, in case it happened again. Not that she expected to have a problem, but . . .

Melody went upstairs and knocked on Logan's door. She heard a giggling, "Dad," or two from Shane before Logan answered with a crease in one red cheek, his eyes barely focused, wearing floppy socks, faded sweats with peek-a-boo knees, and trying to smooth an endearing case of bed-head.

Stuffed suit, humanized. Have mercy.

Good thing Shane came up behind old Dad, or Melody might foolishly have touched the dimple in that unshaven chin. She fisted her hands and gave Shane her full attention.

"Hi, Mel. Ink and Spot have a new bed—come and see."

"I will, later. I came to ask if I could borrow you for a while."

Shane's eyes lit up. "Can I, Dad?"

Logan seemed too fuzzy to assimilate their words.

Melody hid her grin. "I'm nervous about tomorrow," she said. "I thought Shane could distract me."

Logan nodded. "Uh, sure." He checked his watch and regarded his son in that speaking way only a father could. "Bedtime in one hour," he said. "*One* hour."

"Hooray!" Shane shot down the stairs, nearly knocking them over.

Melody grinned. "I don't think he wants to."

She got out the construction paper, Popsicle sticks, glue, markers, and crayons she kept on hand for when he stayed over, and put him to work. "Hey Buddy, remember that dinner we made the first night you came over, and everything went wrong?"

ON the day of the first *Kitchen Witch* show, the whole of New England was under a hurricane weather watch, which made getting to the station early a bit of a challenge. Nevertheless, Melody drove her beetle convertible and ignored the wind whistling through its tattered top.

Not only were the seas along the eastern seaboard threatening to spill over, Wardrobe had done something horrible while cleaning Melody's favorite forties shirtwaist, and a spillover of another sort threatened. Gardener and Logan came into her dressing room as Melody tried valiantly to tuck her breasts back into her bodice.

"Leave it, Mel." Logan gave her a wink. "I like the way it fits."

"You would." Melody blew the hair from her brow.

Gardner laughed and handed her a black witch hat with red polka dots to match her dress. "I had one made for each of your outfits for the next six weeks."

"I'm touched," Melody said. "Shocked, but touched."

"Witch hats instead of chef's hats. I'm brilliant," Gardner announced, since no one else bothered. "I mean, if we're going for a wild and sexy cooking witch here, we may as well go all the way."

"Right." Melody only hoped the show didn't get anywhere near as wild as she feared it could.

Her frizzing hair had seemed to triple in volume, and the perspiration on her face reflected the light, like a mirror aimed at the sun, but hairdressing and makeup fixed both—mostly. Her dress stuck to her, despite the air-conditioning—

in ninety-nine percent humidity, nobody stayed dry—and the preheating ovens did nothing to help her cause.

Before she knew it, Melody stood offstage, trembling, while Woody raised his hand and gave her the signal as he mouthed the countdown. "Three, two, one . . ."

Lights, camera, action, Melody thought. Nerves, butter-flies, nausea. "I think I'm gonna throw up."

Logan chuckled from behind her and squeezed both shoulders. "Knock 'em dead, gorgeous."

Until he spoke, Melody hadn't a clue he was there, but his presence, more than his compliment, calmed her in a way she'd thought impossible.

She flattened her hand against her quivering midriff, as the announcer began. "Welcome ladies and gentlemen. Let's give a huge round of applause to Salem's own 'Saucy' Kitchen Witch, Mizzz Melody Seabright!"

Melody's heart leaped as she took the stage, the applause track drowning the lukewarm reception from her sparse studio audience.

LOGAN watched, dazzled all over again, as Melody beamed, found her mark, stage left, and flicked her wand toward the orchestra, stage right. On cue, they struck up a jubilant rendition of "Do You Believe in Magic?"

In her black and red polka dot dress and hat, with red spikes, and her amazing hair cascading to her waist, Melody made her hip-swaying way across the front of the stage to approach her set from the opposite direction. "Swing it and show it off," Gardner had instructed her, and so she did. Man oh man, could that woman swing it.

Once Melody stepped up to the island counter where she would do her preparations facing her audience, she gave the orchestra another magic flick of her wand, and they stopped mid-beat . . . like magic.

The audience ate it up.

Behind Mel, as if suspended in midair, white cupboards hung on a night-blue sky—actually a high-tech video wall—splashed with a tasteful sprinkle of gold stars—techno magic at its finest. Two high-definition plasma screens stood off to each side for live close-up shots of food preparation.

In a move that surprised Logan, Melody reached beneath the island for a sign. Attached to a Popsicle stick stuck in a wooden spool, and printed in colorfully bold block crayon letters, the sign read, "Caution! Ditzy witch at work." The letter z had been printed backward, and the slant to the left-handed letters looked amazingly familiar.

As Melody chatted, smiled, and generally dazzled her viewers, Logan's respect for her grew. She moved like a dancer in and around the props and ingredients she had begun to sort. Damned if she didn't seem as if she knew exactly what she was doing, thank God. He'd been more than a little worried.

After she placed everything in a certain order, she sashayed around toward the front of the island, raised her shoulder, tilted her head, and bent her knee in a way that showcased her dress's sexy center slit as well as a fine pair of legs.

Raising her wand, Melody drew three flaring swirls above her ingredients and chanted as she circled back to where she began.

> *"Sugar and apples to sweeten it twice*
> *Salt sprinkled gently to tease and entice*
> *Cloves and mustard to spice the meat.*
> *Give us the skill to cook the treat . . .*
> *And friends and family to share and eat!"*

This time, in-house applause drowned the applause track.

Melody began to prepare her cider-baked ham with no less flair than she put into the spell itself. She covered it with a mixture of brown sugar, bread crumbs, and a little dried mustard. "Did you know that mustard seeds are believed to carry the magical properties for courage and faith?" she asked.

Logan hadn't expected her to improvise on her dress rehearsal, nor had he expected her to bring real magic into the show, though Gardner did say she needed to "play" every angle.

"Cloves," she said, a minute later, as she began to stab whole cloves into the ham, "are used to stop gossip, protect children, and foster kinship."

Okaaay . . . it's okay, Logan thought when he saw that a couple of people in the audience seemed to be taking down her every word. Melody was simply delivering the kind of magic they were looking for.

Everyone, including the crew, seemed to be . . . in love, bottom-lining Melody's appeal in two simple words. Melody Seabright "made love" to the cameras, and, oh God, Logan thought he might be falling as hard as the rest of them. Yes, her show had the makings to be a winner, but with all her talk of herbs and magic, he might be in more trouble than he originally suspected.

After she put the ham in one of the ovens, she took out the ingredients for the hashed squash, set a cast-iron skillet on the stove, placed a slab of bacon inside, and turned on the heat.

Everything was going so well, Logan thought a few minutes later, he wondered why he'd been nervous. Mel was acing the show. She'd been baking the ham, peeling the squash, and wrapping her audience around a small manicured finger, all at one time. He couldn't believe it.

As if her every move had been choreographed, she buttered the mold, so her brown bread wouldn't stick, poured in just enough batter, placed the cover on the mold, and put it in a kettle on the stove's back burner to steam.

When the timer that played the intro to "Do You Believe in Magic?" went off, her smile surely won a host of new viewers. "Time to remove the ham from the oven," she said, using her own unique brand of sex appeal to do something as simple as open an oven.

Logan caught her expression at the precise moment her veneer of self-confidence cracked. It happened when flames leaped from the skillet on the stove, set off smoke alarms, and set Melody herself on what might very well be a quick downward spiral.

Adrenaline had Logan set to run to her rescue, but he stopped short of charging like a freaking knight on a damned white horse. What the hell? She could handle this, he told himself, as he grabbed a fire extinguisher.

"Have no fear," Melody said, with barely a waver in her smile. "I know what to do." She donned oven mitts as if suiting up for battle, grabbed the skillet, and slipped the pan of fire into the sink. She took her wand in one hand, and a huge box of baking soda in the other. Pour the soda, flick the wand, pour and flick, until the flames disappeared.

Then she flashed that hundred-watt smile, pulled the soda-coated skillet from the sink, and raised it like the spoils of war.

While her audience cheered, she placed the pan on the counter, produced another sign, and set it down, smack, beside it. "Yikes!" it said, in bold blue and red crayon.

The audience roared. Everywhere Logan looked, somebody was smiling, nodding, applauding. The only sober-faced observer stood in the wings opposite: Gardner.

The Ice Man returneth.

During the fire fiasco, Melody had left the oven open, her dish of ham still sitting on the extended rack, so she completed the task of removing it. As she carried it to the flat-top stove, Logan could see that the ham in the glass casserole dish appeared hot and crusty, maybe a little too dark a crust, but not bad.

Fine, Logan thought. She'd gotten back on track. Maybe. Probably.

In any event, he made his way toward the back of the audience where he would remain standing, so she could focus on him, make eye contact. Perhaps he could send good vibes her way and help strengthen her wavering confidence—not that she appeared daunted, not quite.

She placed the dish of ham on the stovetop. "We'll give it a minute to cool," she said, turning back to her audience, a new glisten to her brow. Okay, so she was a bit frazzled, but she appeared in full control, and no less stunning, as she crossed the set to stand behind the island and face the cameras. "Let's make a glaze with some of the cider we used to marinate the ham, shall we?"

That's when she saw him, Logan knew, because she raised her chin and squared her shoulders the slightest bit, and he nodded, telling her without words that he had faith in her.

She thanked him with bright eyes and an easier smile as she took out a saucepan into which she poured half the cider. She'd put floured raisins in the brown bread earlier, and now she put the rest in the cider. "In the world of magic," she said, placing the pan on a burner and beginning to stir the glaze, "sauce is often used to solve a difficult situation. Focus on your challenge as you swirl your spoon in the mixture, and stir your problem away. If your sauce turns out lumpy, you've still got a few bumps in the road, but you're on your way to settling the problem. If it comes out smooth, your difficulty will be easily resolved."

Despite her trial by grease fire, Melody hadn't lost her

audience. They hung on her every word, proving her assertion that when it came to the bottom line, showmanship was everything, even on a cooking show.

Logan caught the scent of frying ham at about the same time Melody's head came up. "Did you hear a crack?"

She whipped around. "Duck!" she yelled, diving for cover while audience and crew did the same.

Another crack, like ice on a winter pond, and the casserole dish shattered, sending glass shards in every direction, leaving the ham sizzling on a bare burner . . . and Gardner sizzling in the wings.

Eleven

"COAST clear?" Melody asked as she rose to a mixed-bag reaction—a bit of grousing, but a bit more humor, from the audience, and Gardner's seething exit from the wings.

Logan watched with awe, his stomach clenched on her behalf, as she gathered her wits about her and turned the burner off under her sizzling, glass-peppered ham. She chose a wooden spatula to scrape the charred carcass into a pan then place it on the counter. "One fire was enough," she said. "Two, would be showing off."

She got a couple of chuckles, three would have been better.

Logan couldn't imagine the strength of character required to face a room of strangers, never mind the viewers at home, who had witnessed her fall. Damn, he was proud of her.

She wiped her hands on her apron in a slight gesture of insecurity. "Everybody, okay?" she asked, examining the faces of her audience as if speaking to each personally, another winning talent. "Do we need to call the EMTs?" She looked around again, caught the shrugs, waited. "No? Good?" She smiled with apparent relief and placed a hand on her heart. "Guess that was one *smokin'* ham!"

Laughter came slowly, but it came and lasted for a few promising beats.

"You know what I did wrong, don't you?" she said. "I forgot to turn the burner off after the bacon caught fire. Hard to tell a burner's on with a stove like this, but that's no excuse." She wagged her finger at them. "Here are your two most important lessons of the day: "One: *Never* place a glass casserole dish on a hot burner. Two: Turn the burners off when you finish cooking."

The sign she whipped out this time said, "Warning! Don't try this at home." The skull and crossbones, Shane's signature design, confirmed Logan's suspicion about the artist.

As the show progressed, only two more signs were necessary. Her gloppy baked beans got a, "Yuck," her soggy brown bread, an, "Oh no."

When the show ended, perhaps in more ways than one, Melody took off her hat and combed her wild, raven mane of black magic from her face. "Thank you for joining me for our first ever *Kitchen Witch* show, and thanks for being such great sports during my 'Don't Cook Like This' segment."

"In parting, I'd like to give you a centuries-old recipe for Happiness Cake that I promise can't go wrong. Take a handful of good deeds, a tablespoon of thoughtfulness, a cup of consideration, and blend with a flagon of forgiveness. Fold in seeds of faith, tears of joy, and a never-ending supply of love . . . and be happy."

She raised her wand and waved it over the audience with a bright parting smile. "Until we meet again, may your lives be filled with bright blessings and shining stars." Then she zapped the orchestra into a triumphant rendition of "Do You Believe in Magic?" and exited with the same flair and flamboyance with which she'd made her spell-binding entrance.

Logan shook his head in amazement and applauded as her audience gave her a standing ovation . . . as if she'd cast a spell on the lot of them. "Unbelievable," he said. "Un-freaking-believable."

"I know," Tiffany said, suddenly beside him. "Daddy's not going to be happy."

That's true, Logan thought, searching for a bright side, which he'd need for his postshow meeting with Gardner anyway. "At least Melody knew where she went wrong and shared her lessons with the audience. Some of her more naive viewers might even have believed she planned the 'Don't Cook Like This' segment. She did produce the signs."

"Right." Tiffany smiled knowingly. "Give me a call, why don't you, when you're looking to replace her?"

I don't think so, Logan thought, because he realized there could only be one Kitchen Witch—Melody Seabright. And at the end of the day, it didn't matter whether her audience believed her or not, they adored her. She even got a couple of wolf whistles as she left the stage. One guy hung around so long afterward, Logan went to see what he wanted. "Can I help you?" he asked.

"I was waiting to meet Miss Seabright. Do you think she'll come out to see her fans?"

"Not today," Logan said, grinning despite himself. Fans?

"But I'd like to get her autograph," the oily character said. "I'd be happy to wait while you ask her."

You want more than her autograph, Bozo, Logan thought, hackles rising. It was all he could do not to throw the jerk out like a bouncer in a strip joint. Good thing he usually drove Mel to and from work. She might need that kind of protection now. Maybe she should tone down the sex appeal on the next show—if there was another.

"Logan," Woody said, coming up beside him. "Gardner wants to see you in his office. Pronto."

Logan glanced at the teleprompter to catch the final credits. "Signs by Shane. Wardrobe by The Immortal Classic." He shook his head, at a complete loss. He didn't know how to deal with a woman like Melody Seabright. Beat her, or kiss her, or get the hell away from her, while escape was still possible.

As he approached the office where Gardner paced like a lion ripe for the kill, Logan wondered how he was supposed to extract Melody from a mess of her own making, without any of her sexy tricks at his disposal.

"Do you want me to fire her?" Logan asked as he entered, hoping to deflect Gardner's ire by taking the teeth from his bite.

"You said she could cook, damn it!"

Logan didn't know why he should be surprised. No way would Gardner admit to being taken in by anyone, not even the sexiest witch in the East. "I said she couldn't, actually. I kept trying to warn you—"

"Don't give me that! You brought her in to interview for a cooking show. That pretty much implied that she could cook."

Damn, he had a point.

"Besides," Gardner said. "Everybody knows you two have the hots for each other. You wanted her around, and you intended to make it happen."

"Like hell, I—" *For each other?* "You think Melody is attracted to me?"

Gardner growled, and Logan backtracked, while his head remained attached. "If it's any consolation," he said, "the audience loved her. They could have cared less whether she could cook or not."

"You call eleven people an audience?"

"The phones are ringing nonstop," Logan said, "and most

of the eleven bought tickets for next week's show before they left. As have thirty-two others, and that's only in the time it took me to walk up here. I checked with ticket sales on my way up. Want me to check again?"

Gardner growled.

Logan poured them each a scotch, and with a grunt, Gardner downed his in one gulp.

"I repeat," Logan said, after a thoughtful sip of his own. "Do you want me to fire her?"

"Yes, damn it!"

Not the answer he was going for. That was that, then, he thought with regret, as he punched a couple of numbers into his cell phone. "Nathan," he said. "Stop selling tickets to *The Kitchen Witch* show— What? More than a hundred? This fast? Doesn't matter. The boss wants to pull the plu—"

Gardner yanked the phone from Logan's hand. "Never mind, Nathan. Keep selling them." He slammed Logan's antenna down so hard, it snapped.

Logan slipped his broken phone into his breast pocket, while squelching an urge to make slush out of Ice Man. "Do you, or do you not, want me to fire her?" *Not,* Logan wanted to hear, though he wasn't sure why it should matter so much, except, he had a feeling that Melody had finally found her calling.

"I'm warning you, Kilgarven, if that woman can't cook a decent meal on next week's show, I swear to God, you'll both be out of work."

Logan opened his mouth, thought better of telling the boss where he could shove his job, and regrouped. "Mel has such a compelling stage presence, she doesn't need to know how to cook. Why don't we just hire somebody to cook for her?"

"No! Positively, not! You will not, I repeat, not, spend another dime on that woman. She's already cost us too much in salary and residuals."

You're the one who cost us, Logan thought, though he remained prudently silent.

Gardner slammed his empty glass on the bar. "Start using your brain where Melody is concerned, and see that she gets some cooking lessons."

Look who's talking. "Cooking lessons?"

"Yes, and you'd damn well better manage it without spending any more of the station's money, or, I swear, you're finished."

"Right. Free cooking lessons," Logan groused, as he walked away without looking back. "Piece of cake."

LOGAN stopped in the doorway of their office when he saw Melody slumped on the sofa in dejection, her breasts overflowing her dynamite dress, her bare feet curled beneath her, half a bottle of champagne on the end table, and half a box of chocolates in her lap. Oh, brother. If both containers had been full when she started, she was in big trouble.

Logan stepped quietly into the room, shut the door, and turned the lock to give her some privacy.

Mel looked up when she heard the click, the dry tear trails in her makeup giving her away. She held up her champagne glass. "Join me."

Logan unbuttoned his suit coat, loosened his tie, and sat beside her, close beside her, because he thought she might need someone about now.

"I hope Daddy wasn't watching," she said, closing her eyes as if the notion exhausted her. "I hate when he's right."

Therein lay the root of the problem. "If Daddy thinks he was right," Logan said, "that's his interpretation, not mine."

Melody snorted in disdain. "He was. He always is." She poured herself another glass of champagne. "But when he has proof, like today, he's hell to live with, not that I've ever had to live with him long."

Logan poured himself a glass of champagne, if only to empty the bottle and stop her from finishing it, and handed her a ticket sales report.

"What's this?" she asked, setting the report aside and going for another chocolate. "My walking papers?"

Logan took her hand and directed the chocolate to his mouth, instead of hers.

Surprised at first, Melody watched him take a bite.

In his attempt to draw her attention from her failure, he'd turned it toward himself in a way that heated his blood. He'd sat too close. She smelled too good.

Ah, who was he kidding; she smelled of smoked ham, and still she enticed him.

"More?" she asked, her voice low and sultry.

Oh yeah. Lots more. No way to take the other half of that maple cream without touching his lips to her fingers. Bad move, he warned himself, even as he opened his mouth and sanity evaporated.

She squeaked when he nipped a finger and held it to his mouth, as he licked every bit of chocolate from it. Then he drew her hand to his nape, pulled her into his arms, and drank champagne from her lips.

When her mouth opened on a moan, Logan went in for a greedier taste. In the process, she climbed into his lap, or he lifted her there, as he sunk deeper into the cushions, Melody practically on top of him. The kiss went on, their hands exploring, hers, his, everywhere.

Logan found the slit in her dress, and Melody squeaked again as his palm rode her inner thigh . . . until he felt an embarrassing wetness on himself, as if he'd— "Jeez," he said, sitting up and nearly throwing her over. "Damn." He grabbed her hand to keep her from falling off the sofa and pulled her back. He looked down at his unbuttoned pants, more grateful to see the unbroken champagne glass between his legs than the embarrassing stain the dregs had made. "Jeez."

Melody giggled when she saw what happened.

Logan swore. He looked as if he'd had an unplanned spill of his own.

"Take off your pants," she said.

Now why hadn't she suggested that before sanity slapped him upside the head? "I don't think that's such a good idea," despite the fact that he was growing hard before her staring eyes. "Mel, the more you watch it, the worse it's gonna get."

"Oh." She looked up at him, face pink. "I meant for you to take your pants off so I could use my hair dryer on them, unless you want me to blow—" She blushed pinker. "Blow them dry while you wear them."

Logan chuckled. "Yeah, warming an erection always helps." He brought her face to his neck, so they wouldn't have to face each other over his words. That would be too much like admitting they wanted each other. It was safer avoiding the issue, he thought, as they'd been doing. "Never mind. I keep a spare pair in the bathroom. I'll change in a bit." He picked up the ticket sales printout from the floor and handed it to her. "Read this."

"I don't need to. I'm finished, and I know it."

"What makes you say so?"

"Please, I was a disaster."

"You usually are." Logan earned a halfhearted swat for that, but when her eyes filled, he pulled her back into his arms. "Talk to me," he said, tracing his way up her spine in small circles.

"Woody told me that Gardner wanted to see you," she confessed, her discouragement clear, her voice muffled against his neck. "I know Gardner's mad. I know I'm fired."

"I won't kid you." Logan pulled away enough to look at her. "He thinks you should learn how to cook. He's hard-boiled that way."

"He didn't fire me?"

"Nope. Learn to cook, and you're in."

Melody sighed and shook her head. "It's no use. I'm gonna hang up my broom before I make everything worse. Daddy was right."

Logan tapped the paper in her hand. "Read that, will you?"

She did. Twice. "Next week's show is sold out? How can that be? There isn't going to be a show next week." She sounded almost relieved.

Had her father programmed her to give up before she could succeed? Did quitting afford a level of comfort? Logan didn't know how to get around the habits of a lifetime. He knew only that she had failed repeatedly, and, if this time was any indication, she did it with panache. Despite her flair, talent, strength of purpose, she gave up anyway—unless someone needed her, of course, like a small boy, a friend, unwed mothers, stray kittens.

Logan smiled inwardly when realization hit, and he played his ace. "There has to be a show next week, unless you want Shane to go hungry."

"What does Shane have to do with this?"

"If you don't take cooking lessons ASAP and come back to prepare a dynamite dinner next week, Shane's father is going to be out job hunting beside you."

"Gardner's a rat!" Melody's hackles rose in indignation as she "cut the cord" and moved from his comforting embrace. After a minute of hard pacing, she raised her hands in an expression of helplessness. "Okay, damn it, who's the lucky duck who gets to give me cooking lessons?" She shook her head after a thoughtful minute. "Do we know anybody that stupid?"

* * *

SHANE in tow, Logan and Melody made the rounds that night of likely prospects. Jessie welcomed them with enthusiasm, proceeded to show off her second hearse and introduce the D.A. who would be driving it now that her business had doubled. Logan and Melody were forced to say good night early, though, because the judge and the D.A., who had sparred their way through three decades in court, had dinner reservations.

"So much for Jess," Logan said as he herded Shane toward the Volvo. "Let's go ask Grandma Phyl to teach Mel to cook."

Shane beamed. "Yes! She bought me Rockin' Cruiser Bruisers today."

"What?" Melody asked.

"Video game," Logan said.

Ten minutes later, Melody gaped when Logan pulled into the parking lot of a tired tenement building with peeling paint and missing windows.

"It's seen better days," Logan said, watching her.

"At the beginning of the last century, maybe."

"She won't move!" Logan shouted. "Sorry," he said, when he startled her. They got out of the car. "You don't think I've tried? I've begged her to retire and move to a better place. Stubborn thing."

"You're just like her," Shane said as he emerged from the backseat. "Gram says 'You're stubborner than a nor'easter.' "

Logan cupped his son's head playfully as they walked, and brought him close for an affectionate tussle. "And you take after both of us."

Shane giggled. "Right!"

They found Phyllis Kilgarven packing dishes in moving crates, which stopped Logan dead, while Melody stared openmouthed, in the same shocked state, at her father, his shirt sleeves rolled up, tie askew, hands . . . dirty? "Daddy?"

"Hi, Mellie Pie. Saw your show today. I told you not to do it."

Melody sighed and felt herself grow smaller before him. She saw Logan bristle on her behalf, and because he did, Shane did as well, which made her feel a bit better, actually.

"I'm about to satisfy your fondest wish," Logan's mother said, filling the awkward breach, as she kissed her son, then her grandson.

"You're finally ready to move in with me?" Logan said, his relief apparent. "Thank God."

Melody's father gave one of his abrasive belly laughs. "Sorry, son. She's moving in with me."

"You're taking Shane's grandmother to Palm Beach?" On some vague level, Melody knew she was chiding her father—a first—and it felt good.

"Palm Beach!" Logan snapped at his mother. "When the devil were you going to tell me?"

"Gramma? Do you have my Rockin' Cruiser Bruisers game?"

"We're not going to Palm Beach," her father said. "Not until after Christmas. I bought the old Endicott place for the rest of the year. Phyl's only moving across town."

"You mean the Captain Joshua Endicott mansion?" Logan asked, "the one on the register of historic places?"

"Yeah," her father said, "which would be a real pain if we wanted to change anything, but Phyl loves it the way it is."

"Jeez, I'll bet she does." Logan looked at his mother as if he'd never seen her so clearly. "From a tenement to a mansion, Mom?" There was nothing complimentary about his tone. "And it took a stranger to move you."

"Hardly a stranger, son," her father said, but Melody didn't want to hear that any more than Logan did. She dropped into the nearest chair, at a loss.

"Let me fix some tea," Phyllis said.

"Didn't you think I might like to know?" Logan followed his mother into her kitchen, and after a minute of strained silence between Melody and her father, she joined them.

LOGAN laid rubber as they drove away.

"You never asked her to give me cooking lessons," Mel said.

Logan swore beneath his breath. "They're going to freaking Cancun for a freaking jaunt. She's abandoning her housecleaning customers, people she once claimed depended on her so much she couldn't quit. For years I've been trying to get her to retire, and this self-centered prig comes along and—"

Shane looked from one of them to the other. "Is he a bad man, Dad?"

Logan slammed the wheel. "He's, he's—"

"My father," Melody said, not sure why the truth about him should bother her.

Logan did a double take and sighed. "Sorry."

"I can tell."

"It's just that he—"

"Got her to relax and take time off, move to a better neighborhood, everything you wanted for her. You're just pissed you weren't the one to accomplish it. You weren't looking out for your mother's welfare as much as you wanted your own stubborn way about it."

They drove in silence for some time after that, until Logan looked at Shane in the mirror. "When Gramma told you about the Rockin' Cruiser Bruisers game on the phone at Jessie's, did she give you a message for me?"

Shane thought about that for a minute. "Oh yeah. She needed to talk to you about somethin' 'portant."

At Logan's raised brow, Shane drooped a bit. "Sorry, Dad."

"Try to remember next time, okay, sport?"

" 'Kay . . . but who's gonna give Mel cookin' lessons if Gramma can't?"

"Hell if I know," Logan said. "I think we're fresh out of likely candidates." Logan regarded Melody, for the first time since she'd reamed him for his selfishness. "You were right," he said. "The truth is, I'm glad my mother's going to take life easy for a change, no matter who made her do it."

"Good for you." Melody nodded in satisfaction. "Take a left at the next light. Vickie's grandmother might teach me to cook."

Vickie let them in. "Nana's been confined to bed since she fell last month," she said, so when Logan and Melody went in to say hello, they didn't mention cooking lessons. Before they left, the old lady took Melody's hand. "Did my hashed squash work out all right for your dress rehearsal, dear?"

Cat out of the bag, Melody thought, as she assured Nana it was wonderful, while ignoring Logan's heated gaze.

The minute they drove away, Logan called her on it. "You tricked me."

"Get real. You knew from the beginning that I didn't know how to cook."

Logan gave her a dark, warning glare, because she was right, Melody thought. She hid her smile for as long as she could, until she burst into laughter.

"It's not funny," he said.

"Trust me, it is."

"Dad, I know who can teach Mel to cook."

Melody stifled a new chuckle. "I know, too."

Logan narrowed his eyes and looked from one of them to the other, his shoulders tense, his look guarded. "Who?"

"You!" they said together.

"No, no, and no!"

Twelve

IN Melody's opinion, Logan kicked and screamed his way to the inevitable. "How about a professional cooking instructor?" he suggested, even as he pushed her shopping cart of cookware and small appliances through a gourmet specialty shop.

He found a food processor that should clean the house, it cost so much, and placed it in her cart.

Melody took it out. "I can't afford it, and I don't need it."

Logan put it back. "You need everything."

She stopped fighting him. She'd return it later.

In the cookbook aisle, she showed him a copy of *Cooking for the Saucily Impaired.* "Sounds perfect," she said.

Logan took it from her hand and put it back on the shelf. "You're saucy enough."

To prove his point, she chose *101 Uses for Strawberry Jam,* read the title, and winked.

Logan crossed his arms. "Are you turning up the heat?"

"I like to 'cook' fast."

"Slow is better." He chose a copy of *Chocolate Orgasms for Beginners,* put it in the basket, and grinned.

Melody took it out, shook her head, and walked away.

"Don't turn up the burners, if you can't take the heat," he said, and as she turned to respond, he tossed the book, like a gauntlet, back into the cart.

She'd return that, too . . . maybe.

At the checkout, he took her credit card from the clerk's hand and replaced it with his own.

Though Melody didn't want to make a scene in the store, she left steaming. "Whatever happens," she said, on the way to the car. "I'm paying you back, and don't forget it."

"After what I saw on the show Wednesday, I'll have my money back in no time."

"Are you making fun of me?"

"Judging by ticket sales, no, I'm not."

GARDNER wanted to stick with the New England theme for the second show, and Logan wanted a one-pan meal, since less could go wrong that way. They settled on an Indian Pot Roast with dumplings, and cherry slump for dessert. The menu became the curriculum for Melody's first cooking lesson, and for however many lessons it would take for her to master that meal before the next show.

On Saturday morning, Melody felt like a domestic goddess. She enjoyed using her new garlic press almost as much as she enjoyed Logan taking over her kitchen in sweats, stocking feet, and a bib-apron.

She sautéed the garlic in butter, while Shane got so enthusiastically into rubbing the pot roast with salt and flour that he didn't want to stop when it came time to braise the beef.

Melody sliced the onions and laughed because she was crying, so Logan kissed her brow, causing a hum and shiver in her spine, and all she wanted to do was kiss him back. "Keep it up, Kilgarven, and my lessons will be more dangerous than flying glass." She turned to Shane. "Some chaperone you are."

"What's a chaperone?"

"Somebody who's supposed to keep people from kissing."

"I like it when Dad kisses you. Kiss him back."

"Good idea," Logan said.

"Great," Melody said.

"No, the kid's right. It's only fair." For Shane's benefit, Logan closed his eyes, puckered like a fish, and reached for her . . . and Melody raised the peeled onion, smack, to his lips.

Logan's eyes flew open. "Yuck!" He saw the onion, made a face and little spitting noises, then he grabbed a clean towel and wiped his tongue.

"What were we supposed to do with the onions?" Melody asked to Shane's continued laughter.

"You'll get yours," Logan said.

Melody could hardly wait. "What next?" she said, reminding him where they were. "Although, I did find a spell to make a recipe come out. Want me to try it?"

"Don't do anything weird, just cook."

"Then I need to know what to do next."

"Right. Spread the onion slices on the bottom of the Dutch oven, and put the sautéed meet, garlic, and butter on top," he said. "After that, we'll add the spices and rum."

Melody nodded, but when she tipped the skillet, so she could slide the meat into the Dutch oven, the roast fell hard and plopped, with a one-two bounce, splashing garlic and butter all over her. "Oops!" She put the skillet in the sink, wiped her cheek, and licked her finger. "Mmm."

Logan wiped a splotch off her temple the same way, and before either of them could react, he'd rescued a chunk of garlic from her cleavage. After the fact, they stilled and regarded each other, and Melody understood how her bacon had burst into spontaneous flame. Prickles radiated in waves from where he'd touched her between her breasts, puckering her nipples, and bringing a sullen heat to root deep within her. Logan's blue, blue eyes focused on her so totally, she thought he might guess what was happening inside her.

"Silly Mel," Shane said, breaking the spell.

Her laugh sounded hollow, even to her. "Yep, silly, that's me." For wanting what she couldn't have.

Logan nodded, looking dazed, wiped his hands on a towel, then ran a hand across his face, as if to test his day's growth of beard.

Melody raised a disconnected hand and found his unshaven jaw prickly soft, as silky as it was rough. Endearing. A lot like him, rough on the outside, as if to hide a warm, soft center. "You should try growing a beard," she said, stepping away, seeking a modicum of normal.

Logan shook his head as if to clear it. "Makes me look like a street punk."

"You could never look that rough."

He laughed out loud. "Right. Let's get to whipping up those dumplings."

"Then dessert?" Shane asked.

Logan ruffled his hair. "After we make the cherry slump, I'll go get some ice cream to go with it."

MELODY was relieved when Logan left her to clean up while the roast simmered, and Shane went to play on his swings in the back where she could watch him. She needed space, time to herself.

What a mess. Twenty pans for a one-pan meal. Did that make sense? There had to be an easier way. And a faster one. She checked the roast. She was starving, and it was hours away from being done. She shrugged, turned up the burner, and began to do the dishes.

She liked that Logan didn't shave on weekends. The concept eased the whole "suit-and-tie" stigma. It made her want to curl up with him . . . and the Sunday paper . . . in bed.

An unexpected cry caught her attention. She looked out the window, and ran.

Shane was hanging upside down from his swing set, one of his legs bent at an odd angle. Oh God. Melody got him down, as Jess came running. "Call 911," Mel said. She didn't want to jar his leg, so she held Shane with his head on her lap until the ambulance arrived.

She was so focused on him, the paramedics saw the smoke pouring from her kitchen windows before she did, and they called the fire department.

Logan arrived home to find two fire trucks and an ambulance blocking his driveway. He came running and shouted, "No!" when he saw Shane on the stretcher. He fell to his knees. "You okay, sport? Where does it hurt? Tell Dad."

"He's okay," Melody said, already beside him. "It looks like a sprain. We were waiting for you to go to the hospital. Dinner burned, and my kitchen, too, I think."

"But nobody's hurt, thank God." Logan squeezed his son's hand, and at the paramedic's signal, he stood, taking Melody up with him. He slipped an arm around her. "Hold on a minute, will you?"

Melody did, happy for the support, but the force of Logan's trembling required her to do the supporting. "Woe, you're not gonna pass out on us, are you?"

"I never pass out."

"Really? Yet you couldn't be more white if I threw a bucket of paint at you."

The paramedics made Logan sit down so they could check his vitals.

A fireman stood to the side, waiting patiently for

Melody's attention. "Sorry, Ms. Seabright," he said when she turned to him. "There is some damage. I wouldn't sleep in there for a few days, if I were you."

"Hey, Mel, you can bunk upstairs with us," Shane said as they lifted his stretcher into the ambulance.

"That's the spirit," Jessie said, laughing.

"Mel saved me, Dad," Shane said, as Logan climbed in after him. "Like she saved the kittens."

"Tell me you weren't playing in traffic."

Shane giggled. "I was hanging from the swing set," he said, "the way you taught me, remember?"

Shane wanted Melody to ride in the ambulance with them, but that was against regulations. She followed in Logan's car, instead, so they'd have it for the return trip.

Within the hour, Shane had been checked out and released, and Logan had been given smelling salts, twice.

Every window in Melody's apartment sat open, the smoke and fire damage in her kitchen . . . fixable.

"Don't forget to pack your pj's," Shane said, as Melody went down for an overnight bag.

She and Logan regarded each other, unspoken possibilities filling the taut atmosphere. Pj's. Bed. Logan.

"What can I get you, sport?" Logan asked his son.

"Ice cream and cake."

"The cherry slump fried," Logan said, "and the ice cream melted."

"How about we get Keg-a-Chicken for dinner?" Melody suggested. "Your dad can pick it up and stop for dessert on the way, so we can have cake and ice cream later, okay?"

LOGAN made Shane laugh through dinner by making fun of Melody's favorite takeout, but despite the distraction, Shane had been given pain meds at the hospital, and he fell asleep before the cake and ice cream.

"Bed for you, sport," Logan said as he lifted his son from the chair and took him to his room.

Once they'd tucked him in, Melody stood beside Logan watching Shane sleep. When Logan gave a ragged sigh, Melody saw that he was trembling again. "C'mon. The doctor said he'd sleep for hours. Time for Dad to relax." She took his hand and led him to a big comfortable chair in the living room, the one she guessed was his favorite. "Sit," she said, pushing him into it.

He fell back, as if he had no choice, his face ashen.

Melody took off his shoes, because he seemed more comfortable in stocking-feet, then she poured him a glass of scotch, which he accepted and sipped gratefully. "Sorry about that," he said.

"Delayed reaction. He is okay, you know."

"Thank God, but all I can think of is what might have happened, because of me."

"You didn't teach him to hurt himself. You taught him to have fun. That's what good fathers do. He had an accident, that's all. It wasn't your fault. If anybody thought it was, social services would have been asking questions in the emergency room."

Logan sighed again, leaned his head back, and closed his eyes, his mouth tight and grim.

Melody watched him, ached for him. She remembered how she'd felt the first time she'd seen him, how she'd wanted to lower his stress by pushing him into an easy chair and draping something warm over him. But his stress that night, her initial need to calm him, had been nothing compared to this.

Melody eased herself onto Logan's lap, aware he might reject her, thinking it likely, when he stiffened for half a beat before relaxing to accommodate her. He sighed when she rested her head on his shoulder, her hand at his fast-beating heart. "He scared me, too," she said.

When Logan closed his arms around her, Melody knew she'd made the right move. He needed her as much as she needed him.

"Thank you for being there," he said. "For moving fast and forgetting everything but him."

Melody stroked Logan's jaw with her fingertips, playing with the scratchy-soft dichotomy of textures. "All I could think about when I heard him cry was getting to him. Jess was the one who called 911. I didn't even have the presence of mind to grab the phone before I ran out."

"Did Jess bring her phone?"

"No, she ran back to her house to call."

"See?" Logan raised his head and looked at her, for the first time since she'd climbed into his lap. "Your instincts were fine. You were great. The best."

"Then stop imagining the worst," she said. "He's fine, too."

Logan shook his head. "I can't tell you what it did to my heart to drive up and see . . . I didn't know which of you—"

"Jess tried to call your cell, so that wouldn't happen."

Logan groaned. "I forgot to take it."

Melody raised her head. "Wait a minute. You thought it might be me? And you were worried?"

"Of course. Jeez, what do you take me for?"

"What did you think could have happened to me?"

"I . . . guess I thought you'd turned up the heat and burned yourself or something."

Melody tried to look innocent, and Logan shook his head. "You did turn up the heat, didn't you?"

She raised an annoyed brow. "What makes you think so?"

"The expression you're wearing; it's one I'm beginning to recognize. You use it when you're up to something. I saw it first when you and Shane tried to cook, then during your interview with Gardner, during dress rehearsal, and the other night when Vickie's grandmother gave you away."

"Smart ass."

Logan kissed her brow. "God help me, I'm beginning to find the look—" He became serious, but hesitated, as if waiting for something.

Melody wet her lips, parted them, and his mouth came for hers with a hot rush of need. Nothing slow and building; the kiss started fast, hard and open-mouthed. Hot and greedy. He wanted her. She wanted him.

Logan adjusted his hips, parted his legs.

Melody raised her knees, curled into him, pressed her bottom against his erection, teasing the tiger.

He held her face as he sipped from her lips, cupped her bottom, kneaded it even as she moved against him.

Melody slipped her hand beneath his shirt to sift through the mat of silk on his chest. He took his mouth from hers, gazed into her eyes, blue piercing gold, hot need meeting hotter. With unspoken permission, he slipped his hand beneath her blouse, into the cup of her bra, searing her as he touched her.

At the first sizzle of contact, his fingers to her nipple, skin to skin, she groaned and surged, and he did the same. He nipped at her lips, her neck, matching moves, sending wild electric sparks to and from every needy corner of her body.

He removed his hand and she cried out at the loss, but he turned her in his arms, spread her legs, and tucked her knees on either side of him, until she sat open and throbbing against him, nothing but the fabric of their clothing between them as she straddled him in the chair.

"I want to see you," she said against his lips when he took her mouth again. "I want to hold you in my hands."

Logan groaned and surged the more, his movements as involuntary as his hard, thickening length.

Melody barely remembered him opening her blouse, before his lips closed over her nipple and he suckled her. As he did, he began a slow-building rocking rhythm against her that quickened over time to a hard, heavy thrust . . . and she came . . . to her shock and his delight. And though her face burned, he found her center, and he made her come again, and again.

Melody felt his rapid heartbeat, heard his ragged breaths, and went for his zipper.

"Dad? It hurts, Dad!"

Thirteen

MELODY sat in the rocker in Shane's room and accepted him from Logan's arms. It was time for more medicine, so they gave it to him, then she rocked him while Logan sat on the floor beside the rocker and held an ice pack to his son's bruised and swollen ankle.

After a few minutes, Shane closed his eyes and drifted off, and Logan placed his hand over Melody's on his son's leg. "Thanks," he said.

It took about an hour before they could settle him in his bed again, without him crying out.

Melody stood back and yawned.

"Tired?" Logan asked.

"Bushed," she admitted.

"Me, too." He took her hand to lead her down the hall. "Come on. I'll tuck you into bed."

Melody pulled up short, caution riding her, afraid he'd want to go farther than was prudent. "Bed?"

"Yeah, you can have it; I'll take the sofa."

"Oh."

Logan gave her a suspicious look. "What did you think I meant?"

Melody firmed her spine and resisted temptation, strong after her meltdown in his chair. "No offense, Kilgarven, but I'd rather have the sofa."

He raised a brow at her sudden change in attitude and shrugged. "No offense taken, Seabright, but you slept like a dream in my bed the last time you stayed over."

"Yeah, but I didn't like the dreams I had there." She'd liked them too much.

Logan warmed, remembering what he'd almost done, afraid her dreams had been more real than she knew. With a deal of guilt, he headed for the living room. "Suit yourself," he said. "But the bed's yours."

FOR Melody's second show, Logan remained standing behind the audience from the beginning, aware, as he had not been before, that his decision had to do with her making love to the cameras. He wanted her looking at him when she made love, in the same erotic way she had looked at him the other night straddling him in the chair.

As if she understood his intent, she played to him throughout the show, made love, not to the cameras, but to him.

Did she realize it? Did she know that they were reliving every hot and sexy moment in that chair on live TV, with no one the wiser?

The meal was a success, pot roast, dumplings, and all. Her cherry slump came out on the under-baked side, but the hungry crew testified to its success, nevertheless. Gardner grumbled about the dessert, but he never mentioned the great pot roast, though he ate enough for two.

Melody made that night's headlines. "Sexy witch turns

up the heat." So much for nobody being the wiser, Logan thought.

WHILE Melody paced with outrage the next morning over the critique of her show as "a cheap try at sex in the kitchen," Tiffany came by the office to give Mel the evil eye and invite Logan to lunch.

FOR the next week, Melody taped "spots" for the show in and around New England. One day, she shot a promo beside Boston Common, another in a swan boat, then later, on the deck of *Old Ironsides*. The following couple of days, she headed for Mystic, Connecticut, and Newport, Rhode Island.

Logan barely saw her. He missed her during the day, but now that her kitchen was finished and she'd moved back downstairs, he missed her more in the evenings. Tiffany was trying to fill in the gaps, keep him from being lonely, he thought, since she turned up just about everywhere he went that week. Having Tiffany pop up became so common, it made Logan wonder if one of the secretaries wasn't giving her his schedule.

Logan honestly wished he missed Tiffany when they were apart in the same way he'd missed Melody the past few days.

For two more interminable days, Mel shot commercials at Plymouth Plantation and on the *Mayflower*. Later, they would return to the plantation to shoot her Thanksgiving show. Gardner had decided to tape that one, since she would be cooking off-site.

She returned to the station for the first time that week just as Logan was leaving the office on Friday afternoon, but if Tiffany had not waylaid him with a poor excuse for an excuse, he might have missed Mel altogether.

Logan realized, as he saw Melody's surprise at coming face-to-face with him, that she had been avoiding him, likely because he'd made her come three amazing times in his favorite chair. He got hard every time he sat in it now, and if she remembered the experience as vividly, she must surely be running scared.

Melody Seabright, running scared. Logan almost grinned.

"Hi, shark bait," she said, recovering and breezing into the office. "What are you still doing here?"

"Shark bait?" Logan followed her in, glad for a reason. "Excuse me?"

"Since 'Daddy's Girl' has been chasing you like a shark after blood, I think the term applies."

"Is nothing sacred in this place?"

"Hey, why are you still here? You were supposed to pick up Shane again tonight, remember?"

"Just running a bit late," he said. "Let's go pick him up *together*, like the old days."

Melody looked at the clock, grabbed her purse, and scooted him out of the office. "A bit?" The echo of a scold entered her voice as she started down the hall. "He's going to be frantic. Why did you wait so long?"

"It's not that late." She'd all but accused him of neglecting his son, damn it. Prepared to argue, Logan checked his watch, but it was late. Terribly so. Almost an hour later than usual. He stopped, struck by the fact that Melody was acting more responsible than him at the moment. "I did call down to say I was on my way." He caught up to her. "Thanks for worrying about him."

God, he wished she was the stable sort, a woman around whom calm, rather than chaos, normally revolved, a woman like Tiffany—but *not*. Tiffany, who, this very afternoon implied they already had some kind of date, except, Logan's senses were too full of missing Melody to care.

To hell with Tiffany. He was with Melody now, finally. Alone.

When the elevator doors closed, Melody didn't know who reached first, but she found herself pinned against the wall, the rail at her back, not that she cared, because Logan's mouth was opening over hers. A mouth she'd craved for days, his taste, his touch. God, she'd missed him.

They devoured each other, starved, she thought, as if they hadn't touched in years, when it had only been a week. Seven long, frustrating days, during which they'd passed like ships in a fog, circling but never meeting, searching but never finding.

"Oh," she said, when he placed his lips to the vee at her blouse and cupped her so close to her core, she nearly came. "Maybe if . . ."

"I know," he said. "I think so, too."

"I meant—"

"What?" He brought her so close, she felt his need pulsing against her, his thumb teasing so near, she "wept" for more. "What did you mean?" he asked, skimming her center, as if learning the shape of her were as important as touching her.

"Never mind," she said, afraid to voice so clichéd a notion as getting it out of their systems, afraid he'd take her up on her offer, afraid he wouldn't.

"You think we should go for it, scratch the itch and be done with it?" he asked.

Better she should play dumb, make him think that was his idea. "It?"

"Us, sex, 'it.' "

"I see your point."

"I know you do. Because it was your point first."

"What makes you think so?"

"I'm psychic." He cupped the back of her knee, the one she held against his erection, and rocked it against himself the way she had been doing, and Melody blushed, even as she flowed with the electrifying sensations.

"No strings, no commitments," she warned.

"Absolutely," he agreed.

"Do you think once would be enough?" she asked as she bit his ear and tugged on his lobe with her teeth.

"However often it takes," he said. "I'm willing to go the distance."

She looked up at him, and they kissed, an exhilarating new awareness vibrating between them, until the elevator signaled their imminent arrival and Logan groaned, loathe to relinquish the charged moment.

They righted their clothes in time for the doors to open, barely, and Melody walked out first, like a shield, Logan one step behind . . . until he saw the look on his son's face, a look twisted with something like panic but—

Shane charged Melody, launched himself into her arms, and buried his face in her skirt, so Logan couldn't see him. Even when he asked what was wrong, he got a negative shake of his son's head. Since Shane had missed Mel this week as much as he did, it made sense, really, that he should stick to her. And when she got him laughing right off, Logan knew he'd mistaken the look.

Then he got caught in the snare of Melody's gaze over Shane's head, innocent, yet seductive, no longer full of promise, but regret. "Bad idea," she said.

Logan denied the statement, with a slow, determined, shake of his head, shocking her, but arousing her interest. "Sooner or later," he said, leaving her to interpret his meaning, and just as he wondered whether she understood, she blushed and lowered her lashes.

"I don't feel like cooking today," Shane whined, in the same contrary mood that had been driving Logan crazy all morning. Ever since the night before, Shane had been clingy one minute, uninterested the next. Logan couldn't figure out what was wrong with him.

After discovering how much Shane liked creating Melody's signs, Logan had instituted a father-son crafts night the evening before, which had ended rather abruptly when Shane super-glued his hand to the dining room table, a family piece that would now need to be refinished.

This morning, he'd knocked the pot of ivy he'd watered without permission off the coffee table. To make matters worse, he'd blamed Ink and Spot for the mud on the carpet.

Logan hated the ivy anyway. Melody brought it up the night before, all homey and bedtime cuddly in bunny slippers and a pink "stir my cauldron" T-shirt. Refusing his invitation to come in, she'd handed him the freaking plant and announced that Ivy stood for friendship. Then she'd turned to take her fine little backside right back down the stairs.

Logan wondered what had prompted her to give him a friendship gift, after they'd all but decided to consummate their lust. Well, after she'd seemed willing, anyway.

That was it; she was running scared, again. He'd bet the bank on it. He'd be able to prove it, if he knew how much chunky doodle ice cream she'd eaten since they got home from work last night.

Logan grinned. He rather liked the scenario. It intrigued him that she might be as scared of the sizzle between them as he often was.

God knew he didn't want to be "friends" with Melody any more than he wanted to cook with her, well, not cook food anyway. But the fact remained that they still had to prep for next week's show. And he should be friends with her, because anything more than friendship with a load of dynamite spelled suicide.

"Da-aad." Shane tugged on Logan's sweatpants. "I don't wanna cook. I wanna go fly my kite."

"And I wanna go to the Sox game, but neither of us is going to get what we want. We're going to teach Melody to prepare a Boston Tea Party, because we want to keep our job."

"I don't want a job."

"Well I do. Today we cook. I don't have a choice, and neither do you."

"Yes, you do," Melody said, standing there trying to hide her bruised feelings.

"Damn it, Mel."

"Don't act like I did something wrong. Last night you said I didn't have to knock, but you just proved that I do. I don't feel like cooking, either," she told Shane as she kissed his head and turned to go. "See you both later."

"I wanna go with Mel."

Logan rolled his eyes. "All we have to cook today is dessert," he said, speaking to Melody and Shane's sweet tooths. "Cakes," he said enticingly now that he had their attention. "With icing. Chocolate."

"And breads," Melody added, losing Shane's interest and earning Logan's censure.

"All of which we could have with ice cream," she said with a sigh of resignation.

"Ice cream?" Shane asked, doubtfully.

Melody regarded Logan. "Sorry about your baseball game."

"Sorry about what I said, the way I sounded. I had no plans for the game."

Melody smiled, but Shane was acting as if he couldn't trust either of them, which bothered Logan. Something was bugging his son, something had morphed him into a first-class brat this weekend, and Logan wanted to know what.

Melody took their aprons from the hook in the broom closet, handed one each to Logan and Shane, and donned her own, then she took out bowls and mixing supplies. She liked Logan's kitchen with its bright blue counters and yellow cupboards. She liked the cozy lived-in feeling that her remodeled kitchen lacked.

She watched Logan open a well-worn oak recipe file, ruffle through the index, with his too-big hands, and take out a dog-eared card that made him smile with some long-ago memory. The only family memories she had were with Logan and Shane, she realized. She was making them now. Logan placed the recipe on the counter and tapped it. "This one first. Butterballs."

She would always remember this. "You sure the Indians who threw tea into Boston harbor made butterball cookies?"

"It's a tea party. Make butterballs."

"Okey-dokey." Melody read the card, admired his mother's neat hand, and saw her corner note: "Logan's favorite." She held an open palm toward Shane and ordered, "Eggs," like a TV surgeon.

With a shrug, Shane took a dozen from the fridge, set the box on the table, and, with a good deal of interest, watched her struggle to get the first one out. "Slippery little sucker," she said before breaking the egg on the edge of Logan's ancient blue-striped pottery bowl.

"I'll help," Shane said and flipped the box of eggs on its side. From across the room, Logan shouted, "No!" and dove, but it was too late. As if in slow motion, but too fast to be caught, one, two, three eggs hit the floor. Splat, splat, splat!

"Damn it, Shane!" Logan snapped.

Melody's heart tripped when Shane froze, his eyes dulled, and his little hands fisted.

She didn't know which of them seemed more upset; she knew only that she hated the fear on Shane's face and the helpless self-loathing on Logan's.

As Shane directed a yearning gaze toward his father,

Melody threw an egg at the refrigerator. Splat! "Eeeyyewwww," she said. "Look at it slime its way to the floor." She high-fived Shane. "Don't you love the sound it makes when it cracks?"

Logan regarded her with a look of horror as Melody's next egg hit Shane, square, in the chest. She dusted her hands with pride. "Good shot, Seabright."

"Okay, Mel, that's enough," Logan said, grabbing for the roll of paper towels. "We get the picture."

Splat. "Shane's egg hit Melody at the base of her throat. She screeched, and Logan whipped around in time to watch raw egg slip into her cleavage.

Shane raised his arms in an athletic dance of success and crowed.

Melody squeaked and yiked as she tried to dig it out, but the broken yoke kept slipping between her fingers. "Yuck!" she said, though Shane's helpless laughter made her laugh as well. "It . . . it—" She looked up at Logan. "It slipped through my bra!"

Logan looked like he might like to go after it . . . until he saw Shane with the refrigerator door open, holding a second box of eggs. "Don't you dare!" he shouted, and made for his son.

Melody stepped between them, and Logan stopped, startled, slipped in the slime, teetered, and hit the floor with a thud.

Shane dropped the eggs.

Melody dropped to her knees. "Logan? Can you hear me?"

He opened his eyes and narrowed them as fast. "What, do you think I broke my ears? Of course I can hear you."

"Are you okay?"

He raised himself on an elbow. "Could be, but I'm not betting either of you will be when I'm finished with you."

Melody took Logan's empty threat as a good sign. She

gave Shane a thumbs-up, but he didn't seem inclined to celebrate as yet.

"You sure you're okay?"

"I'm sure," Logan said grudgingly, attempting to sit up . . . until Melody knocked him back by breaking an egg on his forehead.

Fourteen

LOGAN'S shock at getting egged was comical, but while they waited for his further reaction, Melody rose and stepped toward Shane.

The belly laugh, from somewhere deep inside Logan, took them all by surprise, even Logan. As his laughter erupted full force, Melody pushed Shane forward, until he lost his balance and fell against his father's chest, and the two of them got into a wrestling match, there on the egg-slimed floor.

Their laughter sounded like music to Melody, until Shane's morphed into something different, and suddenly he was sobbing with deep, soul-searing grief.

Melody watched, throat tight and aching, as Logan sat up and took his son in his arms to rock and shush him. "What is it, sport?" Logan asked gently. "What's the matter? You've been upset since yesterday. Tell old Dad what's up, will you?" he begged. "It's killing me seeing you so unhappy."

Shane shoved his father roughly away and rose to stand over him. "You forgot me!"

"Forgot you?"

"At day care, like Mom used to." Shane swiped his eyes as if he were too old for tears, too strong. "She used to forget me all the time, and I had to sleep at the sitter's." He stepped closer to his father, stood straighter. "I won't sleep at day care," he said. "Pretty soon, you'll be giving me away like Mom did. I don't want you anyway. I hate you!" he shouted, and launched himself at Melody.

Logan looked stricken.

"Oh, baby," Melody said, bending to Shane's level, trying not to cry all over him. She smoothed his hair and hugged him. "Don't cry, sweetheart. Your dad loves you so much, and he knows you don't hate him. He would never give you away. He doesn't even like to let me borrow you, remember?"

Shane pulled from her embrace and regarded his father. "You gotta let her borrow me sometimes, 'kay?"

Gut-punched by the turnabout, Logan sobbed, and that was all it took for Shane to step back into his father's arms, the younger Kilgarven now soothing the older.

Melody rose and left the apartment. As she made her shaky way down the stairs, she wiped her eyes, aware she was in deep trouble. Not only did she love Shane, she was deathly afraid she was falling, and hard, for his workaholic father.

She could love a man who wept for losing his son's love.

Logan Kilgarven was the best father she'd ever come across. The kind of dad she'd wanted for herself. The kind she'd want for her own children, if she wanted children.

Deep trouble, and to save herself, she needed to turn her energy in another direction.

* * *

MELODY'S "Boston Tea Party," her third *Kitchen Witch* show, was a huge success, especially her Wild Rose Faery Jam, a symbol of the goddess, Melody told her audience, though which goddess that was, Logan didn't know.

Melody wore a navy silk nautical pants suit from the thirties and looked as delicious as any of the iced confections on her tiered silver serving tray.

She baked Gloucester Blueberry Cake, Vermont Pumpkin Cake, and Connecticut Dabs. To top it off, she served every kind of tea imaginable, from spiced full leaf, to organic loose tea, to modern herbal tea bags.

Logan noticed that she hadn't quite made love to the cameras this week, so the two of them hadn't been as much in tune during the show, probably because she hated the sexual innuendo in the press. But as she sipped her tea during the final roll of the cameras, Logan managed to snare her gaze, over the rim of her cup. Saucy, he thought. Stormy. Sinful. Seductive. He wanted to take her to bed, carry her off the stage while everybody watched and screw them all. Screw her most of all.

"I wonder where your mind is?" Tiffany said at his shoulder, startling him and drawing his focus from Melody.

Logan tried not to show his annoyance. He thought he might have managed a smile. "Tiffany. Good show, wasn't it?" He looked back at the set.

Tiffany touched his jaw and turned his face toward her, capturing his gaze. "Don't forget our date tonight." She let the words settle while Logan raised a brow. "The dinner show at the Wang? You remember, a local group is putting on *The Witchling* for charity. You told me weeks ago that you'd come."

Ah, the phantom date. Logan was so disconcerted by Peabody's beaming approval, from across the room, that he didn't dare beg off. "What time should I pick you up?"

"Sixish?"

Did people say that? "I'll be there at quarter of."

Instead of going back to Daddy, as Logan hoped she would, Tiffany slipped her arm through his and gave him a smile filled with promise. Jeez, he thought, he hadn't said he'd sleep with her. He looked at her father to make sure the boss understood as much, but all Logan got was an approving smile. Son of a—

He tried to untangle his arms as he looked to see if Mel saw Tiffany get her claws into him, and though the audience milled about and the crew sampled her Boston Tea Party fare, it seemed as if Mel's broom had long since departed.

Aware that he should be glad Tiffany had made a move on him, Logan felt uncomfortable. God knew he'd been thinking about approaching her. She was a safer bet than Melody, though perhaps a bit too cozy. He should be looking forward to an evening with a reasonably stable, down-to-earth woman, instead of pining for a magical loose cannon.

Tiffany was a freaking poster child for home, hearth, family, stability. Forget that she chased him, "like a shark after blood," as Mel had so snidely phrased it, Tiffany appeared to be everything he should want. Calm. Organized. Orderly. No stopping traffic or rescuing kittens. No food fights, no food fires. No sparks or smoke of any kind. No chaos.

Tiffany would make a good mother. As a wife, she would be low maintenance, low disaster, low . . . sizzle. No sizzle.

Logan, the businessman, sighed, ignored his selfish tendencies, keyed into his years of retraining, and figured the equation again. After a serious minute of weighing the results of a wildfire, compared to good breeding and a degree in early childhood education, he nodded in satisfaction. Sizzle was overrated. Tiffany bore no resemblance to

Melody, whatsoever, making the tote board heavy in Tiffany's favor.

LOGAN didn't know where Mel had disappeared to after the show, but she had not returned to their office. He sat there trying to call his mother to ask her to baby-sit, but she didn't pick up. He sure wished she'd carry the cell phone he'd given her.

Jess answered on the first ring. "Hey, Jess, how are you?"

"Running on fast forward, as usual. I love it."

"Too fast to watch Shane tonight?"

"Why, where are you going?"

"I have a date. You said I should start dating again."

"You're finally showing some sense. How is Mel?"

"Er, Mel's fine. Why?"

"Isn't she the one you're taking out?"

"I'm taking Tiffany Peabody to a charity benefit. Her father's the station owner. So, can you sit?"

"I take back what I said. You're not showing any sense."

Logan regarded the phone as if it malfunctioned. "What did you say?"

"I'm working tonight." She hung up.

Logan sat staring at his phone until Melody returned to the office at the last minute before picking up Shane. In silence, she grabbed her purse and briefcase and walked back out. "We'll meet you in the car," she threw over her shoulder, almost as an afterthought.

Logan felt as if he'd missed something. He liked fetching Shane with her, but he supposed they shouldn't spend any more time in the elevator.

Ten minutes later, he pulled the Volvo up in front of the day care entrance and watched Melody, still silent and introspective, strap Shane into his seat, before getting in herself.

On the way home, Shane, his usual chatty self, gave them a blow-by-blow description of his day, thank God.

"Teacher cut Nathan's hair today," he said with a laugh.

Melody turned in her seat. "Teacher cut it?"

"Why?" Logan asked.

Shane did a double take, branding his father's question as pure stupid. "'Cause Torrie got her gum stuck in it, of course." He may as well have started with, "Duh."

"Ouch," Mel said. "Poor Nathan."

"Aw, he acted like a big ole' baby, just 'cause he gots a bald spot."

Logan cleared his throat with a bit of difficulty. "Where exactly is his bald spot?"

"Where Torrie stuck her gum." Another unsaid, "duh" resonated in the air.

"Of course," Logan said. "But, I mean, where on his head?"

Shane made a big circle with his fingers and laid it dead center, above his forehead as he rolled his eyes. "Torrie had 'a mother of a gum wad,' teacher said."

Silence held for half a beat before Logan and Melody burst into laughter. When they calmed, Shane shook his head as if he would never understand them. "It's not that funny," he said. "Can we make caramel apples for Mel's Halloween show cookin' lesson tonight?"

"Supper tonight." Logan ran a hand over his face. "I knew I forgot something."

"Are we still gonna?" Shane asked. "'Cause you promised, Dad. You said we gotta 'cause Mel needs lessons for the show, and we need a job."

"I'll manage," Melody said, turning to look at Shane. "It's okay, sweetheart. If you and your Dad have plans tonight, I'll make caramel apples with you tomorrow, okay?"

Logan glanced at Melody, then he faced his son, in his

rearview mirror, his guilt intensifying. "I'm afraid I made other plans, sport."

Shane and Melody regarded him, Logan thought, with identically accusing looks, while the silence stretched so long, his tie got tight. If someone didn't cut the spell soon, he'd break into a sweat from the heat of their looks alone. "I have a dinner . . . meeting."

"For work?" Melody asked.

"Well, not entirely. I've been invited to a dinner theater fund-raiser, with old man Peabody."

"And Tiffany," Melody said, her smile so eloquent, he wished he could deny it.

"You have a problem with that, Seabright?"

"Why should I? I have a date, too."

"Like hell you do."

Melody raised a brow.

"Until ten minutes ago, you thought we were cooking tonight."

"Obviously we're not, and since I turned Woody down for dinner, so we could, there's no longer any reason not to. I'll just call and tell him we're on."

"What about me?" Shane asked.

When Logan said nothing, Melody frowned. "Logan, who did you ask to watch Shane while you go out on this date?"

"It isn't a date, not really."

"Who?"

"Mel, listen—"

"Jess? Or your mother?"

"They're both busy tonight."

"So you were going to do what?"

"Ask if you would."

"Hooray!" Shane drummed his feet with enthusiasm. "We can make caramel popcorn, too."

"Wait a minute, buddy," Melody said. "Your dad hasn't asked me yet."

"Mel, can't you just—"

"What? Give up my love life for yours? Fat chance."

"Love life?" Logan scoffed. "With Woody?"

"You think that's more absurd than you and Daddy's girl? Is she out of college yet?"

"Look," Logan said as he pulled the car into their garage. "This isn't getting us anywhere. Peabody owns the station. I can't just break it off at the last minute, and you don't actually have a date. Please, Mel? It's for charity," Logan said as he came around to her side of the car. "You're always doing stuff for charity."

"What charity?"

"I forgot to ask."

"Hah. It's probably, Liposuction for the Alimony Challenged."

Logan almost smiled, Melody saw, before she noticed Shane, looking as if he thought neither of them wanted him. "Go get your pj's, buddy. We're doing a weekend sleepover." She poked Logan in the chest. "You can't have him back until Sunday. We have plans. We're going apple picking, then we have a pumpkin to decorate, and a costume to get."

"Yahoo!" Shane yelled as he raced for the house.

Damned kid wouldn't even miss him, Logan thought as he dressed for his date, a scant half hour later, the irritating sound of his son's laughter drifting up the stairs.

Why irritating? he wondered. Because he couldn't share it? Or because Melody could? Didn't matter. He'd only be one floor away most of the night, but still, why a sleepover? Did Mel expect him to invite Tiffany for the night or something? Jeez.

*　*　*

MELODY tried not to let her anger at Logan show as she and Shane planned a fun and easy Halloween-type supper, similar to the one Logan had promised. Before they went up for Shane's things and changed into comfortable clothes, they filled a powder-free synthetic glove with lime punch, fastened the wrists with a twist-tie, and stood it in the freezer. They would cut the glove off the ice later and float the severed hand in a "bloody" cherry punch.

After they changed, she washed a medium-sized pumpkin. She'd gotten a recipe from a secretary at the station for stuffed pumpkin. It looked easy to make, and since Colette had brought a sample for lunch the other day, Melody knew it tasted delicious as well.

"All you have to do," Melody told Shane, after she cut the top off the pumpkin, "is dig out the seeds and the stringy glop with a spoon. Think you can do that? Then we'll stuff the pumpkin with the meat and rice."

The skillet of sautéed ground beef, onion, garlic, sage, and thyme began to smell great around the time Melody's doorbell rang. "Good grief, who could be— Daddy?" she said as she opened it.

"Gramma!" Shane called. He jumped from his chair and threw himself at Phyllis. "What are you doing here?"

"Didn't Logan tell you he invited us?" Phyl Kilgarven asked Melody.

"Er, no, he didn't." Melody tucked her frizzing hair behind her ears and smoothed her stained apron, aware that, as usual, she must look a fright to her father. "He invited you for . . ."

"A preview taste of your Halloween dinner."

"Really?"

"Dad has a date," Shane said, unaware of the reaction his resounding revelation engendered.

"The son of a—"

"Chester!" Phyllis snapped.

"Station owners," Melody inserted into the breach. "He's having dinner with at least one of the station's owners." She blew the hair from her brow. "Business." Of the monkey variety, she failed to add.

"You can eat with me and Mel. See," Shane lifted the pumpkin for his grandmother to look inside. "Glop's almost gone. We're cookin' it."

"You're cooking glop for supper?"

Shane giggled. "Nah, we're throwin' that part away. We're putting meat and rice in this pumpkin and baking it, aren't we, Mel?"

How proud he looked. Melody smoothed his cowlick. "Sure are, buddy."

"And we're having pumpkin soup and eyeball eggs and spider cake and blood punch with a cutoff hand."

"Er, er, I'm afraid we're not—"

Logan's mother gave Melody's father a "look," and his bluster came to an abrupt halt. Imagine that.

"We'd love to stay," Phyllis said.

Fifteen

"PARLOR," Melody said. "Drinks!" But to her dismay, Phyllis Kilgarven and her father sat right down at her faded, flea-market table and mismatched kitchen chairs to "visit," while she and Shane cooked. At least in her living room, her cabbage rose slipcovers gave the illusion that her furniture matched.

Her father picked up his glass of cider and stared at it as if looking for answers. "Er, Mellie . . ."

She looked up from browning the meat and rice.

"I've, er, arranged for the Little Treasures division of Goose Creek Furniture to provide cribs to The Keep Me Foundation." He sipped his cider. "Your fault," he said, his gaze slipping from hers.

Melody fumbled her stirring spoon like a football. It bounced off the red-hot burner and sizzled a second, but she caught it and put it aside. She gave her father a tentative smile, blinking away tears. "I got splattered," she said, as an excuse for the tears, and he sighed in relief.

Logan's mother rose, winked, and rubbed Melody's arm on her way to inspect the pots on the stove. "Mmm," Phyllis said. "Smells good."

How could Logan remain so dense to the wonder of life, after having been raised by a mother who sensed a rare and uneasy moment of unspoken love? Not only had Phyllis sensed it, she embraced it without turning it into a weepfest. No wonder Phyl and Jess were friends. One of these days, Melody thought, she might be moved to hug Phyllis Kilgarven.

Someday, she might even get up the courage to hug her father. For now, she would settle for having him enjoy the dinner she cooked.

When the stuffed pumpkin was almost done, Phyllis and Shane set the table, while Melody's father watched her with a kind of studied concentration. She had never been the recipient of so much of his attention before.

Both alerted and warmed by it, Melody set a bowl of pale creamy orange soup before him, and waited, almost with baited breath, as he dipped his spoon in and took a taste.

"I wanted to call it puke soup," Shane said, "but Mel wouldn't let me."

Her father choked as he swallowed. Phyllis handed him a napkin, and Melody slapped his back.

"Lift up his arms," Shane said. "That's what Dad makes me do."

When her father recovered his breath and a croak of his voice, he squared his shoulders and agreed to taste it again, under Phyl's encouraging eye, but he warned Shane with a look to keep his comments to himself.

"It's good," he pronounced before taking another taste.

Melody allowed herself to breathe. "It's creamy pumpkin," she explained. "Shane's trying to give everything I cook a spooky name for my Halloween show."

Her father raised a brow and looked down his nose at

the boy. "Yeah, well, puke soup sounds spooky, all right."

Shane gave him a half-smile, aware he'd goofed, and Phyl burst into a fit of laughter. She leaned down to kiss Shane's brow. "Love you, pup."

Shane beamed under the reprieve. "Love you, too, Gramma."

"Oh, Melody," Phyllis said with her first bite. "The stuffed pumpkin is delicious. You're going to have to teach me to make it."

Melody hooted. "I never thought I'd see the day."

"You must have a good teacher; you're really making progress."

"Dad's teaching her."

"Is he?"

"But he didn't teach her this. She made it all by herself."

"We made it, you and me, buddy, and I think we should get a gold star."

"Paint one more for each of us on your door," Shane said.

Phyllis grinned. "So Logan's teaching you to cook . . . he didn't tell me, the scamp."

Yep, Mel thought, *he's a real scamp.*

TIFFANY'S father did not attend the dinner gala or the performance of *The Witchling* in Boston that night, as Logan had been led to expect, so it was just he and Tiffany, until he saw an old school chum and his wife and invited them to make a foursome.

It didn't take ten minutes to realize that in Tiffany's eyes, he'd goofed. Nevertheless, Tim Henderson had been a good friend, and it turned out that his wife, Sue, had lived down the street. He remembered her from third grade, so dinner conversation flowed smoothly, comfortable and safe. The three of them had gone to public school together, but Tiffany had gone to private schools. They mowed their own lawns, vacuumed their houses; Tiffany had servants. Much to her dismay, they found no middle ground in tennis, yachting, or yoga, either, but when Logan mentioned *The Kitchen Witch*, everyone had plenty to say, all good, except Tiffany. After dinner, they watched the performance of *The Witchling* in silence, and he and Tiffany drove home the same way.

In her driveway, however, Tiffany must have decided to forgive him, because she tried, with her kiss, to turn him on, while Logan tried to get turned on, if only to forget Melody.

"I knew we'd be good together," Tiffany said a long few minutes later, blind to Logan's hopeless struggle to participate in the seduction . . . blind whenever it suited her, he sometimes thought.

"Want to come up?" she asked.

"Up?"

"I have my own apartment upstairs. Separate staircase and everything." She ran a finger down his lapel. "No one would know."

"I would know." Logan almost said his son would know, too. Did Tiffany even realize he had a son? He wished he remembered so he could ease her into the knowledge, if need be. Better bide his time, he decided. If she knew about Shane, she'd mention it before long; if not, he would.

"Maybe next time," he said in response to her invitation, thinking he'd knock on Mel's door when he got home, make sure she and Shane didn't need anything. He walked Tiffany to her private entrance and kissed her once more, clearing his mind and giving the kiss his attention. "Night," he said as he left her standing there watching him.

Before he climbed back in the car, he found himself speculating as to what Mel's T-shirt might say tonight, considering her penchant for double meanings.

When he stepped from his garage fifteen minutes later,

Logan met with a sight that stopped him cold—his mother and Melody's father coming down the porch steps. He stepped back into the shadow of the garage when he remembered that he'd invited them to sample Mel's Halloween dinner. Damn. Because she'd improved so much, he'd wanted her father to see how well she cooked. Give her a sense of accomplishment. Of course, he'd expected to be there to support her.

"Why did you do that?" his mother asked, and it took Logan a minute to realize she was talking to Mel's father, not to her recalcitrant son.

"Do what?" Seabright asked.

"Offer her money to buy decent furniture. You do realize that in doing so, you implied that she could not provide decently for herself. You put her down, Chester, and after that nice meal."

Logan grinned. *Go Mom.*

"I did no such thing. Mel is my daughter. I brought her up in a mansion with servants, and I hate to see her brought so low. I was just trying to be a good father."

"Bull. You don't try. You write checks, instead, because it's easier. You don't know how to be a father, good or otherwise. Money doesn't show love; it shows you're willing to give your daughter what you have in abundance. Try giving her some of your precious time for a change. Some understanding. Did you ever have a conversation with her about what she wants from life? What she enjoys? Do you have any idea?"

"Teach me, Phyl." Mel's father kissed his mother in a way that made Logan fist his hands, firm his spine, and close his eyes, so the sight didn't imprint itself on his brain.

"Fine," his mother said, somewhat breathless. "I'll teach you how to be a good parent, and you can teach me to enjoy life."

"Deal," Mel's father said. "Let's seal it with a kiss."

Jeez, give it a rest, will you? Logan rolled his eyes, aware that the enjoyment his mother planned probably consisted of more than the sedate retirement-type recreation he'd envisioned for her.

He watched them drive off, wondering if they were sleeping together. *Don't go there, Kilgarven. It's not your problem.* His problem lived downstairs, drove to work with him mornings, and invaded his sleep at night. And he owed her a big apology for forgetting to tell her he'd invited guests for dinner.

Logan checked his watch by the porch light. "Damn." Ten o'clock and they'd been here since when? Six, he thought he'd told them. Mel must be exhausted, and depressed by her father's ability to pull her down, and she must be ready to kill him.

Logan stood on the star-sprinkled side of her door and shook his head. Once, he'd been put off by those stars. Now he couldn't wait to open the damned thing, even if she threw a pot at his head. The stars seemed inviting, now, in a warm, nurturing sort of way.

He knocked softly and expected the door to drift open. When it held, he tried the knob. Locked . . . against him. Mel never locked her door.

He knocked again. Louder. Jiggled the knob. Only silence greeted him from the other side, a suspicious silence that included a strip of light flowing into the hall from beneath the door. She had not gone to bed.

Logan grinned and removed the loose plug of corner molding from the bottom left of her doorjamb, found the key, exactly where Shane had found it when he swept the stairs, and used it.

Melody stood leaning against her kitchen counter, all long shapely legs, one bare foot warming the other, eating devil's food cake from a crystal pedestal plate. "Hey, shark bait," she said, barely looking up when he came in.

Logan stifled every emotion, from a wince to a rush of lust. Her scarlet "come fly with me" T-shirt bore a witch on a broom crossing a bright butter moon, and ended pleasantly short of modest. "I'd give Shane hell for eating from a serving dish like that."

Melody narrowed her eyes and held her fork like a weapon as he approached.

"What, are you gonna do, fork me?" Logan grinned.

"I'd give Shane hell for inviting people to dinner, then taking off for a night of sexual frolic without telling anybody they were coming." She shot her golden dagger-eyes his way.

"I can explain," Logan said as he reached over to finger a glob of chocolate icing dangling from the bottom of her fork.

She swooped and licked it off his finger, about knocking him on his ass, and he froze, all systems on alert.

"Go ahead, explain," she said, shoving a fork full of cake into his mouth.

Explain what? he thought, before ecstasy took over. "Damn, this is the best thing I've tasted all night."

"You're trying to get on my good side," she said. "No fair," but her grin of pleasure derailed Logan's train of thought once more, and he decided to savor both the cake and the sexual energy arcing between them.

"Lousy dinner?" she asked.

He shrugged and remembered where they were in the conversation. "Tasted like sawdust. Where's the punk?"

"Out cold in my bed."

"Your bed? Where will you sleep?"

"Daybed in the parlor. I'll be fine."

"You sure?"

"I want to keep him for the weekend. He's my bud."

"Thanks," Logan said, opening his mouth for the cake coming his way. "Special recipe?" he asked, looking for another bite.

"Yep, Fallen Angel-food Cake. It's Devilicious."

Logan's eyes danced even as he savored.

"Chocolate cake and icing," Melody said. "A spider web piped in white on top, occupied by three licorice spiders, all consumed by one four-year-old, I might add, who let their legs dangle from his lips as he chewed. Grossed my father right out, not for the first time tonight." She told him about the puke soup.

Logan chuckled. "Looks like you aced the meal, without your talented teacher. What did you choose for the main course?"

Melody listed the menu, even showed him the leftovers, she was so proud. "My father ate almost everything, even the eyeball eggs. I think he was afraid your mother would scold him if he didn't."

Logan scoffed. "She's a woman of untapped talents." He cringed inwardly at the intimacy he'd witnessed. "So you and your father got along okay?"

"He was nearly on good behavior." Her gaze softened as she explained his donation of cribs to The Keep Me Foundation.

Logan thought she never looked more beautiful. "Sounds like his best behavior."

"Not quite. In the end, your mother shoved him out the door before I could kill him."

"Hey, are you shivering from the cold or from another brush with your father's criticism?"

"Puleeeze, I don't care enough about what he thinks to be affected by it."

"Right. Go climb into the daybed. I brought something that'll warm you."

Melody nodded and took the cake and fork with her into the living room, while Logan went out to the landing for the bottle he'd left on the bottom step.

In the living room, he found her on the floor, in front of

the blazing hearth, arms wrapped around her knees, some kind of blanket-thing, made of colorful yarn flowers, tucked over her feet, the cake forgotten on the coffee table.

"A woman with a sweet tooth is gonna love this," Logan said, as he put down the pair of stemmed wineglasses he'd scrounged from her cupboard and uncorked a private label split of dessert wine, the fund-raiser favor.

"Don't you have any socks?" he asked as he handed her a glass of the pale, tarnished gold wine and sat on the floor beside her.

Melody made a concerted effort to ignore his question, as she regarded the contents of her glass and questioned him with a look.

"Give it a taste. It's a dessert wine from the Rhone Valley. I conned an extra split out of the waiter for you."

"Sure you did."

"I did."

"Why didn't you bring it in earlier, then?"

"Because I didn't want you to toss it at my head and ruin a perfectly delicious bottle of wine."

"You *knew* you'd screwed up!"

"I forgot until I saw our parents leave."

"You didn't bring me the wine as a peace offering, then?"

"It's a sweet wine; you have a sweet tooth. I brought you the wine as a gift, just because—"

"Because I kept Shane while you went out on a hot date." Melody shrugged and sipped the wine thoughtfully.

"He loves you."

"He's a great kid, Logan, and I love him right back."

"You should have a couple of your own."

"Kids? Hah. No thanks. I come from a long line of screwups. No kids, no husband, that's my motto. I've got all I can do to take care of me." She took another sip, raised the glass. "Great stuff."

"Can you identify the taste?" he asked.

"Apples? No, maybe pears . . . or honey. Apricots!"

"According to the waiter, it's supposed to taste like a funky fruit salad."

Melody took another sip and smiled. "Yes, fruity, and delicious. And your presence tonight helped to raise money for? . . ."

Logan shrugged. "Hell if I know. Venture capital for private vineyards?"

"Which the poor always need."

"I'm sorry I forgot our cooking lesson. Thanks for watching Shane."

Ink and Spot came barreling in, frolicking over Melody's lap, all frisky energy and short, spiked tails. As Ink leaped on Logan's shoulder, Spot landed in a more delicate location. Logan grunted, grimaced, and gingerly removed the lap-leaper before he could do permanent damage.

Melody howled with glee.

"Did you pay him to do that?"

"Please, I'm ashamed I didn't think of it. Sheer anticipation would have kept me sane through dinner."

Logan chuckled, and the kittens left the room as fast as they'd arrived.

"When did you bring them down?" Logan asked.

"When Shane started to worry they'd be lonely. Last I saw, they were sleeping behind his knees like one black fur ball."

"They woke up."

"With a vengeance," Melody said, "and batteries charged, ready for fun. Hey, speaking of fun, did you have a nice date?"

"I wouldn't exactly call it a date."

"Oh." She took another sip. "Why not?"

"I think I blew it early on, though I haven't dated in a while, mind you, so I'm not positive."

"What happened?" Melody asked, her shoulders relaxing.

"I saw an old school chum, two actually, because they married each other, and asked them to join us for dinner."

Melody hooted. "Good move, Kilgarven. You get an F-minus in Dating 101."

Logan finished the wine in his glass. "I surmised as much from the pinch Tiffany gave me before I'd completed the invitation."

Melody rose and got the bottle off the coffee table to refill their glasses. "Were you afraid that you'd screwed up?" Melody asked, when she sat back down. "Or did you screw up on purpose?"

"Beats the hell out of me." Logan looked deep into his wine as if for an answer, knowing only that he was having a better time now, with Melody, than he'd had all evening. He looked up at her, firelight painting silver blue lights in her raven hair. "You got a theory, Seabright?"

"Not one I'm sharing."

Logan shrugged. "No fire," he admitted, not sure Melody would understand.

"Bummer," she said.

"You really don't mind, do you?" he asked. "That I went out on a date, I mean."

"Of course not. We don't have an exclusive; we don't even have an understanding. I'm no better for you than you are for me."

"Care to explain?"

"No offense, but you're not exactly my dream man."

"Right." Logan took another sip of wine. "Then what do we have, because this . . . energy between us is . . ."

"Fire," Melody said. "Sex."

"That's what I thought." Logan took her glass, set it on the floor, and framed her face with his hands. "You are aware of the old adage, are you not, Mizzz Seabright, that if you play with fire, you get burned?"

Sixteen

"BURN me," Melody said. "I dare you."

Logan groaned and opened his lips over hers, starving, desperate to become a part of her, mouth to mouth . . . for a start. They glided to the rug, face-to-face, the blazing hearth at his back, the taste of honeyed apricots and pears, and the promise of sex fresh on their mating tongues.

The world disappeared. Their bodies met, quivered to flame. Hands and hips moved in a building rhythm, exploring, arousing.

Body to body, they lay, absorbed in the taste and texture of each other, barely breaching the barriers, when a wet splash of fruity droplets, a fiery hiss, and a wash of shattering glass brought them to their senses. They heard a mewling screech before a bedlam of cool damp paws scurried over them.

They sat up to find a chaos that gave the furry culprits away.

"Oh, the poor things," Melody said. "They might be hurt."

Logan rose, self-conscious, in total and embarrassing discomfort, and went looking to make sure the kittens hadn't been cut by the glass they broke. But no, they had become sleepy fur balls again, that fast.

When Logan saw that Melody was limping, he made her sit on the edge of the tub and put her foot in his hands. He washed the cut, placed an antiseptic ointment and a cartoon Band-Aid over it. Then he found her socks, put them on her, and carried her to the daybed in the living room, before he cleaned up the shattered glasses and spilled wine.

"Let me help you," she said.

"My cats; my mess." He straightened when realization hit. "Though, now that I think about it, I seem to remember that I didn't acquire those pesky little critters on my own."

Melody smiled sheepishly and snuggled down into the bed, probably more tired from a nerve-wracking evening of entertaining her father than she thought. Logan felt like a rat for leaving her to do that alone.

By the time he went to tuck Melody in for the last time, she'd grown sleepy, but she smiled at his playful lips on her cheek, her brow, her earlobes, her fingers, until she giggled drowsily.

Logan said good night, heard her satisfied sigh, and watched her curl into his favorite ass-up pose. Then he checked his son, kittens and all, kissed his brow, covered him to his neck, and went upstairs.

MELODY was not entirely disappointed when Logan showed up early Saturday morning to go apple picking with them. "I can be the tree climber," he said, "since you cut your foot last night." He bent on his haunches before his son. "Is that okay with you, sport? Or are you disappointed not to have Melody to yourself all day?"

"Nah, you can come, too. But I get to climb trees, too, 'kay?"

"Deal," Logan said. "Mel?"

"I guess we can stand having you along," she said, turning to grab a backpack so as not to reveal her pleasure over the satisfying turn of events.

When they went to the shop for Shane's Halloween costume later, Melody and Shane proceeded to try and talk old Dad into renting a kilt, jacket, tam, and tasseled kneesocks for the occasion. Though it took some coaxing, he reluctantly agreed, with a final, "absolutely not" to the bagpipes.

"Oh, God," Logan said when he modeled his highlander costume. "I'm going to look like an idiot."

No, Melody thought when she saw him, and her heart did a ten-point flip, *women are going to be chasing you around Salem Common.* But she kept that opinion to herself, sure the truth would put a final end to his participation.

Melody rented a genuine witch costume, both for her Halloween show, and to go trick-or-treating with Shane, and she modeled it for them.

While Shane and Logan chose a pumpkin to carve, she went for a final fitting on the gown she'd ordered for the station's annual Salem by the Sea ball the following Friday. No vintage outfit this time, but an up-to-the-minute fashion statement—a curve-flattering, full-length corset dress that her mother would have loved. This, she did not model, because she wanted to make a "splash."

When they got home, Melody and Shane designed and transferred a scary face to Shane's pumpkin. "Hey, Mel," Logan said as he began to carve it into the semitoothless ghoul they'd envisioned, "why don't we drive to the ball together next Friday? That way, we only have one car to park." He looked expectantly up at her.

As an invitation for a date, if that's what it was, it ranked right up there with an appointment for a root canal, but the expectant way Logan watched her made her think that he almost cared about her answer.

"Why not," she said, in keeping with the style of the question, "but who's going to watch Shane that night, if we're both going out?"

"When I got the job at the station they told me I'd be expected to attend the ball, so that's all arranged. He's doing a sleepover at my mother's, aren't you, sport?"

Shane grinned. "Yep. We're gonna rent movies and make popcorn balls and pond scum."

"Pond scum?" they said together.

"Gramma told me about 'em. Lime jigglers with gummy worms and spiders and ugly stuff like that. Yum."

ON Sunday, Logan tasted Melody's leftover stuffed pumpkin, eating two servings to decide whether it would work for the show. Finally he agreed it would be perfect for her "Haunted Pumpkin Patch Halloween."

"Works for me," he said. "Fix that with your creamy pumpkin soup and the bloody punch Shane keeps talking about."

"We could make a berry pie and call it Old Gooseberry Pie," she suggested.

"I don't know; I make a hell of a pumpkin cheesecake."

"Ooooh, that sounds yummy, but I'd want to decorate it with a chocolate icing web, and licorice spiders, and give it a spookier name."

"Spider cheesecake, it is."

"Dad you should carve a hundred pumpkins and put candles in 'em for Mel's show."

Logan groaned.

The following day, Gardner loved the candlelit jack-o'-lantern idea. Fortunately, he ordered them precarved.

Melody's Halloween ratings hit an all-time high for the

station, and clips from the show got picked up by one of the broadcast biggies for a national pre-Halloween news segment. That's when stations, other than their own affiliates, began to show a great deal of frantic, last-minute interest in carrying Melody's Thanksgiving show.

As a result, Gardner held an after-work "social" in his office, with waiters serving champagne to half the staff and crew. "To Melody," he said after calling for silence and raising his glass. "Without your style, your showmanship, spells, and sex appeal, we would never have gone this far this fast." He raised his glass higher. "To Melody Seabright, our own winning Kitchen Witch."

Tiffany walked out.

SALEM by the Sea, a lavish, Friday night, dinner dance extravaganza sponsored by WHCH TV, and held just before Halloween, had become a world-class event, with tickets coveted by broadcasting "names" from New York to Montreal. Salem hotel rooms, already at a premium as Halloween approached, sold out the night of the ball. Because Salem's Kitchen Witch, a hot new property, would attend this year, ball tickets sold out earlier than usual. Though Melody laughed the whole thing off, Logan retained a great deal of awed respect for anyone or anything in the business that created a buzz this loud.

Peabody called an impromptu meeting in his office early on the morning of the ball. Logan and Melody took the stairs, after a mutual, though silent, decision that stairs were safer than elevators. "I've got a nagging in my gut," Logan said as they climbed. "Something ugly is brewing in Witchtown."

Melody scoffed. "If I were shark bait, I'd have a paranoid gut-ache, too."

Logan climbed faster, but Melody kept up. "I'm guessing Max plans to make the most of his marketing dollar tonight." She hesitated at the door when she saw Tiffany holding court.

Logan placed a hand at her back, both propelling and guiding her inside, offering an unspoken bit of protection as well, and he could almost see Tiffany's hackles rise as he did. He hadn't called after their date. She must realize that she held less appeal for him than he did for her, which is probably what made her so mad.

"Come in, come in," Max said, rubbing his hands together. "Coffee, Kilgarven? And what about our little star?" Peabody took Melody's arm and steered her toward the coffee, apparently so his daughter could approach him, Logan thought, because Tiffany came over as if she'd been expecting the opportunity.

Aware he was the center of attention, Max poured a cup of coffee for Melody and took a sip of his own. "I guess you'd all like to know why I called this meeting. The fact is, Marketing thinks we'd be stupid if we didn't use the Halloween ball as an opportunity to promote the *Kitchen Witch* show, and I agree."

Melody gave Logan an "I told you so" nod. He raised his cup in a silent salute, to which Tiffany frowned.

"Since the national news picked up *The Kitchen Witch*," Peabody continued, "Mel's a hot property, and we want to take advantage of that. That's why I plan to escort our star myself tonight. Logan, you can take Tiffany, and Gardner you can take . . . whoever. Any questions?"

Melody caught Logan's stunned expression and Tiffany's satisfied grin. "I think it's pretty clear," she said, slipping her arm through Max's and smiling up at him. "It's a work night, after all, which means the station buys my dress, right?"

"You know, I hadn't thought about that," Max said. "But you're right, since we'll be making a promo out of it." He gave his daughter a look and turned back to Melody. "Whatever you want, Mel."

Melody grinned and made for the door. "Is that it, Max? Anything else? Will you be picking me up or sending the limo?"

"I'll come for you in the limo," he said. "Seven o'clock sharp."

"I'll be ready."

LOGAN caught up to her outside their office. "I thought you already bought your dress."

"I ordered it, but I haven't paid for it. If little Miss I-want-my-way is going to manipulate us through Daddy, then she can damned well pay for it."

"Wow, you're catching on to life in the television world pretty quick."

"Quicker than you think, buster."

"Hey, don't lay this on me."

"Who else should I lay it on? You're the one who went out with her in the first place."

Logan stepped back at her ire. "Are you jealous?"

"Screw you."

"Melody Seabright, jealous. I'll be damned."

"Melody Seabright is pissed," she said without thinking.

Logan raised a chiding brow. "Temper . . ."

"Go to hell," she said as she left him standing there.

BECAUSE Shane slept all the way to his grandmother and Chester's place, after day care that afternoon, the atmosphere inside the car hung thick, icy, and dead silent.

"Look," Logan said to Melody after they dropped Shane off. "I'm sorry you're pissed at me, but I really wanted to take you to the ball, not Tiffany."

"Max obviously thinks you and Tiffany are perfect for each other, so go for it. He'd make a mighty generous father-in-law."

It bothered Logan that he'd once thought the same thing. Worse, he'd thought Tiffany would make a more stable mother than Melody, when really, there wasn't much stability between them. For Logan's money, though, Jessie had been right in the first place. Melody was a nurturer, even though she thought differently. "I've decided I won't be thinking about in-laws for some time yet, if I ever do."

"Tiffany isn't going to be too happy about that."

"Tiffany has no say in the matter."

"I suppose Max doesn't either? Don't look now, but it almost seems like . . . if you don't screw Tiffany, you're screwing the boss, not that Max would think so, but Tiffany might."

"Thanks, just what I needed to hear. Son of a—" Logan shook his head. "I sure wish you'd stop being pissed at me. I wanted to dance with you tonight. I still want to."

"I might not want to dance with you."

"Okay, let me be frank for a change. More than I want to dance with you, I want to hold you in my arms, damn it."

Melody's heart skipped. "Oh."

"Is that all you can say?"

"Oh boy?"

Logan parked in the driveway, got out, and slammed his door, but he swore when Melody got out before he could open her door for her. Ticked, he allowed her to precede him to the landing, then he ran upstairs without a word.

THREE hours later, about ten minutes before Max planned to pick her up in the limo, Melody heard Logan leave. He knocked on her door on his way out, but she didn't answer. She had chosen her knockout, sea green gown with pleasing him in mind, idiot that she was. But now that he was escorting Tiffany, she wanted him to get the full effect in the surroundings she'd dressed to complement—beneath the shimmering opalescent glow of a dozen crystal chandeliers.

He might think she was still mad, of course, but let him stew for a while longer; she'd disabuse him of the notion soon enough.

SALEM by the Sea represented a whimsical, watery fantasy of a teal green ocean, enhanced by colorful coral sculptures, fairy-lights that mimicked water bubbles, and a wall of tropical fish in colors so bright, they seemed fake, except for the way they swam through their aquatic world.

Melody had looked over the plans and talked to the set decorators assigned the job of creating the aqua vista. Then she chose a gown designed to accentuate the fantasy—a straight-fitted, low-cut, strapless confection with pearlescent opaque sequins over pale teal that mimicked the shimmering illusion of a mermaid beneath the sea.

Max about had a heart attack when she opened her door to him. "Melody, you take my breath away," he said, though she knew that nothing touched him beyond money and power, and that however she appeared, however possessive he seemed, it was because she reflected well on the station, its ratings, and his bottom line.

When they arrived at the ball, Gardner greeted them and followed them like a toady. "What did you do to your hair, Mel?" he asked. "It looks as amazing as the rest of you."

"Melody always looks amazing," Max said. "Tonight she simply looks enchantingly amazing."

"I'm glad you think so, Max, because Lily and Dwayne, from Makeup and Hairdressing, made house calls." Dwayne had contained and tamed her buoyant hair with an opaque, luminescent sea green ribbon woven around and through her natural waves. Then he'd pulled the shimmering mane forward to cover a breast and patted it into place until she'd had to move his hand away. He said she looked like her hair was being shaped by the movement of the sea. "I told them to send you the bills."

Peabody squeezed her hand on his arm. "You're worth every penny."

Melody hoped Logan would think so, too.

She had been told that most attendees would wear classic black evening wear, men and women alike, and when she entered the ballroom on Peabody's arm, she saw that few had strayed from tradition. She didn't blame them for conforming, but that was not her style. As a child, when she saw how easy it would be to disappear altogether, she knew that to survive, she must be visible.

"You look as if you belong to this magic world," Max whispered near her ear, almost like a lover.

That's when Logan and Tiffany walked in.

Although it was difficult to tell which of them seemed more taken aback by the sight of her and Max in intimate conversation, Melody couldn't help but realize that all their attention was focused her way.

Logan looked as if he might like to devour or beat her.

Tiffany seemed bent on . . . murder, either because Melody had played up to Daddy, or because she'd stolen Logan's regard.

Either way, Melody thought with a smile, who cared?

Seventeen

IGNORING Melody, Tiffany kissed her father. She had broken with classic black as well, to gain Logan's attention, no doubt, which is no more than Melody had done, of course, but Tiffany had worn red. Too bad that with her coloring, red made her look as if she were ill.

Logan took Melody's hand and brought it to his lips, while his gaze captured hers and she read a great deal of promise in the sea blue depths of his eyes.

"Witch," Tiffany said, almost, but not quite, beneath her breath.

"Our very own," Max said with a cautioning smile.

"Shark," Melody said, in the same low biting manner.

Tiffany stiffened, and Logan began to cough.

"Over there," Melody said. "In the aquarium, isn't that a shark?"

Max grinned, patted Melody's hand on his arm, and led her toward the pressroom, as if to steer her from harm's way. Melody did not miss the warning look he gave his daughter before they left.

The minute Mel entered the pressroom, cameras started rolling, lights flashing, and reporters shooting questions, three at a time. When someone asked how old she'd been when she first started cooking, Melody laughed while panic rose inside her, until Logan stepped up, took her arm, and introduced himself as her producer. "I hardly remember Melody when she wasn't cooking," he said.

Disaster averted. Whew.

For the rest of the interview, Logan fed the reporters the information he wanted them to have, diverting questions she shouldn't answer toward himself.

Later, as Logan led her from the pressroom and back toward the ballroom, Melody wondered where he'd chained Tiffany, because Daddy's girl would never have let go long enough for him to come to her aid with any incentive less than a sturdy lock.

Everyone else had deserted her by then, even Max . . . everyone but Logan. "That was exhausting," Melody said. "Thanks for the rescue. You're a regular knight in shining armor."

"Tarnished armor, you mean. I'm sorry I lost my cool earlier. Did I get a chance to tell you how incredible you—"

"There you are, darling," Tiffany said, coming up to them and threading a possessive arm through Logan's. "I wondered where you'd gone off to. Melody, dear, I'd like you to meet Brian Westmoreland. Brian, this is Melody Seabright, our very own Kitchen Witch, and Logan Kilgarven, my producer at WHCH. Brian produces our evening news in Albany," she told Melody.

Melody extended her hand toward Brian with a smile, but he pulled her into an embrace and kissed her cheek. "Mel and I are old friends," he told Tiffany . . . which, Melody thought, was a bit of a stretch, since they'd met exactly once, on the day she was hired, though not as great a stretch as Tiffany's solo ownership of the station.

"Dance with me," Brian said, sweeping Melody onto the dance floor and making her laugh. "You do realize," he said, as they began to waltz, that you're the most beautiful woman in the room, the whole of Massachusetts, New England, even."

"But not New York?"

Westmoreland blushed.

"I think Miss Peabody would take exception to your statement," Mel said with a laugh, though she enjoyed his compliments and his fascinating stories of life in TV news. After their dance, they went out to the balcony for a leisurely drink.

She should not have been surprised to find herself paired with Brian for dinner, Melody thought an hour later, though she was surprised to find the two of them sitting at the table with the New York station crew rather than her Salem colleagues.

Her ostracism didn't last long, however. The commotion at Max's table, as people jostled for position—and extra place settings and chairs appeared—meant something stunk in Station-town. When Max came for her and Brian and told her that room had been made for them at his table, Melody knew that the only thing reeking at the moment must be Tiffany's temper.

Pointedly ignoring Melody, Tiffany monopolized Logan's attention through dinner, but shortly before dessert, when the orchestra began playing a waltz, Logan managed to catch Melody's eye and ask her to dance.

Tiffany turned his way, as if with surprise, and accepted with blushing grace. How unexpected, Melody thought, that the shark should mistake the invitation as her own. She should get a freaking acting award for that one.

Though Westmoreland remained by Melody's side like

a smitten pup, her energy and enthusiasm waned. Yes, she had dressed for her role at WHCH, and for an appearance in the papers and TV, because *The Kitchen Witch* was a hit, and she wanted the world to know. But she had also dressed to knock Logan on his metaphorical ass, except that he'd been too busy entertaining Daddy's girl to notice.

She felt like a child fading into the woodwork and hated the struggle for acknowledgment, as desperate as the struggle for air. As much as she'd once wanted her parents to "see" her, she wanted Logan to see her now. She wanted . . . to be held in Logan's arms and waltzed across the floor, as if she were the only woman in his world, even for a little while. She wanted him to "see" only her.

She was an idiot.

On the outside, Melody felt like a princess, as she used to in her mother's dresses, but she wasn't as smart now as she had been then. Back then, she'd at least known better than to believe that dreams could come true, if only for a few hours.

They were a bad mix, she and Logan, and Tiffany proved it. Tiffany was a shark, Melody, a mouse. And let's face it, a shark could swallow a mouse whole. So let the businessman have the schemer. *She had herself,* Mel thought.

She was a witch who whipped up magic on TV. She wasn't a failure—in the career department, anyway. She'd known from the start that she and Logan had no future. She would have to look for a new place to live, soon.

Melody made an excuse to Westmoreland, pretending she was going to the ladies' room, and began to make her way toward the cloak room. She'd had enough for one night.

AFTER their unexpected dance, Logan fisted his hands so he wouldn't jump the table and strangle Tiffany. He wanted to slip away to find Melody, whisk her into his arms, and dance with her until tomorrow. He wanted to touch her, talk to her. He wanted . . . everything.

He caught the flash of sequins, the milky-teal of her gown, and saw her duck, literally, into the cloak room.

Wondering if she was okay, Logan rose to go to her.

Tiffany caught his sleeve. "What's the matter, darling?"

"I need to take a walk, Tiff."

"I'll come with you."

"To the men's room?"

Tiffany's blush failed to hide her fury, but who cared? He got away.

The cloak room appeared empty but for a curtain of top coats and evening wraps. "Mel?" Logan called. "Melody, are you in here?" From the ballroom, he could hear the orchestra above the hum of voices. In the cloakroom . . . silence.

She couldn't have gone back out. He wouldn't have missed a shimmering sea green mermaid. He hadn't taken his eyes off her all evening, nor had he lost sight of the cloakroom door since she came in. He looked for another exit, fought his way through a layered jungle of coats and wraps on a snaking mechanized rack, and came up against the back wall. "Damn!"

He felt his way along the wall. "Melody?" he called. "Are you back here somewhere?"

He smelled orchids just before he heard a sigh.

"Mel, for God's sake, speak to me," he whispered. "This is the first minute we've had all night, and I don't want to waste it."

"Logan," she said, wistfully, and from so near, he swept her finally into his arms, so that they danced in place to the new piece the orchestra had begun.

"They're playing the theme from *Practical Magic,*" she said near his ear, a smile in her voice, holding him almost as tight as he held her, as if neither would let go any time soon. Fine by him.

"It's perfect," he said, pulling her closer, if possible, as they swayed to the slow, enchanting beat. "You're perfect."

She chuckled, low and seductive. "Perfect . . . because I'm a witch?"

"Because holding you in my arms is like a fantasy come true, I wanted it so much. Because I like the music—slow, but vital and alive—the way I want to make love to you."

Melody gasped, buried her warm face in his neck, and Logan savored the scent and feel of her permeating and enveloping him, raising him beyond the moment, as if they were destined to float in the watery illusion of the evening.

The rhythm changed; the dance turned seductive. Their lips met, frantic, the way he'd felt all evening, as if his heart would stop, if he didn't get his hands on her soon. "I missed you. I missed touching you, holding you. Let me hold you now, just for a while." He nuzzled her ear, whispered everything and nothing. "You're so beautiful. Did I tell you how beautiful you look tonight, like a virgin mermaid waiting only for me."

Her low laugh caught, as if on a sob, and Logan frowned. "What's wrong?"

"How do you know what a virgin mermaid looks like?" She smoothed a lapel on his tux, ran a hand over his shoulder, threaded her fingers in the hair at his nape, possessive, perhaps, but a bit afraid to show it. He liked the notion almost as much as he liked the feel of her hands in his hair.

"I expect a mermaid would shimmer like you do," he said, sexual energy replacing his concern. He caressed and stroked her, in a bold, possessive mood of his own. "Though no mermaid could feel as great as you do in my arms."

"I don't think I'm so much in your arms as my ass is in your hands."

"Oh, yeah. Just where I like it." Logan swallowed her squeak with another kiss, longer, hungrier. He couldn't stop exploring and stroking, learning every turn and curve of her luscious, long-legged body. "Good grief," he said, pulling back. "The side slit on your gown goes all the way to your waist. Why didn't I notice this sooner?"

"Magic . . . and a graduated overskirt of the same fabric."

"Watch it, Seabright, that's fodder for a hidden weapons charge." Logan slid a hand beneath the slit and encountered nothing but the bare skin of her perfectly rounded bottom. "I think I'm gonna have a heart attack."

"Whatever for?" she asked, feigning innocence.

"'Cause somebody stole your underwear."

"Nah. I'm wearing it, and its design is most appropriate to the evening's theme."

Logan touched his brow to hers, felt his heart pound in his head, the skin of her buttocks against his happy hands. "I'm afraid to ask . . . and . . . don't mind that rocket in my trousers."

"A fishnet thong, of course."

Logan made a strangled sound.

"Are you all right?"

He peeled her dress back to expose the front of her barely there thong to his seeking fingers, touched the triangle of net, and inched it aside. "No, but I'm gonna die happy." The heat of her about scorched him as he found and stroked her—warm, moist, ready. "And go straight to hell for what I'm thinking."

Melody squeaked when he breached her, sighed, and rode a sensual sea wave of unexpected pleasure. "Oh." She bit her lip. "Oh, Logan." He felt her, wet and swollen, against his fingers. "Not here," she said. "Not . . . yes, there. Oh, oh no . . ." She came, and Logan groaned near her ear, bit the lobe, adjusted himself against her to accommodate his pulsing fullness.

Quick on the uptake, Melody turned her attention outward. "Fair's fair," she said, unzipping his fly. "Don't guess

I'm gonna be as lucky as you. I suppose you're wearing briefs?"

"Jeez, yes, I'm sorry, but don't worry, I'm gonna break out of them in a sec."

"Promises, promises."

The "big guy" did a happy dance.

"I'm goin' in for the goods," Melody said.

Logan released a full-throated groan of both shock and ecstasy when she took him in her hand. "Surprise me like that again, and I might spoil that amazing dress."

"Then let's contain the spill, shall we?" Without warning, Melody took his fully cocked self and slid him home as if she were a slick silk glove made to order.

"Jeez," Logan said aghast, trying to keep from coming. "Wait! Don't freaking move. Don't even breathe." He raised the flat of his hands to the wall behind her, closed his eyes, and took three deep, steadying breaths. "Get a grip, Kilgarven," he said.

Those words, more than anything else, gave Melody an indication of his personal struggle. Her smile grew so wide, she was glad he couldn't see it in the dark. "You okay?" she asked, even as she moved to slide herself along his length and test the strength of her power.

"Oh, God. I'm in heaven. You're so tight, I feel as if you're milking me— Oh please don't tell me you were still a virgin."

"Of course not, not technically anyway."

"Technically?"

"I tried it a few times, mostly aborted attempts. Messy business, isn't it? Didn't seem worth the fuss."

Logan cursed even as her unbidden movements forced pleasure to course through him. He tried to stop her one minute, rode her the next. "Stop!" he said. "Wait. I'm not ready. Well, I am ready. Dangerously ready, but . . . how long ago?" He kissed her, a gentle kiss, both more and less sexual than his previous kisses. "I just want to make it good for you, Mel."

"It happened in college," she admitted. "Every time."

"Years?" he gasped. "It's been years?"

"Logan?" Tiffany called. "Are you in here?"

"Do you get the feeling," Logan whispered in Melody's ear, between gritted teeth, "that the world is trying to keep us apart?"

"I'm telling you, Daddy, I don't know what to do with that man."

Melody rested her head against the wall and closed her eyes. "Fate."

"No, goddammit." Logan kissed her with a new and desperate hunger.

"He'll find us, kitten," Max said. "Come back to the table."

Logan broke the kiss and released a long, deep breath. "God bless Max," he whispered.

"No," Tiffany said, sounding so near that Logan jumped. "I'm not going back until I scour every inch of this place and drag his sorry ass back where it belongs."

Melody felt Logan's body stiffen even as his erection wilted.

They heard movement in the clothes racks, and Melody's heart rate doubled. Logan pulled her into the midst of the coats, pressed her up against the frame of the structure, and the motors began to whirr.

"Damn," Logan whispered, and Melody twisted around to find the button she'd pushed with her backside. He grabbed her hand to stop her and pulled her against him.

"Now see what you've done," Max scolded.

"I didn't do anything," Tiffany whined.

"You must have, and frankly I'm tired of paying for your messes. Let's get the hell out of here."

"Daddy!"

"Out!" Max said. "Now."

Tiffany's whine faded while racks of clothes glided past, and Logan and Melody extricated themselves from the tangle.

Melody indicated the switch, and Logan shook his head and held up a hand for her to wait.

They put themselves back together and after a few minutes, as her heart returned to normal, he hit the button and stopped the whirring racks. They both listened before speaking.

"Close call," Melody said. "I'm sorry."

Logan ran a hand through his hair, though the coats had already done their worst. "Don't you dare be sorry. I'm the one who's sorry, because I have no choice but to go back to that damned table."

Melody's heart fell. She didn't know what she'd expected, but maybe she thought he'd go home with her and finish what they started. Yeah, right. "Well, I have a choice," she said, leaving without another word. She headed for the ladies' room, hoping Logan went back to Tiffany with his hair still scrambled.

Ten minutes later, after fixing her hair and makeup, Melody left the ladies' room and ran smack into Brian Westmoreland, literally. So much for an easy escape. Giving up, she asked him to take her home. He did.

They talked until four in the morning, about everything and nothing. Brian was a good listener. After a chaste kiss, he spent what was left of the night on her daybed.

Melody lay awake until dawn, waiting, listening for Logan's return, but he never came home at all.

Eighteen

IN the light of day, memory and mortification got a stranglehold on Melody, so that her face stayed red and her ears remained hot for hours. Though they had not "gone all the way," she had slept—er, stood up with—Logan in a public coat closet. How tawdry was that?

Stupid is what it was, incredibly so. "Idiot," she called herself. "Fool." What had come over her? "Raging hormones," she said, slam-dunking her fishnet thong into the hamper. "Nothing more. Horny, that's all, and I wasn't the only one." She stopped picking up the mess she'd made in her bathroom the night before and remembered how good Logan had felt inside her, how good she had felt when he was. "Oh, God." Then she got a look at her calf-eyed self in the mirror and grimaced in disgust. "Get over it, already."

All right, they'd had a close call. Half a second more and— She groaned. "No protection, no brains, but lots and lots of sex drive." Another couple of minutes, and she might have needed The Keep Me Foundation for heaven's sake. "Jeez," as Logan would say.

Melody made herself a bracing cup of Chai, with extra whipped cream, to take the edge off her frustration, and she took the hot drink to the computer in her bedroom. She hit the power button and turned on her monitor. She would check her E-mail for fan letters. Adoration calmed her.

Logan had adored her . . . with his lips and with his body. He had— "Screw Logan," she said. "Think of something else." But what? The fact that he'd spent the night with Tiffany instead of coming home to her?

"Brian," she said, prodding herself out of her pity-fest. Brian was a great guy, she thought as she waited for her PC to boot up. If she'd met him first, instead of Logan, who knew?

Maybe she would say yes the next time he came to town. When he'd kissed her good-bye at seven, he'd said he would come back, and soon, and he promised to call her. Brian was safe, and judging by his stories, he didn't seem to be a workaholic. True, he had ambition, but he was nowhere near as uptight as Logan, though Logan had been anything but in that cloak room last night. Hard is what he'd been. Big, thick, and hard. Ready. "Wow."

Staying away from a man who made her crazy-stupid made sense, but staying away from her producer, and neighbor, would take a bit more than the usual amount of creative avoidance. To make matters worse, she'd promised to go trick-or-treating with him and Shane tomorrow night. The poor kid would be devastated if she didn't go, so she guessed she didn't have a choice. Shane had had enough disappointment in his short life. He didn't need her providing any more.

However, her life, and Logan's, diverged, and they must, she would make a point of staying in touch with Shane.

For now, at least until tomorrow night, she needed to

keep a safe distance. Since silence reigned upstairs, a good indication that Logan and Shane had not returned, she'd walk over to Vickie's shop on Pickering Wharf and see if she needed help. Maybe later, or tomorrow, she'd attend some of Salem's otherworldly undertakings.

Melody donned a vintage seventies red crepe bell-bottom pantsuit and a pair of red suede ankle boots, the sturdiest walkers she had, in preparation for the only way to get anywhere in Salem during its busiest weekend. She tucked her long black wool cape tight around her and stepped outside to brave the brisk October wind whipping off the harbor. She loved the smell of pine from the crushed needles beneath her feet and the red, yellow, and orange leaves that crackled and shushed as she walked.

At The Gables, on the street parallel to hers, the line waiting to take the famous house tour whip-tailed into the yard. At The Pig's Tail, the pub where she, Kira, and Vickie liked to meet for dinner, a similar line had formed.

Pickering Wharf, a great tourist spot, and a prime location for Vickie's Immortal Classic, bustled with the weirdest of the weird. On Wharf Street, where Vic's shop was located, wandering warlocks, pirates, and ghosts terrified, amazed, and fascinated children and adults alike, as they handed out spook show brochures. A clown on stilts making balloon animals, and a dark and broody vampire both waved as she walked by.

"Hey, Miz Mel, what's brewin'?" the vampire asked.

"Magic menus, haven't you heard?"

"Everybody has. Good on you, kid."

Witches sat in herb gardens and sold brooms, gave psychic readings, and taught children of all ages to make colorful, star-streaming magic wands. Melody knew a great many of the vibrant characters, vampire and witch alike, some of them actors, many the real thing. She loved them all. She loved Salem . . . especially at this time of year.

Melody shouldered her way into The Immortal Classic, glad to warm her cold nose, and when Vickie saw her, she squealed and gave her a welcoming hug. "Now, what's a famous witch doing daring the chaos of a Salem Halloween? I saw you on the news this morning, by the way. You looked awesome. Too bad you didn't get that ball gown here, though. You could have given the place a plug." Vickie raised a mock-chiding brow.

Melody laughed, hugging her back. "I thought you might need a hand today."

"Holy Hannah, do I . . . come on." Vickie tugged Melody through the throng. "Excuse me, 'scuse, please," she repeated, "famous witch coming through. Make way for Salem's Kitchen Witch."

Melody laughed when they reached the safety behind the registers. Vickie stood on a chair to get the crowd's attention. "Ladies and gentlemen, I know you've been trying to be patient, but help has arrived! Melody Seabright, our own TV Kitchen Witch, is here to save the day. Just get in line at her register, and she'll be glad to ring up your purchases."

Melody's line was out the door before she realized what an awesome businesswoman her once-shy friend had become. "You're going to owe me big time for this one, Cartwright," Melody said when Vickie passed her to go into the back room.

"Don't I know it," Vickie said with a giggling wink. Before long, Vic had put a sign in her window, notifying passersby of the star within, and the shop filled to capacity. Vickie continued to help customers make their selections, all the while assuring newcomers that the Kitchen Witch was indeed there. "Just purchase something, and she'll ring it up for you."

Melody could only imagine what the sign said. She helped out from ten that morning until they shut the doors at eight that night, two hours later than normal. "Good thing I've had experience, or I'd never have survived," Melody said, dropping into a sturdy old Windsor chair.

"Want to do it again tomorrow?" Vickie asked.

"You're paying double what you paid me last year, right?"

"I could pay you triple, and I'd still make a profit. Thanks, Mel. Really."

Melody pulled the sign from the window, read it, and laughed. "Come in and get your Immortal Classic receipt autographed by Melody Seabright, Salem TV's own Kitchen Witch. No wonder I have writer's cramp."

"You always said I had a good head for business. Will you let me buy you supper?"

The knock at the door startled them both, especially since the "Closed" sign had been hung up for the night. At first Melody didn't recognize Shane, because it was so dark outside, and he was in costume, but when she did, she was pretty sure the shadow behind him must be Logan. She opened the door and let them both in, though she did consider closing it on Logan. Judging by his tentative step inside, she thought he must feel as uncomfortable as she did.

"Hey, Mel, we been lookin' for you all day," Shane said, lifting his face for a kiss.

Melody's heart melted. "I never moved from this spot." She added a hug to the kiss. "Where did you look?" she asked, still kneeling in front of him, not meeting Logan's brooding gaze.

"We looked on the Hair-Raising Hayride, and on the Spooky Trolley, and at that place where they tell scary sea stories, and um, oh yeah, where we ate a chop suey sandwich. We want you to come on the Phantom Ghost Ship with us tonight. Will ya, huh?"

"For him," Logan said.

Melody stood, since Logan had finally spoken, though what he had not said rang louder. Shane wanted her, but he did not. "How did you finally find me?" she asked.

"We followed the star-struck crowd."

"Cute," Melody said.

"Yeah, people been talkin' 'bout ya, and Dad asked 'em where you were, and how you looked, and if you were alone or with a man, and did you—"

Logan put his hand on his son's shoulder. "It's okay, sport, Mel gets the picture."

Maybe I do and maybe I don't, Melody thought.

"Come with us," Logan said. "Please. He really wants you to."

Melody wished she could ask if he wanted her to, glad he appeared at least half as uncomfortable as she felt. Spending the night, for heaven's sakes, with that bitch Tiffany, after what happened between them, well . . . he should feel uncomfortable, damn it.

Melody ruffled Shane's hair. "Okay, buddy. Let me get my cape and bag."

Logan and Vickie shared small talk while Melody gathered her newest purchases, including a vintage ivory satin blouse with leg-o'-mutton sleeves, a lapis sequined bolero, and a pale pink angora sweater, merchandise she'd rescued from Vickie's arms before it got to the customers.

Melody kissed Vickie before she left. "What time tomorrow?"

"I love you! Eight?"

"See you then."

WHILE they waited on the Phantom Ghost Ship for the cruise around the harbor to begin, they sat on deck chairs, while Shane recounted his day for Melody, minute by minute. She was grateful, as it filled the dead space between her and Logan.

"You're in a mood," she said to Logan when Shane took a breather to pet a puppy someone brought on a leash.

"Didn't you get enough sleep last night?" She was prodding more than she should, she supposed, annoyed she was letting her jealousy show.

Logan's brow furrowed. "You should talk."

"What's that supposed to mean?"

"It means—" He looked at Shane, slipped his hands into his pockets, slid broodingly low in his chair, and crossed his ankles. "I had a hard time getting my car into the garage this morning with Westmoreland's sitting in the middle of the driveway."

Melody covered her mouth with a hand, guessing she had dozed off toward morning, after all. What should she do, she wondered. Confess? Or let him believe the worst? Why not let him picture her and Westmoreland the way she had been picturing him and Tiffany all day? Damn it, he deserved a good dose of imagination, the rat, for going with Tiffany last night, instead of coming home with her. "What's a witch to do?" she said. "When you're primed, you're primed."

Logan growled—actually growled—and if looks were fire, she'd be cooked.

When the ghost giving the tour began his scare tactics over the loudspeaker, Shane scrambled into her lap.

As part of the cruise, the shipboard buffet gave Melody some great ideas for next year's Halloween show fare, until her mind took a truly creative turn. "You know what might be fun?" she told a brooding Logan as she ate a meringue ghost with chocolate chip eyes. "We could have a contest on the show early next fall for the spookiest and tastiest Halloween suppers, and the winners could get an all-expense-paid trip to Salem for Halloween, maybe tickets to the ball—" She stopped, and her face flamed.

Logan turned to stare out to sea, while need, and something stronger, tightened Melody's chest. If she didn't know better, she'd think there might be a touch of regret in the set of his shoulders as well. She swallowed and cleared her throat. "The winners could appear as guests on the show and help me prepare their winning recipes."

"Actually," Logan said, turning back to her with a grudging half smile, "that's a helluva promotional hook. I like it. I like it a lot. You wouldn't believe some of the lame ideas Tiff . . . came up with. Sorry."

LOGAN watched Melody turn in silence to examine the black, black sea surrounding them. If she hadn't ended up with Westmoreland last night, he might find the winking harbor lights pretty damned romantic with her beside him.

He should be glad their coat closet encounter had been forcefully halted. Ashamed of what had transpired, what might again have begun, if he'd gone home last night, Logan had stayed at his mother's, to protect Melody, while Mel had sought solace in someone else's arms. Which she had a right to do. And while nothing had changed between them as a result of last night, the very air surrounding them felt different.

He wished now that Shane hadn't been so sincere about missing her this afternoon. For the better part of the day, Logan had managed to put Shane off, until it came to the cruise. His son had been right, everything they did without Mel was boring. Her presence alone would have made it more fun, as Shane kept reminding him.

When it came to the cruise, Shane had insisted, vehemently, that Mel come with them, to the point that Logan was forced to either punish him for his surly behavior and pigheaded determination, or heed his tear-filled entreaty. Besides, by then, Logan wanted to see Mel more than his son did.

He watched them together now, their reactions to the macabre journey sometimes trembling and sometimes amused, but always shared. The gruesome ghost guide—in gory dress and echoing speech—had finally "appeared" to the spectators. Now the pirate was telling shiver-laced tales of piracy, witchcraft, shipwrecks, all manner of supernatural events, real and imagined, Logan guessed, that might once have plagued Boston's shore.

"IS it true, Dad?" Shane asked on the walk back to the house. "Do you think it's true what the dead pirate said about a floating head dripping blood on the deck?"

Logan chuckled. "You do realize that he was a live man only pretending to be a dead pirate, right?"

"'A course, I do." Shane snorted. "Pirates don't have cell phones."

Melody laughed. "I didn't see him use a cell phone."

"I heard it ringin' in his pocket. Teacher said people didn't have cell phones in the old days, did you, Dad?"

Shared laughter helped ease the tension.

"What time are we going trick-or-treating tomorrow night?" Shane asked. "Do we gotta wait till it gets dark? 'Specially if we have to have naps first?" Shane tugged Melody's hand as they stepped on the porch. "Dad says we gotta nap tomorrow. Today was a long day. He was tired and grouchy 'cause the guest bed was lumpy last night."

The bulb on the porch threw just enough light so that Logan saw Melody's reaction to Shane's comment. Son of a bitch. She thought he'd slept with Tiffany last night. After what they'd shared in that cloak room? What did she take him for?

Wait a minute. What did he take her for? Suppose she had an explanation for last night. Nah. No man in his right mind could spend the night with Melody without making love to her. But he had, hadn't he, after the fire? Damn. "What time did your company finally leave this morning?" he asked, ticked he was showing his colors.

Melody turned to Shane. "How about we go trick-or-treating around four-thirty tomorrow?"

Annoyed, she wasn't giving anything away, Logan shook his head. "How about we stop with the tricks and give with the treats," he said, miffed he was reduced to playing word games instead of coming out and asking her if she'd slept with Westmoreland. And why did he think she wouldn't have, after her reference to being primed?

"Four-thirty, it is," Melody said. "See you then." She went into her apartment, winked, and shut her door, while Logan stood there watching, expecting . . . something.

"Hey, Dad?" Shane stood waiting at the top of the stairs for his dumbstruck father to unlock the apartment door.

IN a kilt, Logan Kilgarven fed every woman's erotic fantasy, times three. Melody moved her gaze from his splendid physique, cute knees, wide shoulders, and that lock of hair falling on his brow, and she shook her head. Just as well the world conspired to keep them apart. Maybe it was good karma, not bad, that kept them from consummating the kind of lust she'd never before experienced, a lust driving her to distraction.

Surely she was supposed to stay away from him, she thought, even as the scent of wintergreen and cloves surrounded her. He touched her back, and indicated that she should precede him up the steps.

Shane rang Jessie's doorbell as a few stray goblins joined them on the porch. Jess and her retired district attorney friend answered together, all smiles, as they handed out treats to the goblins and watched them leave. "I put some special Halloween goodies together for Shane," Jess said, handing Shane a huge plastic pumpkin filled with more than her treat basket beside the door held for the rest of the neighborhood.

"Cool," Shane said. "Hey, this has little wrapped presents in it. Wicked cool." He stood on his toes to kiss Jessie's cheek. "Thanks, Jess."

"Open them later," Jessie said. "And don't eat too much. And you two," she snapped, raking the Scotsman and the Witch with a disapproving once-over. "All I can say is, wise up, will you? Sheesh!" She kissed Shane's head and Melody's cheek. Then she confiscated Mel's broom and smacked Logan's shoulder a good one. "Idiot."

"Ouch! Hey!" He grabbed the broom in self-defense, teetered, and nearly fell off the porch. "What did you do that for?"

"To knock some sense into you," Jessie said, winking at Shane and shutting her door.

All the way to the next house, Logan complained about "judicial brutality," Shane riffled through his pumpkin, and Melody laughed.

After they trick-or-treated through the immediate neighborhood, they got in Logan's car and drove to their parents' new house. Phyllis gave Shane a video game, instead of candy, and she gave Melody a kiss, and her son, a disgusted shake of her head.

"Why is everybody so pissed at me?" Logan asked as they drove away.

"Who knows?" Melody said, almost as puzzled, though way more entertained, pretty certain his mother and Jess had talked, and that both were annoyed because he'd taken Tiffany and not her to the ball. "Let's go to the Common and watch the witches form a circle. I want to see some of my own kind," Melody said, entertained by Logan's double take.

Nineteen

JESSIE had recently told Melody about Logan's early concern over the "witch" gossip, and since she was still annoyed with him for not coming home with her after the ball, she had decided to taunt him, just for fun.

On the drive to Salem Common, Melody realized that her actions on the night of the ball were not much better than his. She had used Brian to keep her company, at the least, to get back at Logan for not coming home with her, at the most. And though she'd enjoyed Brian's company, they would never be anything more than friends. Fortunately, Brian knew it, too.

In the center of the city, with street parking banned, traffic moved at a snail's pace while everybody looked for a spot to park. Logan used his pass to get them into the WHCH parking garage, and they walked the few blocks to the Common, but the spectacle in progress made the trek worthwhile.

Though most Salem witches would form their circles in

private, closer to midnight, there were often one or more groups who enjoyed forming circles in the Common earlier Halloween night for the benefit of the tourists. A black-robed figure swaying and chanting in one of the circles recognized Melody right away and invited her to join them.

Melody thanked her for the invitation and remained with Logan and Shane, but the woman had drawn the attention of the WHCH news crew filming the circles, and they came over for a quick interview.

At first they focused on their own Kitchen Witch, dressed appropriately for the occasion, which would give the show a nice boost, but then they turned their cameras on the small bespectacled wizard they knew Melody kept in day care.

"Are you going to eat all that candy tonight?" the reporter asked Shane, who was, at that moment, selecting a monster chocolate bar from Jessie's pumpkin.

Shane shook his head and looked up at Logan. "Dad won't let me. Will you, Dad?"

The reporter about swallowed his tongue before he continued, but the videographer kept shooting, and wasn't that the spot they aired the following noon?—Melody Seabright, their own Kitchen Witch, with the wizard she kept in day care calling the WHCH TV producer "Dad."

At about seven minutes past noon, Tiffany came shrieking into their office. Since half the station had been gossiping, making jokes, and asking questions since dawn, Melody figured Tiffany must just be getting into work.

Melody picked up her coffee cup. "Must have missed the break room gossip-fest," she said to Logan before she chose a ringside seat for the "Tiffany in a Temper Show."

Logan poured himself a bracing glass of scotch.

Tiffany's tirade ended with a flat: "I can't believe you married that woman."

"Oh goody, I've graduated. I'm 'that woman' now. I'm so proud."

"Can it, Mel." Logan turned to Tiffany. "Melody. Her name is Melody, and no, Tiff, I didn't marry her."

Tiffany gasped. "Then your son is illegitimate?"

Logan took a furious step in Tiffany's direction, making Daddy's girl step back, way back, until she stood safe behind a desk. *And well she should,* Mel thought.

Logan reined in his temper, more or less. "Don't you ever label my son again."

"Here, here," Melody said, lifting her coffee cup.

Tears filled Tiffany's eyes.

"Weeping crocodile, stage left," Melody warned.

Logan gave her a look, while Tiffany bristled and made a show of ignoring her. "I'm sorry, Logan. I . . . realize how bad that sounded. Truly. I'm just so shocked, and . . . hurt, that you didn't tell me."

"Get real," Melody said.

"Mel," Logan warned.

"Don't you know a flaming case of crocodile tears when you see one?"

Logan took Tiffany's arm and led her toward the door. "This is no place to talk. Let me take you somewhere later. Somewhere private where we can discuss this . . . over dinner?"

"Where?"

Melody heard the victory behind the pout in Tiffany's question, and suspected Logan did, too.

"Your choice," Logan said.

"How about Liberty Station?"

Melody mentally rolled her eyes at Tiffany's pricey choice.

"Okay, sure. Tonight at seven?"

Tiffany sniffed and smiled. "I'd like that."

When Logan came back into the office, Melody shook her head. "Being nice to that woman is like feeding a baby shark so it can grow big enough to eat you."

"She's Max's daughter."

"Who you should never have dated in the first place. Jessie's right, you know."

"About what, precisely?"

Melody regarded the ceiling, aware that sooner or later Logan would remember Jess calling him an idiot as she whacked him with her broom the night before.

"Gee, thanks," Logan said, two beats later.

AS Logan left Shane with Melody that night, he planned to end this thing, whatever it was, with Tiffany. Perhaps if he explained his initial interest in her as a misplaced search for a mother for his son—which was true—she'd see that he'd never really wanted her for himself, anyway. Women wanted to be wanted for themselves, not for their maternal instincts.

In a lot of ways, the excuse was lame, he knew, but it was the best he could come up with, without turning Tiffany's powerful ire toward Melody.

Liberty Station, an old art deco train station, now a landmark Victorian restaurant, overlooked Salem Harbor from the tip of Pickering Wharf. Owing its early twentieth-century ambiance to stained glass chandeliers and windows, Liberty Station maintained a reputation for serving the finest gourmet seafood on the North Shore.

"I adore this place," Tiffany said as the waiter left them with menus.

"I'm glad," Logan said, loathe to point out that she should, since it was clearly the most expensive restaurant this side of Boston.

"Wrong answer," Tiffany said, attempting to charm him with a pout. "You're supposed to say that you adore me."

Ah. She expected him to follow like a lapdog wherever she led. But he'd failed obedience school. "You might have noticed, Tiffany, that I'm not very good at saying or doing the right things. Right, according to you, that is."

"We all have our flaws," she said. "We can work on yours."

Logan smiled, grateful she'd helped strengthen his resolve to break it off. "Before we order," he said, "let me settle a few issues for you and get us on the same . . . wavelength."

"Go ahead, darling. I've been . . . tuned in all along."

Logan ignored the endearment and told her about his struggle for Shane's custody and his concern about station day care ruffling administrative feathers on the new job. He explained how Melody got Shane in without a ruffle.

Tiffany made a sound of pure pleasure, as if he'd given her one of those gaudy diamonds she liked so much. "So Shane isn't Melody's at all? I've never been so glad of anything in—" She bit her lip, her relief short lived. "Wait, why would Melody get him into day care? Why spend Halloween together?"

"Because my son adores her."

"How does he even know her?"

Logan took a sip of water, the words, "none of your damned business" teetering at the tip of his tongue. He placed his glass on the linen tablecloth. "Melody is our downstairs neighbor. Shane loves to spend time with her."

"Oh . . . but that can be fixed."

Whether she referred to the location of his home or the time Shane spent with Mel, Tiffany's statement bothered Logan a great deal. He could see the selfish wheels of manipulation turning. "Before you start trying to fix things, Tiff, hear me out."

"Sure, but order us some champagne first, will you."

Logan sighed, shook his head, and signaled for the waiter.

When the champagne arrived, Tiffany offered a toast, "to us," but Logan purposely left his glass untouched, while he proceeded to reveal a future in which, he pointed out, Tiffany did not figure. "I want to stay in Salem," he said, "buy a house, mow my own lawn, have more children, and work hard to give them a good education. I want to share my life with someone who shares my interests and who doesn't care that I hate to shave on weekends. In other words, Tiffany, I'm not looking for a member of the country club set." There, that about said it all. She might even break up with him.

Tiffany became serious. Twice she began to say something, and twice she stopped, before bracing herself to speak. "You're not saying Melody is that woman?"

"No, of course not. I want someone who sticks to something for longer than a month. You do understand where I'm going with this, don't you? You and I simply don—"

"Yes! Oh, Logan," she said. "Yes! Oh, yes!"

While Logan tried to make sense of Tiffany's skewed reaction, she pulled out her cell phone and hit speed dial. "Daddy! I'm getting married! But I'm quitting the country club."

Shit!

"Logan. I know. Me, too. Sure, here." Tiffany handed him the phone.

Like a fish out of water, Logan kept trying to speak but Max didn't give him a chance. Nevertheless, Logan heard the bottom line: Make my daughter happy, and you win; hurt her, and you lose. As Peabody hung up, Logan saw Shane's, and Melody's secure futures passing before his eyes.

Where had he gone wrong? Shit! "Tiffany," Logan said, avoiding her kiss to finish his drink. "Tiff." He grabbed her hands as she tried to place her arms around his neck. "You don't understand. I didn't mean to propose. I meant to—"

"I know this is not the most romantic place for a proposal," Tiffany said, "but it doesn't matter; I accept."

"You hear only what you want to hear, don't you, Tiff?"

Tiffany grinned. "It's called optimism, and right now, I'm hearing wedding bells."

Logan swore beneath his breath. "It's called stubborn. I'm not ready to get married," he said baldly.

"Fine." Tiffany shrugged and covered his hand with her own. "I have no objection to a long engagement."

"I object to *any* engagement," he said, louder this time.

"Then we'll get married tomorrow."

Logan ran a hand through his hair and decided he was getting nowhere. He'd have to settle this with Max to keep the damage to a minimum, because Tiffany just wouldn't hear what she didn't want to.

Shit! When had he lost control?

He'd tell Max in the morning, explain where he went wrong. Another man would understand, right? When it was settled between them, Logan would . . . quit his job, to save Max the trouble, and get his résumé into the mail. Shit!

Tiffany pouted when Logan dropped her at her door and refused to stay the night, but when he said he had to pick up Shane from Melody's, Tiffany thought that was best and urged him on his way. "Bring the boy over tomorrow night," she said, "and the three of us can have dinner together. He and I need to get to know each other."

Logan waved and got into his car, his heart pounding, his palms sticking to the wheel. "The boy's name is Shane," he snapped into the silence. "I only mentioned it twenty times." He started the car. "Dead meat," he said. "Kilgarven, your ass is toast."

In his garage, he turned off the engine and rested his brow on the wheel. "My life is crap." He got out, slammed the car door, and noticed that Jessie's parlor lights were still on. He ran over. Jess would know what to do. If she could help him beat a theft charge, she could help him beat a life sentence.

She tried to slam the door in his face.

"Hey! Hey, what's up?" Logan kept the door from closing, but she fought him. "Jeez, why do you hate me all of a sudden? I need a friend, Jess."

"No kidding, Bozo." She opened the door enough for him to step in, but kept him standing in the entry. "What's new, shark bait?"

"You've been talking to Melody."

"Ever since we saw the news."

"Wait. I'm confused."

"Once you marry that black widow shark, she's gonna eat you alive."

Logan's stomach flipped. "Marry?"

"Your engagement was just announced on the local news. The station is celebrating. They interviewed Peabody. He promised a hell of a public exhibition of a ceremony, by the way, and nothing less than a full partnership as a wedding gift."

"Damn!" Logan ran a hand through his hair.

"Why do you look so sick? This can't come as a surprise to you?"

"It's a mistake."

"I'll say. Wait . . . it's a mistake? You're not engaged to Tiffany?"

"The announcement's not a mistake. The engagement is." Logan gave her an abbreviated explanation.

Jessie finally showed a bit of sympathy. "Come in and sit down."

Logan's shoulders fell as he followed her into the living room and sat on her sofa.

"I don't know why you dated that woman in the first place, with Melody right there—"

Logan's head snapped up. "You and my mother have been matchmaking from the beginning, haven't you?" He made an exclamation of disgust.

"Wait a minute. Don't get your knickers in a knot. It's not like your mother and I didn't talk before you came home about what a nice couple you and Mel would make, but frankly ever since you got here, Melody's been so vocal about not wanting you that we"—Jess shrugged—"sort of gave up."

Logan ran a hand through his hair. "See," he said, annoyed all over again that Mel didn't want him, though he didn't want her, either.

Jess furrowed her brow. "While I can see why Mel wouldn't want you, I can't figure out why you wouldn't want her."

"Who *are* you?" Logan said. "Thanks a freaking bunch."

Jessie laughed. "I mean, I understand that you seem to have turned into a tight ass with a briefcase, like Mel says, and she's had enough of that with her father. But why wouldn't you want her?"

"Jeez," Logan said, his elbows on his knees, as he rubbed the throbbing in his brow with the tips of his fingers. "Glad I have friends in this town."

He looked up when Jess nudged his arm. She was holding a cup of water and a bottle of aspirin. "Thanks," he said taking the bottle and popping a couple.

"So . . ." Jess sat beside him. "Care to tell me why?"

"Why what?"

"Melody loves Shane; he loves her. I even think you care for each other. Why the hell wouldn't you ask her out and let her see the real you? You're not really the stuffed suit she thinks you are."

Logan sat back. When I date someone, I think of them as potential mothers."

Jess raised her hands in a gesture of incomprehension. "So . . . Melody would make a wonderful mother." She smiled. "Mel thinks it's funny, by the way."

"What's funny?"

"That Tiff sprung the engagement trap and you fell in 'dumb ass over thick head.' Her words."

Logan shot from the sofa. "Melody knows? Jess, I gotta go."

"I thought you wanted to talk."

"Can I have a rain check? I want Mel to understand what happened, and Shane . . . I want him to hear it from me, so he knows the truth—"

"Right, go. First things first. See you tomorrow."

Before Logan made it across Jessie's yard, his mother and Melody's father pulled into the driveway.

Melody came out to greet them. His mother folded Melody into her arms, and they walked inside arm in arm, followed by Mel's father. If any of them had spotted him, and Logan thought his mother had, they didn't acknowledge his presence.

Damn. He hung back a minute, squared his shoulders, went to Melody's door, and rapped it open. The three of them sat at her table, as if waiting for him, their faces set like a hanging committee.

Melody's father stood, his stance protective, and Logan chuckled. "If Mel needs defending from one of us, it's not me," Logan said.

Actually, after the coatroom incident, she did need defending from him, Logan thought, but he hadn't considered that before he spoke. Damn, he had it coming anyway. "Sorry, sir. Do your worst," Logan said.

"Don't 'sir' me. You're despicable."

"Daddy, stop it. Logan and I have no understanding. We've made no promises. He's free to marry any shark he wants."

"It's a mistake," Logan said. "I didn't ask her. She assumed I meant—"

Melody laughed. "She didn't assume; she manipulated you, again, the same way she did at the ball when you asked me to dance and she accepted. You simply played into her hands . . . as always."

"At the ball?" Logan said. "At the ball, she . . . You're right."

"Right," Melody said. She *acted* as if she thought you asked her. Looks like a case of the shark bites twice."

"Hard to believe anybody can be that—"

"Conniving, spoiled, calculating, controlling," Melody supplied. "Guess again, Sherlock."

Logan sat. "I plan to end it tomorrow." He looked at his mother. "Shane and I might have to move, though."

"It can't be that bad," his mother said.

"Can't it?" Melody said. "The station owner giveth, and the station owner taketh away. Tiffany's daddy is used to giving his girl whatever her cold little heart desires."

"I don't know how you got yourself into this," his mother said to Logan, "but I do know that you and Shane deserve someone who loves you."

"I know, Ma."

"I think you should be horsewhipped," Melody's father said, "for leading my daughter on."

"I never—" Logan and Melody looked at each other, and Logan shut his mouth.

"Has Tiffany told you that she'll be a good mother to Shane?" Melody asked. "Because, take it from me, she'll send him to boarding school first chance she gets."

Melody's father regarded her for one enlightened minute, and they seemed to understand each other, perfectly— perhaps for the first time, judging by the surprise, and sadness, on their faces.

"It won't come to that," Logan said. "I won't let it."

"Right," Melody said, shoving him, literally, out the door and slamming it in his face.

"You're mad at me, aren't you?" Logan said from the wrong side of the door.

"Jerk," Melody said, her lock clicking into place.

"I'll take that as a yes."

Twenty

LOGAN guessed his son was staying over again, because he was pretty sure he was standing in the cold alone.

Upstairs in his apartment, he paced. He could fix it with Max, he thought, but Tiffany was going to be pissed when she got it through her thick head that they weren't getting married. If she also figured out that he honestly, hopelessly, cared for Melody, she would do her vindictive worst to make Melody's life a living hell.

Tiffany *was* conniving and manipulating. Mel had been right about her all along. She was a pampered, spoiled brat. Damned early childhood degree had thrown him—probably why Tiff chose it in the first place—man freaking bait.

But why had Tiffany played that game at the ball, unless she already knew he was attracted to Melody. Shit! Maybe he should try and turn the tables before he approached Max, and manipulate Tiffany into breaking up with him.

He might start by not letting her have her own way all

the time. Max would likely embrace that maneuver, plus it would drive Tiffany crazy. He'd have to stop paying attention to Melody, though, to throw Tiffany off Mel's scent.

THEY worked on Melody's "Plymouth Plantation Thanksgiving" on-site for the better part of the following week, which gave Logan a good excuse not to be available for Tiffany to parade him to every fund-raiser and society event she could find. It also kept him and Melody away from Tiffany's scrutiny.

Since Melody had never cooked over an open hearth, her Thanksgiving show became a liberating experience for her. In a thatched roof cottage with a kitchen garden, hideaway loft, and cooking fire, she could admit that she didn't understand how the pilgrims cooked anything, much less the first Thanksgiving. She could be herself, ask questions, and allow her pilgrim guides to teach her.

In costume, Melody gave the word *pilgrim* new meaning. Logan guessed that if any of the original pilgrims had looked like Melody Seabright, the "goodwives" would certainly have considered her a witch, if only because their "goodhusbands" would have followed wherever she went.

The following Monday, after wrap-up and editing, the entire crew watched a preliminary screening of the show.

Because Melody knew how to play to a camera, they had kept an unplanned scene where a lamb wandered into the cottage and stole the show. Mel made it work by kneeling and whispering into the lamb's ear—loud enough for the mikes—that perhaps lamby-pie was not what he'd like them to serve for Thanksgiving dinner. Lo and behold, the lamb had bleated and trotted back out.

They'd kept most of the tourist segments as well. At Melody's suggestion, they had invited some of The Keep

Me Foundation's proud successes to tour the plantation during the shoot.

In one scene, a set of three-year-old twins dressed as Indians had taken to Melody, and she to them, and they'd helped her stir the cauldron suspended over a banked fire in the huge walk-in fireplace, while she chanted a spell for giving thanks.

Mel suggested the video editor add a Thanksgiving request for donations to The Keep Me Foundation to the screen credits at the end of the show. The request rolled over a scene with the girls tasting Indian Pudding and zooming in on their smiles.

When the tape ended, everyone in the viewing room applauded and raved, especially Gardner and Peabody, who called it "magic"—no surprise to anyone. Even Tiffany smiled, though she lost her composure somewhat, Logan thought, when her father praised Mel to the stars in front of everyone, and asked her to do a New Year's Eve special with a larger market in mind.

THE day before Melody's Thanksgiving show was set to go out, Logan got one of those evening calls from the station that he hated so much, but this time the break-in was real. Gardner wanted him there as soon as possible.

"Anything missing? Any damage?" Logan asked, as he pulled a pair of slacks off a hanger in his closet.

"Yeah," Gardner said. "See if you can track Mel down and get her to come, too. We have a problem. I can't find a single copy of her Thanksgiving show. Looks like they've been stolen. Come as soon as you can. I have to get out of here."

Logan went downstairs for Melody. Ice Man didn't seem to know they lived in the same house. Office gossip must be slipping, or the loyalty the staff showed Mel had paid off.

Logan didn't tell Melody that her Thanksgiving show seemed to have gone missing, because he hoped he'd find a backup on the server.

"Who's going to stay with Shane?" she asked from the bedroom side of her closed door.

Logan paced her kitchen, dialing and redialing his cell phone looking for an answer to that very question. "Nobody's answering anywhere," he said.

"Our parents went to the Keys for the week. Didn't your mother tell you?"

"Yeah, I guess she did, and I think maybe Jessie's doing a sleepover with the D.A."

Melody's hoot made Logan grin. Leave it to her to be happy for Jess, though she hadn't acted so excited over their parents.

"Try Vickie or Kira," she suggested.

"What's Vickie's number?"

Melody came out of her room, turned her back on him, and held her hair aside, revealing the unzipped back of an electric blue wool dress, figure-hugging and sexy as hell. "What's wrong with Kira?" she asked.

"I don't know. You tell me."

"No, I mean why not ask her to sit?"

Logan zipped her dress, and Melody turned to face him, still waiting for an answer.

"She's . . . a witch?"

"Not the kind that will shove Shane in an oven and bake him."

Logan winced.

Melody confiscated his cell phone to call Vickie and ask if she could stay with Shane. "Nope," she said a minute later, as she flipped the phone shut. "Her grandmother's not feeling well tonight. She can't leave her. Shall I try Kira?"

Logan sighed. "Mel."

"For heaven's sakes, Logan, Kira was a kindergarten

teacher before she became a fund-raiser. Give her a break."

Jessie had once said the same about Mel. Logan caved. "Call her."

Kira arrived ten minutes later, wearing a quilted camouflage vest over a pair of red flannel pajamas and sporting a playful pair of witch-face slippers, complete with nose warts and pointy hats. "I believe, I believe," Logan said, raising his hands in defeat and leading the witch upstairs.

"I woke Shane to tell him we were going and to make sure he remembered meeting Kira at the tall ships party," Logan said, getting into a warm car. "Thanks for starting it."

"Did Shane remember her?" Melody asked, giving him a sidelong glance.

"You know damned well, he did. Seems he's been to Kira's with you a couple of times."

"Hey, that was before I knew about your irrational fear of witches."

Logan chuckled. "Are you warm enough with all that leg showing? I can't believe you wore a dress. I thought you said this was the new millennium."

"I pretty much dress for whatever mood suits me."

"You know, I figured that out somewhere along the way."

"I like old clothes. The styles are unique, and I can always find something that speaks to the moment. I also feel connected to the people who wore them before me, as if I'm living history. My grandmother—my mother's mother—was the same. She's the reason I fell in love with the clothing styles themselves, as opposed to the dates the clothes were in vogue."

Melody turned in her seat. "Now my mother, she used to buy the latest fashions, the newest designs, and after she wore something once, even for half an hour, she'd toss it. We used to rescue what she discarded and play dress up—me, Vickie, and Kira—I still have a couple of her outfits, and that's how Vickie got into vintage clothing."

"And it's how you stay connected with your mother."

"It is not!"

Logan raised a questioning brow.

"I don't like that theory."

Logan found Melody's hand, squeezed. "If you think about it, you'll see—"

"No." She reclaimed her hand. "I won't think about it. I hate mining for emotions. I'm happy, thank you very much. This is me, everything out in the open, on the surface. What you see is what you get."

Logan regarded her with a heated gaze. "Is that a promise?"

"Don't change the subject. I am not pining for a mother who never wanted me."

"Right, and I'm not like your father."

Melody huffed, then she sat forward. "Wow," she said. "Are those police cars waiting for us?"

In minutes they were embroiled in a search for evidence, only to discover most of the damage confined to the video editor's office. Other than the broken lock on that door, they found no sign of forced entry into the station, or into the parking garage. "Early hypothesis?" said the detective. "A disgruntled employee . . . a stupid one."

A bookcase containing copies of shows in all formats, lay tipped on its side, its damaged contents strewn about. Desk drawers sat open, while outdated cutting and editing equipment had also been smashed.

"The computer's off," Logan said.

"That's odd," Melody said. "Isn't most of the editing done on a computer these days?"

"Yeah, but I don't think our thief realized that."

"Like I said," drawled a cop. "Check employee IQs; might narrow the search."

"Bingo," said one of the cops, taking something from the

rug near the desk with tweezers and placing it into a small clear zipper bag. "Looks like our burglar is a woman." He handed the evidence bag to the detective, who looked at it then handed it to Logan. "Look familiar?"

Logan showed the bagged evidence—a glittering gold fingernail, inset with diamonds—to Melody. Seeing it, the two of them regarded each other for half a beat. "No," Logan said as Melody shrugged and shook her head in denial.

"Where did you find it?" Logan asked.

"Here," said the cop who found it, as he examined the desk. "Looks like the nail broke when the perp forced a drawer open. Unless your video editor is a woman?"

Chuckling, Logan and Melody shook their heads. "Sam Schraft is an ex-jock. Those nails are not his type."

"Cleaning woman, maybe?" the detective said.

"No cleaning woman in her right mind would wear nails like that," Melody said.

The detective stepped closer and lifted one of Melody's hands, then the other, and examined her lavender nails. "Paint these lately?" he asked, brow raised.

"Yep, I grew a new one and painted it right after you called. Look closer," she said. "They're real."

"Hey," Logan said. "Her show is what's missing, remember?"

"It's okay, Logan," Melody said. "He's only doing his job. "Maybe I didn't like my show, right, detective?"

The detective nodded, but Logan saw that Mel had won his admiration, and Logan felt the headache resulting from another adoring male coming on.

"And what about you, Kilgarven? You got anything against the lady's show?"

"Me? That's not my nail."

"No, but you have a history, don't you?"

Logan shook his head. "Not one you can look up. Those

records are sealed, and you damned well know it. Find a record in the past twenty years and come back. The man and the punk are two different animals."

"That's what my father said."

"Your father?"

"Martin Grey. He took you in that day."

"I hate small towns," Logan said, sensing Melody's interest.

They saw the police out of the building, and Logan turned to her. "Don't ask," he said. "And I won't ask why you said you could cook."

Melody nodded. "Fair enough."

They returned to the video editor's office and Logan sat down at Sam's desk to see if anything of Mel's Thanksgiving show had been backed up on the computer. "I'll tell you about it someday."

Again Melody nodded, glad he felt comfortable enough to confide in her.

"Good thing Gardner left," Melody said. "He would have recognized Tiffany's nail, too."

"Right, and since you didn't say anything, either, I guess you agree it's not in anybody's best interest to finger the station owner's daughter—pun intended."

"What happens when the police show Max the evidence?"

"If Max recognizes it, let him deal with her. If he doesn't, well, you can be sure that as soon as Tiffany notices it's gone, there'll be a new and different set of nails on those corrupt hands of hers."

"How do you think Max will deal with her, providing he recognizes it?"

"He'll send her on a world cruise or something. Max is like your father in that he thinks money represents love."

Melody slipped into a chair. "Poor kid." She frowned. "What am I saying? She sabotaged my Thanksgiving show, and it was awesome. I was a freaking domestic goddess in that show."

Logan grinned as his fingers continued tapping at the keys. "A goddess," he said on a laugh. "Let's see if we can retrieve any of it."

Melody pulled up a chair. "I thought you said it was gone."

"The backup copies that were supposed to be shipped tomorrow to the stations airing the show are gone. I don't know if any were sent on-line. I do know the copies on the computer desktop have been deleted, but I was thinking Tiff might not know enough to look for backup on the server, so that's where I'm looking."

"You think the show might still exist?"

"Damn!"

Melody's smile froze. "That doesn't sound good."

"Looks like Sam backed up the raw footage but hasn't backed up the finished product yet. Try calling him at home."

Melody tried. "No answer," she said, closing Logan's cell phone.

"Forget it, then. We can't take a chance that the show exists anywhere in or out of cyberspace. We've got the footage in pieces, and that's a beginning."

"A beginning of what?"

"Turning the raw clips back into a Thanksgiving show."

"You know how to do that?"

"Moviemaking is my first love. One of these days, I'll have to show you my documentaries."

"You have hidden depths."

"Depths and depths of depths," Logan said. "I'll need your help, though. Got a few hours to spare?"

"I do, but I don't know about Kira. How many hours are we talking?"

"With what we've got of the original footage, all the

show needs is a better than average team of experts—that's us—and five, maybe six hours to put Humpty-Dumpty together again."

"Bad analogy," Melody said, dialing Kira. "They failed with the egg."

Twenty-one

* *
* * *
*
* *

"KIRA'S cool with staying over," Melody said, putting the phone aside.

"Thanks for calling." Logan concentrated on the computer, clicking the mouse with the speed of an expert. "Look," he said with a nod, his focus barely taken from his task. "Here's where the lamb walks in and everyone scrambles out of its way." He chuckled. "Sam cut the best part."

"Nah, the best part was where the lamb pooped on my shoe."

"Oh, God. Here it is." Logan watched the clip twice, wiping away tears of laughter when he saw a close-up of Mel's wide-eyed reaction. "Someday we're gonna send that to a funniest videos show."

The next clip showed Mel returning to the scene, shoe clean, smile in place. "Look, here's where you hug the lamb and talk it into leaving."

"But the sound's gone. It's ruined."

"I turned the audio off. We'll put the video together first

then maximize the audio effects by adding sound bites, titles, credits, and special effects later." He found a segment with Melody tasting something, rolling her eyes in ecstasy, and licking her fingers. "I like that part. What were you eating, and why didn't Sam keep it?"

"Baked Indian Pudding. You're kidding about keeping it, right?"

"Maybe, but you do look cute."

Melody reached up and covered his brow with her palm. "What are you doing?"

"Testing you for fever. Me, cute?"

"Okay, so I'm tired. So sue me. Here, let's put that clip after the one where you have a similar reaction to the scent of whatever's in the cauldron, and try a freeze-frame . . . here . . . and here. Logan hit a couple of keys and sighed in satisfaction. Then we can transition to . . . hey, I never saw that gang of kids before; they're adorable."

"Oh, I like that clip. Why didn't we use the kids before?"

"It's not unusual to shoot hours of videotape for a half hour show, and every video editor has his or her own vision of the finished product. It's a matter of visual storytelling. Since there's no time for Sam to recreate the original, even if he could, we'll choose what speaks to us. While our show will be essentially the same as Sam's, it'll be different as well."

"Better, you mean?"

"Nah. Sam's the best."

"He is good, but you're good, too, better maybe, and you love what you're doing right now. I would know, even if you hadn't told me. Why don't you try a career in filmmaking, instead of producing? Wouldn't you rather let your creativity run wild than produce the shows?"

"Of course I would. I love the idea. My documentaries are great, but an independent filmmaking career does not make for a stable income."

"Why are you so afraid to take a chance on life?"

"Hey, I've taken more chances than you can imagine, but the fact is that I would be gambling with my son's future. I can't do that. Every decision I make now is made with my son's well-being in mind. Enough said. Let's just get your show reworked and be grateful we can."

After that, they worked pretty much in silence, Logan revealing an amazing talent, asking for Melody's input and opinions along the way. Sometimes he showed her the difference between one visual and another, one sound and another, so she could make educated decisions. But sometimes he just knew, with the gut instinct of an artist.

In that way, with a new camaraderie and professional respect, they worked for hours without a break, except for the coffee Melody made around midnight, to keep them going.

"Sounds like there's a storm brewing outside," Melody said. "Maybe I should call home again. Holy cow, did you see the time? How much longer?" Melody dialed, using Logan's cell.

"Less than an hour, I suspect."

"But it's two A.M. Kira, it's Mel. Are you guys okay? Sounds rough out there."

Kira told Melody what was happening with the weather.

"But you two are okay?" Melody asked, nodding at Kira's answer. "Okay. Good idea. If it looks like we can't get out, we will."

Logan raised a brow when she hung up.

"Kira says there's a raging sea squall outside with trees and power lines down. On the news, they're telling everybody to stay off the roads. She says if we go out there, we'll get blown away."

"How are they faring in all this?" Logan asked with concern.

"Snug as bugs in rugs," to quote Kira. "They've been

camped on your sofa, but the winds are fierce on the top floor, so they're going down to sleep in my bed. She says that's where we'll find them in the morning."

"Sounds reasonable."

Melody bit her lip. "We might be stuck here for the night."

"We already are," Logan said, turning back to the computer. "Here, what do you think of this?"

BY three A.M. they'd finished formatting and viewing a Thanksgiving show that improved on the original. A work of art, Melody thought. "It's incredible. If I weren't so tired, I'd dance," she said. "Awesome job, Kilgarven. Now, let's go home and get some sleep."

"First," he said, "let's go find an office with an outside window. This close to the ocean, we take travel warnings to heart."

"You're the native."

Five minutes later, they stood at the picture window in Gardner's corner office and counted two cars and one porch with trees crushing them. A bush flew straight toward the window, glanced off as they ducked, and kept going. A minute later, they heard the sound of breaking glass somewhere else in the building. "Oops," Melody said. "Is that going to set off the burglar alarm again?"

"Nah, we didn't reset it yet, but the night watchman is down there. Tony'll take care of it."

"Good thing."

For a while, they watched the world fly by, some debris sailing so fast they couldn't identify it. "This is like the center of a twister. Think we're on our way to Oz?"

"We will be," Logan said, "if we go out there."

A doghouse lost shingles as it rolled across the street below, bounced off of a Mercedes, and continued on its way.

"Ouch!" Logan winced. "No discrimination."

"Yeah," Mel said with a grin. "Poor rich sucker. Ain't it a shame?"

"Hey, that could have been my Volvo."

"Or my vintage beetle."

"Old. Your bug's old. That would have been a mercy killing."

"Hey! I love that car."

"It's older than you are."

"We bonded in the cradle. Hope the dog got out."

"What?"

Melody shrugged. "Hope the dog got out of that dog-house."

"Is that a ship's mast?" Logan asked, stepping closer to the window. Call home again; make sure they're not flooding."

Melody talked with Kira for several minutes before she was satisfied they were okay. "They're fine," she told Logan after she hung up. "Don't worry, the house sits on pretty high ground."

"I'm still glad you told her to take Shane back upstairs if flooding becomes a problem."

"It probably won't."

"I agree."

"Best to be safe, though. Let's go up to our office and see if we can catch some sleep."

In their office, Logan locked the door.

"Why did you do that?"

"Tony knows we're here, but I don't feature waking up to find him watching me when he makes his rounds."

"Good thought."

Logan proceeded to throw the cushions off the sofa, revealing a hidden mattress.

"I had no idea," Melody said. "Did you ever sleep here?"

"No, I requested the sofa bed when I took the job. That was about a month before we hired you. Go ahead, lie down, get some rest."

After her turn in the bathroom, Melody kicked off her spikes and reclined fully clothed on the sheeted mattress, straight as a soldier, arms at her sides, feeling like an idiot with him watching. "This is impossible," she said.

"Sleep, and that's an order."

Melody huffed but closed her eyes while Logan continued to shuffle around the office, driving her nuts. A pillow hit her in the face.

"Hey!" She sat up. "Wow. Pillows and blankets too? Gee, all the comforts." She spread the blanket over herself while Logan moved chairs around, facing them toward each other. "What are you doing?"

"Making a bed for myself. What does it look like?"

"Looks like you're afraid of me. There's plenty of room over here. I won't attack you, you know."

"I'm sorry to hear that."

"C'mon sleep here—the operative word being *sleep*—if you don't think Tiffany will mind."

"You think I give a rat's ass what she thinks?"

"Whatever, but you're safe with me."

"Gee, thanks." Logan threw off his jacket and lay beside her. "Our parents picked the perfect time to take off. Think they're having fun in Florida?"

Mel turned to him and wiggled her brows. "Think they're having sex?"

"Jeez, way to give me nightmares. Give me another picture, fast."

Melody giggled. "Picture my father smiling, then. He does it all the time around your mother. It's pretty scary."

"My mother's the same," Logan admitted. "Until your father, I hadn't seen her smile in years."

"Hell, until your mother, I rarely *saw* my father. Now I

see him all the time. Kind of weird, actually, but they're happy together, and Logan, I don't know if you've picked up on it, but they're hinting that they might get married." She touched his arm. "I think I'm happy for them."

Logan sighed. "I caught a marriage hint once, but I tried to ignore it." He chuckled. "I'm happy for them, too, I guess. Hard to believe your old man is actually good for my mother, but I'd like him better if he were nicer to you."

"Really?" Melody savored the unexpected wash of emotion Logan's concern engendered. "I asked your mother once what about my father attracted her."

"I'm not sure I want to hear this."

"She said he widened her world. I asked my father the same about your mother, and he said she made him focus on the important things, then he kissed my cheek." She touched it. "Here. That was the first time he'd kissed me in years."

Logan stroked the exact spot with the back of a knuckle, a touch Melody felt to her toes. "I like him better already."

She shifted a leg, brought a knee up to touch his. "Our parents balance each other, like Jessie said."

"I suppose," Logan said. "Jess and her balance."

"She's right about a lot of things. Life *is* short. Our parents have said the same. All of them want to make the best of the time they have left. We could take a lesson from them."

He didn't know about the others, but he knew exactly how to make the best of the time he and Melody had left— here, now, tonight . . . in this bed.

He wanted to take her into his arms and kiss her the way he'd kissed her in the cloak room, as if time had stopped and belonged entirely to them. He wanted to slip inside of her and stay for a while, take her on a meteoric rise to the stars and make her weep with pleasure.

Damn! Logan turned on his side and faced away from temptation, wishing his slacks weren't suddenly so tight. "Night, Mel."

She tried another position, then another, driving Logan nuts, reminding him of her provocative presence about every two seconds. And if she touched him, even by accident, with her hand, or her arm, or, God help him, with her breasts or her backside, one more time . . . "I take it you can't get comfortable?" he said, tongue in cheek, aching to suggest a position they were both likely to prefer.

"This dress is too tight to sleep in."

"By all means, take it off."

"Don't be fresh."

"I'm only being practical. Take it off, and I'll give you my shirt." He sat up and started unbuttoning his shirt.

"Wait! I don't want you bare-chested beside me in bed."

"A turn-off, is it?"

"Get real."

Logan grinned. "Okay, then, I do have a spare shirt in a bathroom drawer, all fresh, starched, and folded." He rose to fetch it.

"I want the one you're wearing," she said, padding after him in stocking feet. "It's softer."

"So you want me to be uncomfortable?"

"I want you to be a gentleman."

Logan stopped unbuttoning and held her gaze with his. "Are you certain that's what you want?"

Mel's topaz eyes widened, and her cheeks flushed. She turned her back on him. "Unzip me and keep your smart remarks to yourself. This is awkward enough."

"I still don't know why you wore a dress," he said as he unzipped it. "First dress I've seen you wearing."

"No. I've worn several on the show," she said, turning back and snatching the body-warm shirt from his hand while trying not to gawk at his naked torso. She smacked him in the chest with the starched, paper-banded shirt. "Go put this on, so I can change."

Logan did as told, then propped himself up in the sofa

bed to wait. Melody returned, finally, bathed in moonlight, his white shirt stroking her, from her neck to the tops of her long shapely legs.

He imagined those legs wrapped tight around him and was forced to shift to his side to hide his resurrected arousal. "Can we get some sleep now?" he groused.

Melody finally switched off the light, no less noisy and obvious about trying to find a comfortable position than she had been the first time. "Night," she said, touching his arm. "Thanks for the shirt. Feels yummy."

Yummy. The word brought a renewed surge of discomfort. Yummy, the way she'd taste on his lips, the way she'd feel gloving him.

LOGAN dreamed that something heavy nestled snug against his lap, rode his erection and made him throb. He dreamed a warmth at his neck, a heaviness on his chest, Melody's hair feathering his cheek. Its scent—sin and salvation at one and the same time—enticed him to slip further into the arms of sleep. He dreamed that her hand rode his chest, her knee, his groin.

In sleep, he found her mouth, warm, open, inviting, seeking his kiss. He opened his own and devoured her pouting lips. She gave him an involuntary throat-squeak, a lusty moan, like a babe at the nipple, and a tongue that set him on fire. "Melody," he heard himself say. Greedy. Ravenous. No words could describe his edgy upward spiral, half starvation, half satiation, increasing hunger, soothing spirits, a relentless climb, breathless and unyielding.

They kissed in half-sleep, a dream but not, a ride toward eternity, a need to prolong, yet despite his best efforts, Logan woke. He did not know the exact minute awareness came to him, but it did. It came in winds and waves mightier than the elements that trapped them . . . blessed them. It came with a frisson of panic and a flood of joy. Acceptance. Gratitude. Responsibility.

"I want this," Logan whispered against Melody's ear, sharing the warmth of his breath, offering her his essence, raising her higher still, but not so high that she could miss the underlying question in his voice.

"I want it more than my next breath," he said. "No more pretending this is out of control." Concern laced his voice, worry perhaps, that she did not feel the same. She knew him well enough to know he'd just handed her the choice to make for them both.

As if all choice had not been snatched from her grasp the day she opened her door to him, she thought. "I want it, too," she said, arching against him, fitting her every curve to his every hollow.

"Now tell me you're awake."

She smiled. "I'm awake."

They lay on their sides, facing each other, embracing, as close as two can be without becoming one. "I want you inside of me, Logan. No pretense, no evasion . . . no interruptions. No promises," she wisely added. "No expectations for the future."

Logan nodded. "No promises, no future," he acknowledged to her relief. "We've known it from the beginning, haven't we." Not a question but a statement.

His echo of her thoughts firmed Melody's resolve to grasp this rare pulsing moment in time. No fear of rejection . . . she'd short-circuited every expectation. Free, she felt. Uninhibited, for the first time ever. Ready to welcome the man she had lusted after from the first.

"I have only one worry." Logan regarded her, moonlight gilding his blue eyes to green. "Tell me again that you're not talking in your sleep."

Melody buried her face in his starched shirtfront. "I'm

awake," she said after a minute. "Tell me you're as sure about this as I am."

He surged, almost involuntarily, against her. "Never more so of anything . . . obviously."

"It's not the, er . . . 'Big Guy' talking, is it?"

"Him? Oh, he's never been more alive, whimpering, weeping in anticipation, aching to sing in full-throated glory." Logan chuckled, as he hardened even more, "but my other brain is doing the talking right now. My word on it."

"Alive, yes," Melody said. "Me, too. Like that storm raging around us, gathering energy and momentum. Let's finish what we started too many times to count."

"God, yes," he said. "Now, when the world can't get to us. Take my hands," he whispered on a kiss that lingered as he rose to hover over her.

He held himself apart as they kissed and kissed, fingers entwined.

With no one to interrupt, they could take the kiss as far as they wanted. Farther than the kitchen, the elevator, the cloak room, as far as consummation. Logan stiffened and held himself away from her, nothing but hands and lips touching. Not yet.

"Let me touch you," Melody said.

"No," Logan said on a smile. "I want to make it last, Mizzz Impatience."

"You're going to kill me. I'll make the news. 'Salem's own Kitchen Witch dies of lust. In a spectacular bid for an orgasm—' "

"Shut up!"

Logan kissed her, as hungry, she thought with satisfaction, and as possessive and wildly frantic as she.

Twenty-two

"I'M dying, too," he said. "We'll make it last until we can't bear it. I have protection in the bathroom, then we'll fly away together. No broom necessary."

"Protection! Good. Oh, but hell, we'll have to stop for that."

"It'll slow us down, Mel, make us wait. That's good. It prolongs the pleasure."

"As a multiorgasmic creature, I'll have you know that I plan on seconds, thirds . . . maybe more—"

"Oh God." Logan surged again, as if he'd lost control. Melody arched as well, to meet and tease him.

Logan ravaged her mouth, nuzzled and licked her neck, swooped and let their bodies touch, then he swore and rolled away and off the bed.

Melody gasped and sat up. "What's wrong?"

"Too many clothes." He began to tear at his buttons. "Take the shirt off. No, wait. I want to take it off you myself."

He knelt beside her on the bed, his erection tenting his shirttails.

Melody smiled, undid his buttons while he undid hers. She planned to take possession of that erection the minute she freed it into her greedy little hands. But Logan got to her breasts first, his mouth distracting her, nuzzling her. He teased beside and around her nipples, making them erect, making them ache for the pull and abrasion of his tongue.

"You're torturing me," she cried, nearly weeping with need.

"You've been torturing me for months."

"Hey, you're not the only one."

"Since when?" he asked.

"Tall ships day, my kitchen."

"The first time you opened your door."

"That day," she said. "Yes."

He tongued her nipple, but she wanted to feel the pull of him suckling. She arched and all but put her nipple in his mouth. He chuckled and denied her, kissed her to her navel.

Melody squeaked in frustration. "I wanted to spread something warm over you that first day. Me."

He sat back. "What?"

She reached for his shirt and pulled him back to her. "I lived the fantasy that night in your living room chair, remember?"

"Remember? The sound of you coming in my hand keeps me awake nights. I dream about it, wake up hard, like now."

"Let me see how hard."

He slapped her hand away. "Not yet."

"You have my breasts. It's only fair that I should have something to play with."

"Not yet. Keep talking like that, though, and I'll come before you get a chance."

Melody threw her head back and gave a mock howl of frustration.

"Shh! You'll have Tony up here for sure." Logan chuckled as he freed her from his shirt and threw off his own. He went for protection.

"Bring the box!" Melody called after him. Screw making it last, he'd given her no choice but to take matters into her own hands.

Yes, she wanted instant gratification, damn it. She'd waited a long time to get Logan into bed. Shame on her if she couldn't beat him at his blasted "let's make it last" game.

She'd take him captive, shirtless and hair mussed, pupils dilated with lust, and hard as the proverbial rock.

Melody grinned as she watched him return.

When Logan knelt over her and made to nuzzle her breasts, she slugged him hard in the shoulder.

He reared back, puzzled, speechless.

"Damn it," she said, raising herself on her elbows, arching so as to point her breasts his way and keep him focused. "We've been hot for each other, jumped each other, got interrupted every time, and you want to make it last? Are you nuts? I want hot, fast, fly-me-to-the-stars sex, Kilgarven, and I want it now!"

Logan wanted to laugh, scream in frustration, shout in triumph, and for the first time ever, he wanted to make love. Ignoring the heart-skip the insane thought brought, he focused on the task at hand. "You wicked, impatient witch, you. Hard and fast, you say? Okay, you asked for it." He started to rip off her panties, found her bikinis as royally sexy, and blue, as her dress, and had to keep himself from swooping in for a taste.

"Later," she said. "Hot and fast now, slow and tantalizing later."

"Right."

He kept going, got her naked, then he let her have at

him. She pulled off his slacks with due haste, but stopped halfway to his knees. "Time out. Black briefs. Oh, glory."

"Why, thank you." But while she appreciated, he grew more rigid and uncomfortable before her eyes.

"Yum," she said.

"Too late to savor, Witch, you wanted it fast. You're getting it fast." Logan shed his slacks in record time.

"Oh," she said, still focused on the nest of his arousal. "Just let me feel all that nice soft black cotton . . . and everything." She stroked him through the briefs, took him from his cocoon and into her greedy hands, and turned him into her submissive slave. She handled him with gentle reverence, kneading and nuzzling with fingers and lips, growing him, breath by gasping breath, stroking him against her cheek, nibbling with her lips, until he got so close to coming, he took her down on top of him.

"So much for making it last," he said as he slid into her, in one fast, incredible thrust, burying himself to the hilt, satisfying a longing so sharp, it hurt to achieve, yet felt so wondrous, he could hardly bear it. He wanted the same wild and unexpected pleasure for her, and more. He wanted to make a memory.

She came almost at once, making him slick, easing his heaving way. When he caught his breath, when they both did, he rolled her to her back, still inside her, and rose over her. "That's one," he said.

"More," she said arching, pulsing tight around him as if to help.

"Greedy," he said, rising to the occasion and going for two, pretty certain that giving her as many orgasms as she wanted, before his turn came, would about kill him.

She wrapped those incredible legs around him, taking him in, working him deeper still, with muscles that pulled and swallowed, kneaded and pulsed.

He began to move faster; he had to. She was milking him, wringing sanity from him with every pulsing beat, every rotation of her hips, each stroke of her palm and scratch of her nails.

She came again, thank God, and he'd survived, amazingly. But he was falling deeper under her spell with every involuntary squeak, every explosive orgasm in which she took full and uninhibited pleasure. Have mercy.

When he thought he couldn't take a second more of her torture, when he pumped into her so hard, he was afraid he'd hurt her, Melody reached between them with both hands, cupped his balls, and held them firm against her. Logan groaned and he growled, begged her to stop, begged for more, and he knew in a flash that no other woman would ever mean as much to him as this one.

He cried out, cursed her, and kissed her as if to devour her, and spilled his seed in a climax that made any previous explosion seem like nothing in comparison.

If he lived, he thought—his heart beating in his head like a drum—he would survive to be a hundred, because he was tougher than he imagined.

"Melody?" He pushed himself up in a panic, fought dizziness. "Oh God, I've killed you." He'd pinned her to the bed, crushed her, hair wet, face pale and still. She wasn't even breathing.

He rolled off her, called her name, felt for a pulse at her throat. "Melody? Melody, speak to me."

"Shh." She didn't open her eyes. "I'm floating."

Logan laughed and collapsed, pulled her against him, and buried his face in her neck. "Thank God." He let himself float as well, until the air in the room nipped a chill along his nether regions and the wind outside the window became louder than the pounding of his heart. He grabbed a blanket, pulled it over them, felt Melody's slowing heartbeat, the gentle way she breathed as she slept.

As he warmed, Logan began to replay every incredible fly-me-to-the-stars moment.

Melody woke, feeling his talented hands raising her again toward that star-sprinkled place where he'd brought her before. "Mmm." She stretched like a cat so supremely content it didn't want to move. "Now," she said, all but purring. "Now it can be slow, sensuous, lay me on a cloud sex."

Logan laughed and kissed her. He kissed her slow and easy and with the experience of a lover. "More, she wants, after she's damned near killed me."

"Tell me another one. We have to do it in the shower, too," she said. "I want my fair share. I will not have Nikky one-upping me in the shower."

Logan pretended to pass out from exhaustion, but when she began to lift his eyelids, he laughed and pulled her full atop him. "Good thing I didn't know you were insatiable or that you kept all those tricks up your sleeve, or I'd have been walking around embarrassing myself for weeks."

"That's exactly what you were doing."

Logan chuckled. "I'd hoped no one noticed."

"Everyone noticed. What time is it?"

Logan put on the light to see his watch. "Nearly five."

"Come on, we're running out of time." Melody hopped out of bed and reached for his hand.

Logan groaned and fell back against the pillows. "It's too early to get up."

"Exactly. I have time to make you cry for mercy in the shower."

He opened his eyes. "I hate to admit this, but I think you ruined me."

"That's okay, stud, leave everything to me. I love raising

the devil." She gave him a wink before disappearing into the bathroom.

Logan rose and followed. "How is it that you're so talented, after having so little practical experience?"

She struck a match to light some candles. "I read a lot."

"That must be some reading material. What are you doing?"

"Setting the mood," she said. "Gold is for attraction." She purred and lit a gold candle. "Ruby red is for passion. Start the shower, why don't you? I like it nice and . . . hot."

After Logan got in the shower, Melody lit the indigo candle, for defenses, as in, she would need plenty, because she was falling, and hard, for Logan, "stuffed suit," Kilgarven.

"Books, huh?" he said when she got in and began to soap him up in the most seductive manner she could manage.

She looked up at him. "And I was primed."

"I've heard that before."

"Well, this time I'm telling the truth."

She saw the dawning in his eyes as he kissed her, with relief and passion, and maybe something as frightening as she herself had been feeling. Where was that indigo magic when you needed it?

"You were supposed to let me do all the work," she said, a breathless few minutes later. "Here, hold on to the top edge of the stall on both sides and don't let go. I'll take care of everything."

"Something tells me I'm going to regret this. I don't think I have the staminaa . . . aahhhh."

"Oh, I think you do." She soaped him everywhere, giving particular attention to the part growing in her hands. "Nice," she said, sliding it between her breasts, lathering them both vigorously.

Logan groaned, and he swore, he reached for her a dozen times, and she ordered him to put his hands back where they belonged. And then she knelt before him, but before she realized what he was doing, he had her back against the shower and he'd slipped inside of her, pounding her, raising her so high and so fast, she screamed with her cataclysmic release, and he did the same. "So much for slow," she said, when she caught her breath.

He soaped her, languorously, played every sensitive spot, gave her the same attention she gave him, except that he made her come, not once, or even twice, but four extended times. Now she was the one begging for mercy, as her knees buckled and she slid into his waiting arms.

He carried her back to the bed, and they slept for almost an hour, unmoving, dead to the world, wrapped in damp sheets and each other's arms, until the sound of a honking horn woke them with a jolt.

"Jeez, what time is it?"

"After six," Melody said. "We have to go." Her knees nearly buckled as she rose.

Logan pulled her back down. "The world is about to intrude. Give me one more kiss to remember."

Melody went into his arms, and they kissed as freely as the wind, the way they would never kiss again. He cupped her cheek, she grazed a finger down his fresh growth of beard. "I love your beard in the morning."

"Careful or I'll never shave again."

He cupped her and brought her close. I love your ass, morning, noon, and night. Did I ever tell you that?"

"Er, no, you never did."

"Well, I do. Get some clothes on before I forget we're leaving."

Melody came back wearing her dress, ready to be zipped. Logan accommodated her. "I like this on you."

"I wore it to get your attention."

He turned her to face him. "You always have my attention."

"I wanted to look as nice as Tiffany always does."

"Clothes can't make her beautiful. I saw her face when Max gave you that raise. She's a jealous cat."

"You're insulting Ink and Spot."

Logan chuckled, glad they'd stepped from regretful to playful. Together they put the sofa back together and tidied the office. Mel put the sheets in a bag to take home and wash.

"All set?" he asked.

They looked around, as if they would never see the place again, though they would never view it in quite the same way, and they both knew it. Melody worried about going back to the way things had been between them.

Logan worried about going on without her. He knew what he had to do, and he wasn't looking forward to it.

The Volvo had survived the storm fine in the garage, but it didn't get them far, because a tree blocked the exit. They turned around and tried getting out the other exit, but a bulldozer clearing an obstruction in the road blocked them there, so they abandoned the car in the garage and walked home.

The bracing, storm-clean air smelled of fresh cut greens, and sea salt. Melody and Logan walked hand in hand, not saying much, stopping to kiss a time or two, through the bricked mall, by closed shop windows, wishing it wasn't too early to get a Morning Glory Muffin or the best pancakes in the world.

When they got to Salem Common, in front of the Hawthorne Hotel, Logan asked Mel to sit for a minute. She did, and he braced a foot on the bench to face her. "I robbed a convenience store when I was twelve, got arrested, and was brought before a juvenile judge named Jessie Harris."

Melody nodded. "Not the background of a tight-assed stuffed suit."

"Nope. The past of a man forced to trade in his beat-up

'hog' for a briefcase, his bad-boy image for a job, and care-lessness for fatherhood. I like the me I've become, though. I'm not making excuses, not even for the stealing."

"Jessie told me a bit about the way your father treated you and your mother, but not much."

"He said I'd never amount to anything."

"Hey, our fathers predicted the same for us."

"Nah, yours is mild . . . and redeemable." Logan extended his hand. "Have I shocked you?"

"A bit." She rose and leaned into him. "Makes me like you more."

"No kidding?" He kissed her brow. "Guess I should have told you sooner."

They made their way past Pickering Wharf and The Gables to the street where they lived. With Halloween a memory, Salem was the image of any other sleepy New England town, except for having some of the most beautiful historical architecture Logan had ever seen. A great place to raise a boy, he remembered thinking. Too bad that hadn't worked out.

He kissed Melody on the porch before they went in the house. A kiss good-bye. He believed she knew it as well. Good-bye to intimacy and a future that could never be. They would both move on, move forward.

Logan had a son to raise—none of the choices he made were for himself. Melody had a life to conquer, every choice she made based on survival. Her parents had about crippled her in that way, he thought. His father had nearly done the same to him.

Funny how the past could direct the future, no matter how hard you tried to keep it from happening.

Melody pushed her door open. "Kira, Shane, we're home." She turned to Logan. "They must have gone upstairs after all."

He ran up. "Hey, sport, I'm home."

Melody heard Logan shout. She got halfway up before he came out. "They're not here."

"They're not in my apartment, either."

When there was no answer at Kira's or Jessie's, Logan punched in 911 on his cell phone. "I'd like to report my son missing."

Twenty-three

LOGAN watched his hand tremble as he told the police dispatcher he'd been out all night on a job emergency and hadn't seen his son since five the night before. The dispatcher said the boy hadn't been missing long enough for them to start a search, but when Logan asked for detective Grey, he promised that Grey would be right there.

Logan and Melody walked through the neighborhood calling Shane's name. They rang Jessie's doorbell, just in case, but no one answered. "She should sell the house," Melody said. "It needs a family in it."

"Screw the house; my son is missing!"

"I won't kid you, you're scaring me, but I think you're overreacting."

They woke their neighbors fronting the harbor, but they hadn't seen Shane, and they weren't pleased to be roused, either. Melody came up beside Logan as he looked out over the harbor. "This is stupid," she said. "There's a logical explanation."

Logan said nothing then, but back in the driveway, he cursed. "I can't believe I let you talk me into letting that witch baby-sit. Of all the irresponsible . . ."

"Kira is not irresponsible, and neither am I for suggesting her, if that's where you're—"

"Me!" Logan snapped, "I'm irresponsible, damn it. I've done some stupid things in my life, but this—misplacing my son—is by far the worst. Worse than robbing that store, worse than getting Shane's mother pregnant, worse than allowing Tiffany to believe we're engaged, worse even than taking you to bed."

"Gee, thanks."

"Tonight, I proved my old man right."

"Taking me to bed is not the worst thing you've ever done."

"No, losing my son is."

"He isn't lost. We should try Kira again."

"Do it," Logan said, handing Melody his phone.

He shouted Shane's name a couple more times, to keep from jumping out of his skin. Two patrol cars pulled up at about the same time. His heart skipped, because he thought he heard Shane answer. Detective Grey stepped from the patrol car in time to see Kira and Shane, a frisky beagle pup in tow, emerge through a backyard hedge. "Hey, Dad." Shane ran over. "Wow, cops!"

Logan had never been more grateful for anything in his life than he was to see his son. He lifted Shane in his arms.

"Da-aad, you're squishing me."

"How come the police are here?" Kira asked Melody.

"Logan reported Shane missing."

Kira frowned. "Didn't you read my note?"

"What note?" Grey asked.

"Oops," Shane said, pulling a sticky note and red pushpin from his pocket. "I was s'posed to tack it to the door. Sorry, Kira."

"My fault," she said, ruffling his hair. "I should have made sure you did."

"Where the hell were you?" Logan shouted at Kira.

"We went to get my dog. Shane worried about Spooky all through the storm, so when the rain stopped, we went to get him. I said so in the note."

"Dad, she only lives two streets over. We cut through lots 'a yards, and I was hopin' somebody would yell at us."

"Likes to play with fire," Melody told Detective Grey, "like his father."

"Can it, Mel." Logan thanked the detective for coming, and saw him off, before turning back to Melody. "I'm giving up playing with fire. I can't stand the heat, or the chaos, or the mayhem, that results, and it's not what I want for Shane either." He could see that she knew exactly what he meant. Chaos, turmoil, problems seemed to follow wherever she went.

"I'm settling it with Tiffany, now," he said. "No more fire, no more Mr. Irresponsible. Keep Shane for a while; I'll pick you up for work in about an hour."

Melody nodded, while the welling in her eyes brought a heaviness to Logan's chest.

AT Max's house, Tiffany met Logan at the door in a clingy red silky thing as flashy as her diamond fingernails. "Can't wait to see me, darling?"

He evaded her kiss and took her hands to examine her nails. She hadn't yet bothered to get them fixed. He rubbed a thumb over the single pale nail, minus its glittering fake. "The police have it," he said. "If you care to claim it."

She retrieved her hands and placed the undamaged one on her heart. "I don't know what you're talking about."

"Sure you do. It's called evidence . . . of the breaking-and-entering variety."

"Logan, don't."

"Don't what? What do you want from me, Tiff?"

"Keep this between us? For old times' sake?"

"Old times?" He chuckled. "It'll cost you."

She raised her chin. "Name your price."

"You can't buy your way out of this one, honey, not with me. Here's the deal: We're through, and you tell Daddy breaking it off is your idea. I'll resign from WHCH, and you stay the hell away from Melody . . . from now on. If anything, I mean anything, goes wrong for Mel—her show, her friends, lovers, car, future—if *she* so much as breaks a nail—I'll . . . turn you in to the police, and you get arrested for burglary."

"Arrested? It's my station."

"You want to duke that one out with your father and the police, then?" She paled but said nothing. "I didn't think so," Logan continued. "No more sabotaging Melody's shows, not an unkind word, a snub, or snide remark. Stay clear of her, of the station actually. Yeah, go work at another station—you've got plenty—and no one says a word. Oh, did I tell you that Melody also recognized your nail when the police found it?"

"Logan. I'm sorry, I was . . . afraid—"

He stepped beyond her reach and into the foyer. "Get your father, Tiff. You need to tell him you don't want to marry me."

Max came down in a chocolate brocade dressing gown, looking tired. He asked about the break-in, and Melody's missing show, and mentioned the seven-figure cost to the station if they lost it.

Tiffany lowered herself to the edge of a chair and gave Logan an imperceptible nod.

"After the police left last night," Logan told Max, "Melody and I managed to retrieve the raw clips from the server. We stayed up half the night reformatting. The show's not exactly the same as the original—Mel thinks it's better—but you've got a Thanksgiving show to ship this morning."

"I may not wait for the wedding to make you a partner," Max said as he accepted a cup of coffee from a maid.

Logan turned to Tiffany, who sighed. "Logan and I are not getting married after all, Daddy."

"Your daughter has decided to end our engagement, sir. We wanted you to know as soon as possible. I'll have my resignation on your desk by noon. Though, after last night's save, I'm still hoping for a recommendation."

"Suppose I don't accept your resignation?"

"To be fair to your daughter, I don't think you have a choice."

Max rose with a sigh. "I can't say I'm not disappointed. You've been an asset, and I still think you'd make a great partner." He gave his daughter a different look this time, as if he wondered where he'd gone wrong.

He shook Logan's hand at the door. "Come see me later. We'll see what we can find . . . er, we're not losing Melody, too, are we?"

"No, sir." Logan shot Tiffany a meaningful glance. "You've still got your Kitchen Witch."

"Good, good. I thought, perhaps, er . . . glad to hear it."

MELODY paced half the morning, wondering what Logan was up to. He'd barely spoken to her since returning from Tiffany's. He remained quiet and introspective in the car and worked in silence at his computer after they arrived. Then he went, God knew where, without a word.

He hadn't given her a straight answer or met her eyes once all morning. True, they'd made love all night in this very room, but she didn't think that was the problem. She'd known, of course, that everything would be different once they consummated their lust, but she hadn't expected it to be this different, or this frightening.

Logan returned to the office after about two hours.

"Where have you been?" Melody asked.

"I gave Peabody my resignation, and he accepted it."

"Idiot." Melody lowered herself to the sofa. "What are you going to do now?"

"Work on my résumé?"

"To protect Tiffany? You think that selfish bitch is worth your job?"

"Keep your voice down," Logan said, shutting the office door. "The bitch's father owns your ass."

"You can be such a shit."

"Hey, don't hold back," Logan said, twisting the cap off a soft drink. "Tell me what you really think."

"You jerk," she said, coming to press a finger to the center of his tie. "I'm furious with you."

"Stay that way." He kept himself from raising her finger to his lips. "But tell me what I did to make you so mad."

"You got involved with the boss's daughter, for one thing, then to make matters worse, you quit your job, you dunce."

"You're right. I failed . . . again. If I can face it, so can you."

"You once accused me of failing so I could fulfill my father's expectations. I think you're doing the same."

"No, I'm good at what I do, and I know it, unlike you. I simply have to find another station that needs a dynamite producer."

"You don't even like being a producer."

"I like it well enough."

"Why don't you do something wild for once in your life and send out those documentaries you love making?"

"An independent filmmaker does not make a steady living."

"Will the real Logan Kilgarven please step forward."

Logan raised a brow. "Care to explain that remark?"

"I'm on to you, Kilgarven. You've only been pretending to be a briefcase. You're hiding the real Logan Kilgarven beneath a camouflage suit of pinstripes. You date the women 'the suit' should, you do a job 'the bad boy' hates."

"I'm doing what I have to do to raise my son right."

"Define right."

"In a calm, stable environment. No upheavals, no cops knocking on the door to arrest a wife-beating drunk, no kid going hungry."

"You didn't steal money, did you? You stole food."

"Either way, I turned my mother into a workaholic. The old man spent every dime on booze, and when I . . . brought that to her sad and guilt-ridden attention, we left him, and she got a second job. Sometimes a third."

"You're not responsible for every member of your family. Your mother's a big girl."

"I'm responsible for my son, and as his father, I make choices with his best interests in mind."

"Commendable, but did you ever think that if you were happy, Shane would be, too."

"He is happy."

"He won't be when you leave Salem. You are planning to leave, aren't you?"

Melody's voice cracked, and her sorrow sent a shaft of pain straight to Logan's heart. Before he could stop himself, he took her in his arms and kissed her, with the same intensity he'd kissed her when they were making l—

"No!" He stepped away, took a steadying breath. He didn't need her. "I need to do what's best for my son," he said. As to whether his son's father loved Melody, it didn't matter. No promises, no future. She'd set the rules, and he'd agreed. "I have a lead on a job," he said to ground them both. "Max made a few calls while I was with him."

"Where?"

"Chicago, probably. Keep Shane for a couple of days while I fly out for an interview?" He held her while she cried, his throat aching, so dreadfully averse to letting her go, he wondered if she hadn't bewitched him after all.

WHILE Logan was in Chicago, Melody took Shane to a toy train show in a huge heated tent on the cobbled mall. He fell in love with a Blue Streak circus train and a layout with big top tents, animal cages, even a drawbridge. Not a shiny new train, but a beloved, well-played-with set in muted primary colors, with dents and scratches. The old guy selling it said he had built the layout more than fifty years before. He talked about his sons and grandsons playing with it over the years. Shane asked about the boys and what they liked best about it, and as the old man told his stories, Shane's eyes got to be as bright as his. Shane talked about the boys and their train all the way home.

On the second night, she drove Logan's Volvo to Boston to pick him up at the airport. She could tell by the set of his shoulders, as he cleared the gate, that he and Shane were leaving. After he lifted his son for a hug, he put Shane down, slipped an arm around her waist, and kissed her, thoroughly.

"You got it," Melody said after the bittersweet embrace. "I know a good-bye kiss when I get one."

Logan nodded, and she turned away, so he wouldn't see the sorrow in her eyes. Glory, she was mad at herself for all this emotion, but she was madder at him for being so god-awful stubborn about taking a job he didn't even like . . . halfway across the country.

* * *

THANKSGIVING morning, while Logan went to talk to Jessie, he left Shane and Melody preparing cranberry relish and cornbread stuffing to take to his mother and Chester's for dinner.

Jess's face fell when she answered her door and saw him on her porch. Logan tried not to be hurt that she'd been angry with him for weeks. "Before we get together for dinner later," he said, standing in her foyer like an unwanted guest, "I want to thank you for everything you've done for me and Shane." He gave her the floral arrangement he'd brought.

Jess firmed her spine. "I didn't do anything," she said, taking it. "Melody helped more than I did."

"Don't worry, I'll thank her, too. Those lessons in manners you forced on me finally paid off." His attempt to lighten the mood failed.

Jess shook her head as she walked away. Logan gave a mental shrug and followed her into the dining room. He found her stoically regarding his flowers in the center of her polished mahogany table. "You're mad at me for leaving again, aren't you?"

"For giving up, Logan." When she looked up, he saw that her eyes brimmed with unshed tears. "But I'm not mad, I'm . . . disappointed in you."

"Ouch." Shaken, Logan ran a hand through his hair. "You haven't been disappointed in me for years, Jess. I'm . . . sincerely sorry to hear it. If it's any consolation, I haven't given up. I'm moving forward. I have to, Jess. It's time."

"Can't you see that you're letting your past destroy your future? You make me so mad!"

"Aha, you are mad at me."

"Yes, damn it, and I have a right. I'm mad at your

narrow-minded refusal to accept the flaws in anyone, even in yourself."

"You're the one who taught me not to accept my own flaws."

"Don't lay your stupidity on me. You do know that girl is head over heels in love with you?"

Logan's heart did a ten-point Olympic handstand, an unwarranted one. However Melody felt about him, she didn't want him, and he shouldn't want her. He needed to go, and Mel needed to stay. "Tiffany only loves Tiffany," he said, purposely obtuse.

"Idiot." She rolled her eyes.

"Melody doesn't want commitments. She told me she has all she can do to take care of herself."

"You knew I was talking about Mel!"

"I figured out a long time ago that you and my mother have been playing matchmaker since before I came back to Salem."

Jessie blushed. Another first to add to the swearing and shouting. *A red-letter day for the judge.*

"If Melody lets you go, then her elevator doesn't go to the top floor any more than yours does."

Logan winced at the analogy, considering how chummy they'd managed to become inside elevators.

Jessie watched him with speculation for a minute. "She doesn't know what she wants any more than you do. I'm betting you love her as much as she loves you."

Logan shook his head, a sign he wouldn't answer, before he walked to the bow window and looked out. Shane's abandoned swing set swayed in the winter wind, dead leaves circling in an eddy of predicted neglect. He regarded the turret, empty of its four-year-old pirate, the landing that led to Mel's welcoming door.

He turned in time to see Jess give her table a mean

swipe, as if to eradicate a nonexistent dust fleck. "Bah, the two of you are the only ones who don't see it."

"I won't even ask who else does. Jess, what I want doesn't matter. When I stole from that convenience store, you said I had been thinking only of myself, remember?"

Jess nodded, giving him her full attention, with less ire and more respect.

"You said back then that I needed to consider how my actions and decisions affected other people. Well I've learned to do that. I think of my son now, and only of my son. I put him first, before anyone, even myself."

"He needs a mother," Jessie said.

"He does," Logan agreed.

"So it's the witch thing."

"Not so much anymore."

Twenty-four

"WHETHER Melody is a witch or not, is not the issue. She's not the marrying kind—her words. Besides, she's . . . unpredictable, wacky, as Peabody calls her, a . . . loose cannon."

"Fun," Jess said. "She's fun. Shane says she's 'wicked fun.'"

"Maybe," Logan said, knowing it for an understatement. "But until WHCH, Melody Seabright couldn't hold a job for more than a few weeks. The jury's still out on whether *The Kitchen Witch* is a fluke or not."

"The jury's in." Jessie beamed with pride. "It's not a fluke."

Logan smiled as well; he couldn't help himself. "I think you're right. I think she's found her calling. But even so, Melody . . . plays in traffic. She . . . sets things on fire." Especially him; the thought came from nowhere, and everywhere—his heart, his mind, from deep in his soul. Wildfires, she set inside him. Infernos, in his blood.

He shrugged, blocking further thought. "I don't know, Jess. It comes down to the whole stability thing. Shane's barely had a stable moment in his life, and I should be selfish and give him a walking disaster for a mother? I can't do that. He deserves better."

"But what about Melody? Doesn't she deserve—"

"Melody deserves better, too, better than a thief and a failure. She deserves . . . everything."

"That's interesting," Jessie said, perking up.

"What is?"

"You just admitted that you want Melody for yourself, but you won't give in to your own needs, because Shane and Melody might need something different."

"I did not. Look, I messed up my own life, I am not going to mess up theirs. Besides, Mel has a job in Massachusetts, and I have a job in Chicago. That's life. The situation may be my fault, but facts are facts. Things don't always turn out the way you think they should."

"Just promise me one thing."

Logan gave a half nod as Jess opened her door. "Try to remember that Shane loves Melody as much as you do, and that Melody loves you both. The rest, you and Mel might address together, if you tried."

BEFORE sitting down to Thanksgiving dinner at the Captain Joshua Endicott Mansion, Melody got a chance to see Jessie in her judicial robes for the first time.

In a formal parlor overflowing with fresh holly and red roses, before a claret marble fireplace, Jess performed the marriage ceremony uniting Logan's mother and Melody's father. Before retiring to Thanksgiving dinner, their guests gave the happy couple a standing ovation. Melody had never seen her father look so happy or so proud.

With a hand to her back, Logan propelled her toward

the new Mr. and Mrs. Seabright. She embraced her father, and Logan hugged his mother. Melody and her father parted more quickly, and she envied Logan and his mother's ability to hold on without embarrassment.

"Daddy, you keep close track of this one," Mel said, her heart heavy for so many reasons. "If she wants to go on a trip, you go with her, you hear?"

"Don't worry, Mellie Pie," her father said, patting her hand. "No separate vacations—or anything else—in this family." Her unemotional, brutal-businessman of a father blushed.

"I'm happy for you, Mom," Logan said. "This is everything you deserve, everything I've ever wanted for you. I'm not even jealous anymore that I'm not the one who got you to retire."

Melody and Logan traded parents to congratulate. "Congratulations . . . 'Mom,'" Melody said to Phyllis, and burst into tears.

"If I could special-order a daughter," Phyllis said in her ear, "she would be you."

Though she laughed at her own foolishness, while accepting Logan's handkerchief, Melody couldn't seem to stop her tears. Logan and her father stood in awkward discomfort, silently commiserating with each other—their first tentative bonding experience, Melody thought, and her eyes filled again.

Before digging in to their Thanksgiving dinner, each of the twenty guests shared what they were most thankful for, a touching tradition that Melody thoroughly enjoyed. She embraced the big family Thanksgiving with gusto. She'd never had a family—a mother figure, her father—in her life, a job she loved. If Logan and Shane weren't moving to Chicago in the morning, she'd have everything a girl could want.

Despite the blessings for which Logan was grateful—his new job, a new house waiting in Chicago, his mother's marriage and retirement—he worked hard to enjoy the day. He and Shane were leaving Salem. For perhaps the first time, he realized they were also leaving family and friends, people his son loved. They were leaving home.

Brian Westmoreland's presence did not improve the bittersweet feel of the day. To Logan's shock, Westmoreland had become the new WHCH producer. True, Melody had finally moved into her renovated office, so there would be no sharing, either of office or bathroom space, but they had apparently already become such good friends, Melody had invited him to join them today. What was that about?

She said Westmoreland would have been alone on Thanksgiving, otherwise, but Logan couldn't seem to forget the night the two of them spent together after the ball, even though he knew nothing had happened. Westmoreland did pay a bit more attention to Vickie than he did to Melody, but Logan still wanted to beat the crap out of him, just for the fun of it.

Shane's tears, when he said good-bye to his grandmother that evening, pierced Logan like a knife. Never mind what saying good-bye was doing to him; his son hurt, and there was nothing Logan could do. The newlyweds were leaving on a short trip to Paris for their honeymoon later that night, so they would not be at the airport in the morning, which only made matters worse.

Shane didn't calm down until Logan's mother promised that she and his new grandfather would visit often. Shane nodded, somewhat pacified, and turned to say good-bye to Jessie, who broke down and cried with him, which got Melody and Logan's mother tearing up again.

Logan felt like a creep, a heel, the usual failure, as they made their way to the car.

"I want Melody to ride in the back with me," Shane said on a whine, as he climbed into his car seat. "I want her to come to Chicago with us."

"Shh, it's okay, pup," Melody said, getting in beside him, cupping his head and kissing his temple. "I can't come. You know that. *The Kitchen Witch* belongs in Salem. Chicago isn't the city for me."

Logan started the car, like a freaking chauffer, or an outcast, or the worst father in the world. Talk about screwing up at the highest level. Where the hell had he gone wrong? Shane had barely spoken to him, or laughed at anything, not even Ink or Spot, since Logan told him they were moving.

Tearing Shane away from his friends at day care had damned near finished Logan. He hadn't struggled with a throat that tight since he'd seen his mother walk into juvie and had to face the fact that he'd broken her heart.

On the drive home, no matter what Melody did or said, Shane's mood deteriorated, so Logan put him right to bed. "I don't want you, I want Melody," were the last words his son spoke as he drifted to sleep.

They'd avoided saying good-bye to Melody, because she was driving them to the airport in the morning. He needed to be on the job Monday. Whether her seeing them off would turn out to be a good or a bad idea remained to be seen.

"Damn it," he said, loosening his tie and kicking off his shoes, as he sat on the sofa and picked up the remote. He didn't want to leave Mel anymore than Shane did. To turn his mind from missing her, he channel surfed for a bit, but nothing caught his attention.

He wanted to take her to bed. He wanted . . . one more night of magic. Except that Shane might wake up, which he did all the time, though when he did, he called out, he never got out of bed.

Logan powered off the TV, sat forward, rested his elbows on his knees, and scrubbed his face with his hands, listening for the voice of reason, but the need churning inside him was stronger.

No looking back, he and Nikky had said, and he'd had no trouble looking forward that time. But the night he and Melody made love, he hadn't even been able to use the words, because he knew, he knew deep in his soul, that he would never be able to forget.

One more kiss. A minute more with Melody in his arms. Ten minutes. Not in a bed . . . or on a sofa . . . somewhere . . . where he could hear Shane.

Logan hustled down the stairs in his stocking feet, before he could change his mind. As usual, his knock opened her door. "Get this damn lock fixed, tomorrow," he snapped.

She looked up in surprise. He'd caught her at the kitchen table hugging a gallon of ice cream, still wearing the long, red velvet jumper and white satin blouse she'd worn to the wedding.

"You've been crying," Logan said, going to stand beside her.

Melody raised her chin. "I have not."

"Your nose is glowing like Rudolph's on Christmas Eve."

"Eating ice cream makes it cold."

Logan fought for possession of the chunky doodle, won the tug-of-war, and opened the container. "Pure as newfallen snow," he said. "Nary a spoon-print in sight. How long have you been holding it?"

He put it into the freezer, ran his sticky fingers under the water, and turned back to her as he wiped them on a dish towel.

Melody had rolled up her sleeves and was rubbing her red-cold arms. Her sob rose from nowhere.

Logan hauled her into his arms and opened his mouth over hers, his kiss hungry, rushed. "Come on." He took her hand.

"Don't even think about it."

He stopped at the stairs and turned to her. "I'll never stop thinking about it. About you."

He saw the fight go out of her. He'd said the magic words. She would be his, if he asked. He wouldn't ask.

He hauled her to the top of the stairs, sat, and urged her down beside him. "We can hear Shane from here," he said, "while we say our own personal good-byes. I needed . . . I . . . just kiss me, damn it."

Her tears salted their kiss, compelled them to avarice, to grasp everything they could.

"Let me hold you, just for a while," Logan said when they came up for air, and they calmed, held on, kissed some more, and took to savoring. "Tell me this is just physical," he said, kissing her sad, puffy eyes, her red nose.

"It's physical," Melody repeated, grazing his jaw with her lips, weaving the hair at his nape between her fingers, which he adored. "It really is. We're oil and water, you and I. Pinstripes and polka dots. Wacky Witch and—"

Logan took her mouth again. He didn't want to hear anymore; he needed another taste.

The taste lasted, and lasted, until . . . now he wanted to take her to bed.

"You said no commitments," Logan whispered against her lips, as an antidote to his lust. "Because?"

"Stability," Melody said. "Shane needs it, and I don't have it to give. I'd hate it, if I had it, and I'd hate me, if I failed him."

Logan reared back, his face warm. "Who told you? Are you being sarcastic?"

"Sarcastic? What are you talking about? Who told me what?"

"Nothing." Logan found her echo of his sentiments harsh. It made his reasoning seem flawed and somewhat ludicrous, off-kilter, coming as it did from her own lips.

"He does need stability," Logan said, for his own benefit.

"That's what I said. Besides, I'm not the marrying kind

any more than my mother was." Melody slipped her hands beneath Logan's shirt. "I've told you that before."

"Right," he said on a groan, following her example, undoing her bra clasp, beneath her blouse, and freeing her breasts into his hands. His touch budded her nipples; his lips ached to do the same.

She whimpered when he took his hands away to undo her blouse, but when she saw what he was doing, she went for his zipper.

"This is crazy," she said. "Someone could open the door, step onto the landing, and look up."

"Or we could fall down the stairs."

She freed him and he groaned. "Get on my lap," he said, helping her. "If we fall, we'll fall together."

"This really is nuts," she said as she straddled him and he slipped inside her, but she ended with a contradictory whimper of satisfaction.

"Nuts . . . according to the wacky witch of the east." Being inside her felt so damned good, Logan had to fight coming too soon.

"This makes you as wacky as me, pal. What's wrong with us, do you think? Besides the fact that we seem to have this kinky 'thing' for sex in dangerous places."

"We're . . . horny?"

"Oh yeah," she said, sliding herself along his length. "But only for each other. What's up with that?"

"I know," Logan said, glad she'd brought it into the open. "How soon can you come to Chicago?"

Melody stilled and sat back so she could see his face. "Come to Chicago? For what, an affair? That would give Shane some big-time stability."

"I could get a sitter; we could go to a hotel." Logan knew before he finished that he'd gone too far. He saw the color leave her face. "Sorry," he said. "Other brain talking."

"I want more than that," Melody said.

"You want nothing," he said. "No commitments, re-member?"

"Right." Melody rose awkwardly, turned, and made her silent way downstairs. At her door, she looked up, censure and disappointment in her expression.

"You don't know what you want," Logan said, a bitter echo of Jessie.

"Like I'm the only one?" She went in, and for the second time since he'd known her, he heard the click of her deadbolt.

MELODY drove them to the airport in Logan's Volvo the next morning, under the threat of dark snow-filled clouds.

"I'm glad I'm not going to drive all the way to Chicago in this weather," Logan said. "Flying will be faster and easier. Each of them got lost in their own thoughts after that while Shane went back to sleep in his car seat.

"I know you asked Jess to sell the car for you," Melody said in an attempt to break the tension. "Would you have a problem selling it to me? I'm finally at a point where I can afford a good used car, and I like this one. I know you've taken care of it."

"Beats the hell out of a leaky pink beetle with 'flower-power' fading on the hood."

Melody smiled. "I'm having the bug restored," she said, "by the guy who did Jessie's first hearse. In hot pink. With-out the flowers."

Logan chuckled. "Only you could amuse me at a time like this."

"Only I could make you mad at a time like this. Listen, I'm sor—"

"Sorry about last night," Logan said, unwittingly interrupting her apology.

"But not about the sex," Melody cautioned.

"No," he said. "Never about that."

"Easier to say good-bye when you're mad, though, isn't it?"

He shook his head. "Wreaks havoc on a night's sleep, though."

"Tell me about it."

After helping Logan check his bags, because Shane was still sleeping in one of his arms, Melody walked him as far as security would allow. The urgency in Logan's kiss spoke of longing, need, sorrow. Melody knew hers did the same.

"See you on TV," he said, his voice soft, shaky.

Melody stepped from the embrace. "I'll borrow copies of your documentaries from Jess or your mother," she said, her heart racing, her hands fisted so she wouldn't grab him and beg him to stay.

"Do that," Logan said and carried Shane through security. He turned before grabbing his briefcase off the belt on the other side. "Have Woody make you some copies of your own."

" 'Kay," Melody said through the lump in her throat, raising a heavy hand in a half-wave. She stood rooted, an unseen hoard buzzing around her, as she watched Logan head for the gate. Her heart seemed to slow in proportion to the distance growing between them, until he hesitated, and it fluttered back to life.

He stopped, turned, made eye contact. So near yet so far. Melody raised her hand higher. The wash of tears and the rush of panic came as one. Pain filled her. Logan raised his briefcase, turned, and walked from her sight.

She didn't wait to watch the plane take off; that would be torture. Driving home, she kept tissues handy, so she could see the road more clearly. When she finished crying, because she'd never said good-bye to Shane, she was relieved he'd slept through their departure. She would not have remained dry-eyed so long, otherwise. She had fallen in love with him first, after all.

Twenty-five

MELODY finished feeling sorry for herself about the time she pulled into her driveway. After a minute of watching Shane's swing-set languish, she went next door.

Jess gave her a cup of tea, copies of Logan's documentaries, an obscene deal on his Volvo, a bit of sympathy, and a lot of encouragement on the idea that had come to Melody earlier in the week. At that time, taking matters into her own hands had only been a passing fancy, but the notion had taken root and simmered to a boil on her drive home from the airport.

"You're right," Jessie said, after Melody explained what she wanted to do. "Logan needs to get beyond his past, but he needs a good nudge. Go for it, Mel. I think you're the one who can make it happen."

After hugging Jess, Melody felt better, though she knew that missing Logan and Shane would get harder before it got easier. For a short while, she had hoped deep down that she'd found the love of her life and the child fate meant for her. She'd barely had a chance to come to terms with that frightening seed of hope before Logan and Shane were gone. Now she hurt as if she bore a raw, gaping wound where they'd been cut away.

So much for feeling better.

Even though she had requested the day off, Melody went to the station to put her idea—set to simmering by Logan's parting words—into motion.

She found Woody and offered to pay him for his time and the supplies he used, if he would make her a couple dozen copies of Logan's documentaries. Then she went to see Nikky in Human Resources and shamelessly begged for a copy of Logan's résumé and cover letter.

By the end of the day, she had retyped the letter, altering it to reflect Logan's new address and his cell phone number, and she had added his interest in independent filmmaking and Peabody's recommendation, also compliments of Nikky. When Woody finished copying the documentaries, after work, Melody packaged sets of them, including copies of her Thanksgiving show, with her version of his cover letter and résumé for each of the networks in New England.

She left the station with a great sense of accomplishment that night, and a new realization of her success. Somehow, she had managed not only to keep her job but to turn *The Kitchen Witch* into a winning program. She wasn't a ditz, as her father had always said. She was pretty smart actually, smart enough to win and succeed at a difficult job. Amazing.

She remembered exactly when she would normally have given up, however, and the way Logan had talked her out of it, as if she would be doing him a favor.

Well, maybe she could turn the tables. She wouldn't lie about her motives, even to herself, so of course she hoped that if Logan could have the career he wanted, he might come home to pursue it. But whether he did or not, her efforts would be worthwhile, even if all she did was give him the confidence to do something he liked. She would not fool herself into believing he and Shane might come back. She would instead learn to go on without them, however difficult that might be.

LOGAN left the station in a rush, worried about his son. Shane had been moody and listless for the two-plus weeks since they'd come to Chicago. He didn't want to go to day care, but preferred staying with Celia, his housekeeper-sitter, who said "the boy" never went out to play.

She had called Logan a half hour before, raging about an emergency, and property damage, and how it wasn't her fault. All she did, she said, was go downstairs for ten minutes to put laundry in the washing machine.

It took Logan forty minutes to get to the suburbs from the city, and by the time he arrived, he was tense and ready to give his son a good talking to, until he pulled into the driveway and saw the damage firsthand.

Logan sighed. He had bought them a painted-lady style Victorian with teal, turquoise, and gold gingerbread trim and a backyard big enough for a little boy to play. Obviously, Shane's afternoon play had consisted of getting into the shed where the painters left the touch-up paint, because their teal front door now sported five and a half drippy gold stars.

Logan slammed the steering wheel, guilt riding him, not for the first time since they'd come to Chicago. Shane's message couldn't be any clearer if he'd painted "I miss Melody" on the door.

In the living room, Logan found his son on the sofa watching TV, but the program stopped Logan dead. Melody, dressed as a pilgrim, laughing, leaning over an open hearth, a close-up of her tasting Indian pudding and rolling her eyes in ecstasy. Logan sat down and hauled Shane onto his lap. "You miss her, huh, sport?"

Shane's eyes filled, and he nodded as they continued to watch, mesmerized.

"This is an odd time for the show to be on," Logan said.

Shane shook his head. "Gramma sent me some shows, 'cause I cried on the phone the other day."

"Why did you cry on the phone?"

"Cause Mel wasn't home when I called her."

"How did Gramma know?"

"Celia helped me call her to see if Mel was there, 'cuz Gramma married Mel's dad, remember?"

"I see." His mother had not mentioned the incident nor sending the shows. "What say we call Mel right now?"

Logan got an approving "Whoopee!" and called Melody at the station. Between him and Shane, they talked to her for nearly an hour, each of them going from laughter to sadness in turn. Logan hung up while Shane put another *Kitchen Witch* show on to watch. Talking to her was like riding an emotional roller coaster, Logan thought, both enervating and depressing, and he didn't think it was any easier on her.

Celia, a wiry sixty-year-old, brought them a bowl of fruit for a snack.

"Celia," Logan said. "Call the painters will you, to fix that door, and see if they've got somebody who can paint some gold stars on it." He turned to Shane. "Okay, sport?"

"Okay!" Shane watched Celia go. "She's no fun, Dad."

Logan chuckled. "Don't tell her that."

"It's just . . . Mel made me smile."

Me, too, Logan thought. He was beginning to believe that Melody imbued life with joy, not turmoil, and with love—lots of love.

"Which show is this?" Logan asked as Shane finished putting another disc in the DVD player.

"It's a new one where Mel doesn't put the cover on the blender good and cranberry goop shoots all over her and a lot 'a yelling people." Shane chuckled, jumped up, and demonstrated how Melody jumped out of the way, too late, and Logan realized he hadn't seen his son this animated since they'd left Salem.

He wondered which of them was in worse shape.

"She used my signs again, too," Shane added. "I already watched it once, but I wanna see it again."

AFTER Melody got off the phone with Shane and Logan, she left work early, happy and lonely after talking to them. Her parents and Jess were coming to dinner so she could test the meal for her Christmas program on them, and she needed to shop for groceries on the way home.

LATER, as she basted the small goose she was preparing, she began to think that it might be nice to go to Chicago for Christmas after all. Shane's train had been delivered, and she really wanted to see his face when he opened it Christmas morning. Her father and Phyl were going and had asked her to come along. They would get a hotel suite, they said, with a room for her, which would be good, as it would keep her and Logan from getting into any of the dangerous situations that might arise if she were staying at his house.

God, she ached for a dangerous situation with Logan. She wanted to feel the rough of his beard against her cheek, his hand skimming her waist, his mouth opening over hers, his cool firm lips . . . anywhere.

Melody squeaked as a hot, literal need turned her to jelly. *Get a grip,* Seabright, she told herself. Shaking her head, she cracked open a window and concentrated on her cooking.

* * *

JESS arrived first and admired the plum pudding she'd made the weekend before. "I hear you talked to Logan this afternoon."

"Good grief, how did you hear so fast?"

"Shane told me a few minutes ago. He calls a lot."

Melody grinned. "Me, too. Sometimes, twice a day. I'm thinking Logan hasn't gotten his first phone bill yet."

Jessie chuckled. "Serves him right for leaving. I hope the bill tops a grand."

Melody pretended shock, but they broke down and laughed.

When her parents arrived, her father put a wrapped Christmas gift, about the size of a tie box, on the counter beside her. "That's for you."

"A little early for gift-giving, isn't it?" Melody said, more or less ignoring the gift. "Though I'm happy to see it's too big to be a check." She sighed and wiped her hands on her apron. "While I'm on the subject, I think this is as good a time as any to tell you to stop with the checks. No more. Nada. None. Not a nickel. Got that?"

Her father grinned. "You've ruined the surprise."

"What? This is a noncheck?"

"Sort of," her father said, rubbing his hands together, looking as anxious as a kid at Christmas. "Go ahead. Open it."

Melody rolled her eyes, but she did as he asked, though she didn't understand the papers she found in the box. She saw her name, though, beside an eight-figure dollar amount that floored her. "Wait a minute," she said, looking more closely. "This is some kind of trust fund. Daddy! You didn't! Damn it, I don't want your money. I'm not a ditz. I can earn my own living. I'm getting an awesome salary for *The Kitchen Witch* show—"

"Shh, shh, Mellie," her father said, taking her into his arms, rocking her. "No, don't pull away. Listen to your old Dad for a minute, will you, and let me hug you for more than half that time for a change."

Melody lowered her brow to his shoulder and closed her eyes so he wouldn't see her tears. Once, just once, she wished he'd have some faith in her. "I'm listening."

"I won't be sending you any more checks," he said. "You are doing great on your own. You've proved you're smart and innovative, and to show you I believe it, I've started a charitable foundation in your name. For you to administer, I mean. In addition to your *Kitchen Witch* job, of course. You can give the earnings to whatever causes you choose, no questions asked, and the principal will keep earning more. Phyl and I have decided to continue supporting The Keep Me Foundation, in addition to whatever you do, but that's beside the point. I'm proud of you, Mellie. I believe in you."

Melody looked at her father, not quite comprehending.

"I . . . I love you, Mellie Pie. I'm . . ." He cleared his throat. "Sorry I never told you so before."

"Oh, Daddy." Melody didn't know what else to say. She didn't know how to say the words either, not to him. "It's not like the words are necessary . . . I mean, Mom never used them, either."

Her father raised his chin. "My fault, you know, the way she felt about us. I bought her, really. Lured her with money into marriage and motherhood, neither of which she wanted." He scoffed as he turned to look out the window. "You'd think I would have learned from that, but no." He turned back to her. "I kept making the same mistake with you. It took Phyl to show me where I went wrong. I . . ." He cleared his throat. "When you didn't want my money, I thought you didn't want my love."

"You were wrong, Daddy." She stepped into his arms again. Joy filled her, and yet, with his avowal of love had come a final truth—her mother never wanted her. Melody had always known it, of course, but she had also thought she was like her mother. Now her father had proved her wrong. Her mother accepted money in place of love. Melody did not.

Perhaps, just perhaps, she was worthy of love.

After a successful Christmas dinner, two weeks early, Melody kissed Jess and her parents good-bye at the door. There she remained standing until Jess's porch light went out and her parents' Mercedes disappeared around the corner.

Her father loved her. Learning that had turned out to be as amazing as she had always imagined it would. A miracle. She turned on the landing and went up the stairs to sit at the top.

For the better part of her life, she'd dreamed of her father's love and approval, had thought it was all she'd ever want or need. She had been wrong about that, too.

What she needed to make her life complete, who she needed, lived hundreds of miles away. She, fool that she was, had let them go.

Too bad she hadn't known sooner that she was not a ditz and that she was—hard to believe—lovable. Her father loved her—imagine that. Shane loved her, Phyl, Jess. And she was not like her mother; she would never marry for money. Love, she would marry for . . . if she ever married. Would she? The thought no longer seemed ludicrous.

A smart, lovable, loving woman might be able to offer a boy stability. A smart woman with a career and a once-in-a-lifetime-love might even become the marrying kind.

Melody sighed. Too bad she'd figured it all out so late. She leaned against the cold door, missing the sounds of life behind it, missing Logan and Shane. Mel, the ditz, would have gone after them, no second thoughts, no responsibilities holding her back, but the new Melody, Salem's Kitchen Witch, couldn't afford to screw up the best job she'd ever had.

She would have to find another way.

A few days later, Mel's latest show arrived in Chicago, express mail. Logan and Shane watched it the minute Logan got home.

Melody wore the sizzling electric blue wool dress she'd worn the night they made love, the one she'd worn to get his attention. It worked then. It worked now.

On the set, royal blue candles glowed softly amid potted ivy and mistletoe, and a small potted cedar that twinkled clear light. As Mel prepared a Yuletide brunch, she cast a spell on an artichoke and lemon soufflé, so it would "rise as high as the stars," and when it fell flat, Logan chuckled at the look on her face.

"Apples," she said as she peeled one, "can divine your future mate or restore a relationship." She cut the fruit lengthwise and held it up to the cameras. "See how the seeds form a heart? An even number of seeds means marriage. There are six in this apple." Logan sat straighter as she followed that statement with a spell for unconditional love.

Her Honeycomb Pudding, Apple Fritters, and Rhode Island Johnnycakes all turned out great. When the show came to an end, she came around to the front of the island counter. "From all of us here at WHCH, I'd like to wish you and yours bright blessings and the longing in your hearts during this Yuletide season."

She picked up her wand. "I'd also like to end our Yuletide program with, not so much a spell as a wish, though I rather hope it works like a charm. She waved her wand in a series of graceful arcs.

> *"I have a dream that's dear to me,*
> *A longing in my heart,*
> *A little boy,*
> *A man so tall,*
> *Two cats called Ink and Spot."*

"Da-aad . . ."

Logan hauled Shane onto his lap as Mel swirled her wand again.

> *"I have a dream that's yet to be,*
> *A family made of three,*
> *Come home to me,*
> *I yearn to see,*
> *You both beneath my tree."*

The camera framed her, and as she finished, Melody looked at them with the longing in her heart, there, for the world to see, then she waved her wand and left the stage to the song Logan couldn't get out of his head.

"She wants *us*, Dad."

"I think she does, son." *What if she really is a witch?* Logan didn't care anymore. Melody made magic all right—bright and alive, glittering, energizing magic—love, it was called. She had already given his son more love than his real mother could scrape together in a lifetime.

Jess had been right. He couldn't let the past ruin the future—his or his son's. Yes, Shane missed Melody, but Logan missed her more. He loved her . . . like crazy.

Crazy in love with Melody. That figured. He'd known all along that he'd have to be crazy to fall for her. Logan rose, taking Shane with him. "What say we go home?"

"To Mel?"

Logan nodded. If he hadn't known before, he knew now: Home and Mel were one and the same.

Logan called his mother to say they were coming, then he called Jess, because he wanted her to see how fast he could get a marriage license. She knew the answer already because she and the D.A. were getting one for themselves.

He was still smiling and booking their flight to Boston when he got a call-waiting, from a TV station in Rhode Island, offering a contract for a series of New England documentaries. He was shocked, amazed, flattered, and he would never be able to thank Mel enough. He set up an appointment with them the following week.

Melody had once told him that if he were happy, Shane would be happy, too. A shame, they'd all had to become so miserable before he discovered she was right.

"Now we have more than one reason to go home," he told Shane as they went to get their suitcases from the basement. "Though I don't suppose that even a new job is as important as telling Melody we love her and want her to marry us."

"Yes!"

"Guess that settles it, then."

When they arrived in Salem, Logan went straight to Jessie's, where a "For Sale by Owner" sign sat in front of her house. "How much for the house?" he asked as she opened the door.

Jess screeched when she saw them. "I'll make you a deal," she said, hugging them.

Logan raised a brow. "Make it as good as the deal you gave Mel on my Volvo, and you've got yourself a buyer."

Jessie chuckled, but her cheeks turned pink.

He'd always loved the house, and she knew it. She'd probably put the sign out this morning. "Keep the kid for a while, will you, you old meddler. Oh, and get your robes out of mothballs. Who did you say we have to see for a quick license and blood test in this town? I'm not waiting a minute longer than I have to."

"If Melody will have you," Jessie said on a wink. "She's not the marrying kind, remember?"

"What did you do, miss her last show? I think I can talk her into it." But Jess had a point. Melody could be stubborn sometimes. Then again, her Christmas wish had been clear. A family made of three, or four, Logan thought, anticipating the challenge of a future with Melody in it.

By the time he got to WHCH, she was in the middle of her Christmas show. Oh man, Santa's sexiest helper stood before the stove in red spikes and a red velvet miniskirted dress, trimmed in white fur, looking like something he'd seen in an old Christmas musical. A floppy red Santa witch hat crowned her lush, waving hair. A sight to soothe a longing heart.

Logan wanted to rush the stage, forget the show, and take her into his arms. Instead, he stepped quietly into the wings to watch and wait for Melody to finish. He took in the Christmas set, where a beat-up old circus train circled a huge Victorian tree in the corner, trimmed in cranberries, popcorn, fruits, nuts, and cinnamon sticks. Ruby candles—red for passion, Melody had once said—and matching poinsettias had been set about. Christmas scents assailed him, peppermint, cinnamon, cloves.

A perfect plum pudding dusted in confectioner's sugar and topped by a sprig of holly sat on the counter. Beside it sat a fruitcake and a cut-crystal dish of steaming cranberry sauce.

Melody cast a spell for harmony and good fortune, while she basted a Christmas goose as if she'd been born cooking . . . until she looked up and saw him standing there.

Startled, she squeaked, stumbled over the spell, and overshot the goose by a mile, damned-near basting a videographer, who tried to jump from the scalding liquid, only to trip and take his tripod down with him.

Logan ignored the resulting commotion, the waving director, the chuckling audience, while he held Melody's gaze, and she held his. She dropped the baster into the pan, forgot the goose, and met him halfway across the set.

Screw live TV, Logan thought, as he stepped in front of the cameras, backed his sexy-as-hell witch up to the wall, and kissed her senseless.

Watching at home, Phyllis and Jessie high-fived each other. Shane shouted, "Yes!" and jumped from his grandfather's lap. "Wait! I know that train."

On the show, as their reunion kiss lingered, the orchestra struck up a festive jingle-bell rendition of "Do You Believe in Magic?"

"I believe in magic," Logan said, loving the feel of her curves under velvet. "I'm holding her in my arms." He kissed her again. "I love you."

"Took you long enough to realize it."

"Like I'm the only one?"

Melody blushed. "I love you, too."

"Too bad you're not the marrying kind."

She toyed with a button on his shirt. "I . . . might have been mistaken about that."

Logan raised her chin, saw that her eyes were bright. "I got the feeling that you sort of . . . proposed . . . on your last show, but before you confirm or deny that wild assumption, you should know that I'm about to become an independent filmmaker, not exactly a steady job."

The smile she gave him could rival the sun. "That's all right," she said. "I have a steady job. You can provide the excitement in the family, and I'll provide the stability."

Logan grinned. "In that case, bewitch me, please, for as long as we both shall live?"

Melody unhooked her mike and tossed it. "Hell, yes," she said, "I love raising the devil," and she gave herself up to his kiss.

A roar of approval rose from the audience, and her candied yams came out perfect.

Dear Reader,

Salem, Massachusetts, is a wonderful city to visit, and the majority of the events I portray in *The Kitchen Witch* are available to visitors, some all year long, and others only at Halloween. Owing to my experience as a special events' coordinator, and to the evolving nature of such events, I renamed those herein to fit my story and to protect the actual events from my imagination. Among the figments of said imagination are WHCH TV, "The Salem Museum of Witchcraft," and "The Keep Me Foundation." For more information on Salem, please visit their website at www.salem.com.

ANNETTE BLAIR
www.annetteblair.com

Turn the page for a special preview of
Elizabeth Minogue's novel

The Prince

Coming soon from Berkley Sensation!

* * *
* * *
* *

ROSE twisted through the crowd, sweating in her heavy kirtle as the relentless sun beat down upon her uncovered head. Safe within the press, she dared cast a quick look over her shoulder. As far as she could tell, she had not been followed.

Yet.

Two weeks on shipboard had left her legs uncommonly stiff. The wooden planks rose to meet her, jarring her off-balance. *Clap clap, clapclap*. Heel and toe of her wooden pattens hit the planks more quickly as she found her land legs. She hurried on, breathing through her mouth against the oily smell of fish, thick as fog on the unmoving air. She kept to the most crowded places, head down, meeting no man's eye. Yet still the sailors noticed her.

"Slow down, Jenny—sweeting—*chevra*," they called after her. "What can be the rush? Stay a moment, let me show you—"

Despite the paralyzing heat, she wished desperately for

cloak and hood. The past year of silent solitude had stripped her of defenses. Even before that, she had never been the focus of so many eyes. On the few occasions she was permitted to appear in public, her cousins were always present. The two of them rendered her as invisible as any magic cloak could ever do.

But today Melisande and Berengaria were far away. She was alone in a place where no respectable woman would be seen. No woman at all just now, not in this unrelenting heat. Even the dockside whores had retreated to some shady chamber to wait for evening's cool.

But she could not afford to wait. She must go now, and swiftly, before her absence had been noticed. Eyes fixed on the wooden planks beneath her feet, she concentrated on her destination.

I must be calm, she told herself. *Or,* she amended, wincing as a sailor trod upon her toe, *I must* look *calm.* But that should present no problem. She was good at looking calm; so good, in fact, that those who knew her best would swear she was half-witted.

But *he* must not think that. He must believe her story, strange as it might seem. She would be bold. Bold and firm . . . yet not overbearing. After all, she was a supplicant. Or would be, if she ever got there.

Almost running, she crashed into a bearded sailor no taller than her chest with a broad basket balanced on his head.

"Forgive me—please, sir, could you tell me—"

"Piss off," he snarled, shoving her away.

She took a few stumbling steps toward the edge of the dock, but was halted on the edge by a hand fastened on her wrist.

The moment she regained her balance, her plump dark rescuer released her and turned away, wiping his palm fastidiously upon his flowing crimson robe.

"Wait!" she cried, hurrying after him. "Pardon, sir, but could you tell me—"

"*Channa zayra,*" he snapped, not slowing his pace.

"*Alet amia,*" she answered sharply.

He stopped instantly and turned, one hand moving to his brow. "Forgive me, *serra*. How may I serve you?"

"Can you tell me where the Prince of Venya may be found?"

He shut one eye in the Jexlan manner, a courteous gesture denoting careful thought.

"I have not seen him," he said at last. "And had I done so, I would not tell you."

"But I must find him! Please, *serrin,* it is a matter of life and death."

He sighed. "Daughter, whatever this matter is, you should take it to your family. The . . . one you speak of cannot help you." He clicked his tongue, a *tsk tsk* of disapproval. "To so much as speak his name is to sully your honor."

Perhaps in Jexal; if it were so in Valinor, every maiden in the country was already sullied beyond redemption, for the Prince of Venya's name was shouted out constantly in every market square. Despite a dozen edicts, half the troubadours in the country made their living courtesy of his adventures.

"But I must speak to him," she insisted. "My family is dead; they cannot help me, and I haven't a moment to waste."

He studied her face for a long moment, then gestured toward the row of stalls. "If the Venyans are here at all, that is where you will find them."

He touched his brow again, this time with one finger only. *Why, the man thinks I am a whore,* she realized with a shock as he turned away without the customary bow. *Jehan help me, will* he *think the same?*

I must behave with dignity, she thought, turning toward the stalls. *Dignified, bold, calm, and spirited—*

"Good day, master," she said to the man behind the counter. "Are there any Venyans here?"

"Oh, thou dost not want those sly sorcerers," the man said with an ingratiating smile. "Whatever they have, 'tis no match for what I can offer you. See, here is—"

"I thank you, but only Venyan will do."

His smile vanished. "I cannot help thee."

She tried the next stall.

"Venyans!" A burly man spat at her feet. "I have no truck with their kind. Move off, you're blocking the way."

An hour later she was soaked with sweat and so thirsty she could barely rasp out another question. But all that was nothing to the anxiety gnawing at the pit of her stomach. She started at each footstep behind her, heart leaping to her parched throat. What if he was not here? What if she had misheard or Captain Jennet had been mistaken?

She had no food, no water, not a single coin with which to buy the most basic necessities, let alone passage on a ship. And soon, if not already, she would be hunted.

She dragged shaking hands across her eyes. *I'm not giving up. Not yet. Not while there is still the slightest hope.*

She reached the end of the row of booths and turned the corner. A single stall stood in the deserted stretch of dock. She held her breath as she approached it.

The shelf was not crowded, but what was there drew and held the eye. A knife with a plain silver hilt, two rings, a glittering crystal on a stand of twisted strands of gold and silver. A tiny bejeweled windmill whirred and chirped a merry tune without a breath of air to stir it.

The man who stood above these offerings was no less exotic. He was immensely old, his eyes lost within a network of wrinkles. Hair the pale silver of *carna* blossoms fell nearly to his waist.

"The blessing of the day upon you," she said cautiously in Venyan. The man's eyes lit and he smiled.

"And upon you, *acelina*," he replied in the same tongue, his weathered face creasing in a smile. "How may I serve you?"

He is a mage, she thought, giddy with relief. A Venyan mage. So they *do* exist.

"A *sheeral* ring, perhaps?" he offered. "One for you and one for your . . ." He used a Venyan word that could mean either husband or lover. "It will burn with Leander's fire should he ever be unfaithful, recalling him his vows."

"No," she said, "Not that. I—"

"Then perhaps this knife. Have him wear it for a moonspan. When he journeys forth, it will be a comfort to you. So long as it stays bright, you can rest easily, knowing he is well. Should it rust . . ." He ran a finger across the shining edge. "Is it not better to know than sit and wonder?"

She shook her head. "No—though they are very fine. I am searching for your prince."

The mage carefully replaced the knife in its sheath. "*My* prince? Lady, I am but a simple wanderer without home or country."

"But you are Venyan."

"Ah, you seek Prince Rico? Then I fear you have gone far astray. You would do better to look in Valinor, perhaps at Larken Castle."

She shook her head. "Not him. Your *true* prince."

"I am sorry, but I do not know of whom you speak."

"Of course you do! Everyone knows of him! And he is here somewhere, I'm certain of it. Please, can you not take me to him?"

"I am sorry," he repeated, reaching upward. "I cannot help you."

A wooden shutter rolled down across the opening. She caught it before it latched and lifted it an inch. "He who will return upon the flood tide with all who have been lost," she said rapidly in Venyan. "His cause is just, his followers true, and you shall know them when they speak his name."

She shoved the shutter up another few inches. "Well? I spoke his name, didn't I?"

"You did."

"And I know the words. By right of custom, you must answer me!"

The shutter began to fall.

"I am Rose of Valinor."

It halted.

"And I demand—no, I entreat you to take me to your prince."

The sorcerer bent to peer through the opening, regarding her with hooded eyes. "Venya *has* no prince."

"Until the true prince is restored," she answered promptly. "When Leander's heir returns, the stones will sing and the land rejoice."

When he did not answer, she tried again, raising her voice a trifle. "I *said,* when Leander's heir—"

"I heard you. My silence was an indication of surprise, not failing hearing."

"I know a half a dozen more but I really haven't time. So if you don't mind, I'd like to see him now."

"Wait. I will see what I can find."

NOT another round of questions, Rose thought, *I cannot bear it.* Her last inquisitor, an elderly man with a tired face and piercing eyes, had taken far too long to accept that she would give him nothing but her name. Now she followed him into an alehouse and down a tiny passageway, halfway between fury and despair. She wanted to rage at him, to insist that she be taken to the prince, yet she knew she was utterly dependent on his good will.

"Please," she said, "I have told you all I can and time presses."

"You shall have your audience," he said. He opened a door, stepped back, and with a stiff little bow gestured for her to enter.

The squalid little chamber was stifling and the stench of it made her empty stomach twist uncomfortably. It took her a moment to realize she was not alone. A clerk sat at a tiny writing table in the corner, quill scratching frantically. He looked up briefly when she entered, then lowered his head over his work.

She sat down on a stool, folded her hands, stiffened her spine, and lifted her chin. After several minutes her neck began to ache and her stomach grumbled noisily. She cast a quick, embarrassed glance at the clerk, but he was oblivious to everything but his work.

You'd think a prince's clerk would have offered me at least a cup of water, she thought with an inward sniff, *let alone a crust of bread.*

Standing, she paced the chamber. It only took a moment to go from end to end. A single glance was enough to show her four bare walls of rough planks, a bare floor, and a straw mattress on a wooden frame. Her silent companion still wrote on. He was youngish, perhaps a year or two older than her own twenty-four, dressed in sober black, light hair combed neatly back.

She sidled closer, peering sideways at the page he was writing. A black sleeve moved to block her view.

"Good day," he said, though he did not look up again and the quill did not so much as pause.

"And to you," she answered with a sigh, retreating to her seat again and fixing her eyes expectantly on the door.

Any moment now it would open and the Prince of Venya would stand before her in the flesh. Her heart gave a nervous lurch. He was the hero of a hundred songs and stories, the sorcerer pirate whose name struck terror into every captain on the nine seas. Bold and dashing, wily and clever, the Prince of Venya was as deadly to his foes as he was loyal to his followers. It was widely sung that a single smile had the power to melt a woman's bones within her flesh.

Not that Rose wanted her bones melted, if such a thing were even possible. All she wanted was one small favor. Surely that was not too much to ask of the Prince of Venya, the living embodiment of every chivalric ideal!

"Your Highness," she would say firmly, "you must help me."

No, that wouldn't do. She had a feeling that a pirate—let alone a prince—did not take orders well.

"Venya and Valinor were once allies. Now I offer you a new alliance, one that will work to your advantage."

She nibbled at her thumbnail. That sounded well. The only trouble was, it was a lie. The moment he asked *how* it would work to his advantage, all would be lost. Perhaps something a bit more spirited would catch his interest.

"What ho, Your Highness, Rose of Valinor here. Damned if I'm not in a bit of a spot. Long story—uncle hates me—think he wants me dead. What say you play the hero and get me to Sorlain?"

She groaned, starting on another nail. Spirited, yes. But she doubted idiotic would appeal to him.

"I am Rose of Valinor and I am fleeing for my life. Venya and Valinor were allies for many years and the breaking of that alliance is something I regret with all my heart. Venyans have ever acted with honor toward my people; for that I dare appeal to you to help me to Sorlain."

Yes. That was it. Calm, dignified, yet spirited—if only she could remember it. She drew a breath and closed her eyes.

"Your Highness," she murmured. "I am Rose of Valinor and—and—oh, bloody hell, I've forgotten it already. Where in blazes is he?"

"I'm sorry?"

Her head whipped toward the clerk. "Listen, can you possibly hurry things up a bit? I haven't got all day."

"Nor have I. Your pardon, lady, but the letter could not wait."

For a clerk, his voice was oddly cultured, the words tinged with an accent she could not quite define.

He stood and stepped from behind the writing table. He was clad entirely in black, but now that she saw him fully, she could not call it sober. His flowing shirt was unlaced halfway down his chest and tucked into a pair of sable breeches that clung to the hard muscles of his thighs. Bare feet were silent on the wooden floor as he approached..

This is no mere clerk, she thought uneasily. He must be one of the prince's men. She swallowed hard and sat a little straighter. The Prince of Venya might commit acts of piracy, but he had been driven to such desperate measures by cruel necessity. At heart, he was no pirate, but a nobleman. What she had not considered was that his crew—even his clerk— would be the real thing.

A thin white scar, very prominent against his sun-bronzed skin, ran down one cheek; another through an eyebrow. A gold ring glittered in his ear. Looking into that hard young face, Rose sensed instinctively that this man knew more about survival than she could ever hope to learn.

Or wanted to.

She swallowed hard and stood, taking a step back as he continued to advance. The stool overturned with a small clatter that she barely noticed. Another step and her back was to the wall.

"I suppose an introduction is in order," he said, sweeping her a bow that no courtier could have bettered for its grace. There was nothing of the humble clerk about him now. How could she have ever been so blind as to mistake this man for a servant?

Stupid, credulous fool, she raged at herself, *they never meant for me to see the prince at all. I have been tricked, trapped . . . and sold? Oh, Jehan, not that, not sold. Not me!* But why not her? It happened every day, women carried off by pirates and never seen again. *At least now I'll know what becomes of them,* she thought. She almost laughed, but the sound tangled in her throat and came out as a gasping sob.

She shot a desperate glance toward the door, praying that even now the prince would walk in and rescue her. But that hope died when the pirate spoke again.

"Florian of Venya at your service."

BERKLEY SENSATION
COMING IN NOVEMBER 2004

Miss Fortune
by Julia London
The third book in the Lear sisters trilogy, in which the
last of the sisters must get her head out of the clouds
and her feet on the ground to find love in order to
fulfill her father's last dying wish.

0-425-19917-7

The Demon's Daughter
by Emma Holly
Inspector Adrian Philips' job is to keep the peace
between humans and demons, and he's hated by both
sides. But when he meets Roxanne, a fellow outcast,
he will risk everything for a dangerous love.

0-425-19918-5

Arouse Suspicion
by Maureen McKade
Ex-cop Danni Hawkins must come to terms with her
father's murder and, along with the help of an ex-Army
Ranger, she must track the path to a brutal murderer.

0-425-19919-3

The Prince
by Elizabeth Minogue
Prince Florian wants only to reclaim his throne. But
when he is forced to help Rose of Valinor, he finds the
last thing he ever expected—love.

0-425-19920-7